Book 3 in the
Davina + Quinn
Series

# Love's Games

## Deborah Armstrong

*Children make your life important.*

—Erma Bombeck

Other books by Deborah Armstrong

*Forever Love*
Davina + Quinn book 1

*Love's Promises*
Davina + Quinn book 2

*Love's Challenges*
Davina + Quinn book 4

*Love's Farewell*
Davina + Quinn extra

*Boss*
Game Changer series

# one

**They gazed into each other's eye**s as passers-by made their way around them on the crowded sidewalk. Her heart called out to him. *Kiss me.* He stepped toward her. He was so close to her that she felt the sweet warmth of his breath caress her face. Her bottom lip quivered in anticipation. After all these years of longing and regret, he was finally going to kiss her. She raised her chin toward him as he lowered his face to hers. She closed her eyes and held her breath. His lips pressed against hers with a soft kiss. It was sweet and innocent. She liked this kiss. He'd never kissed her like this before.

His arms wrapped around her waist and pulled her against his hard body. His sculpted chest pressed against her breasts. Her hands gripped his shoulders, letting him know she wanted him to hold her tighter as she rubbed her aching breasts against him. The ache between her legs reminded her of how much she had missed him. She didn't need reminding. She thought of him every day and every lonely night.

*Kiss me harder.* Her mouth pressed against his as her tongue pushed its way past his teeth and played with his tongue. He allowed the invasion and continued to kiss her. Her hands left his shoulders and ran through his thick hair, pulling on the long dark strands that framed his chiselled face. His soft moan vibrated through her mouth in response, encouraging her. Her fingers found his ear lobes and caressed them.

He groaned as he broke their connection. "Come on, Rene, we discussed this. No playing with my ears. French kiss me if you want, but leave my damned ear lobes alone."

"Cut," the director barked. "Rene, what the hell are you doing? That kiss was perfect until you screwed it up."

Rene Adams looked at the famous director, giving him her best sex-kitten eyes. "Clint, I couldn't help it. It seemed like the right thing to do." Then she batted her eyelashes at Quinn. "Sorry, honey, there's something about your ears that I just can't resist."

Quinn Thomas stepped back from Rene as he shoved his hand through his perfect mess of shaggy brown hair and swore. Nine takes for a damned kiss. Everyone knew what she was doing.

"Okay, let's try this again," Clint called out. "Rene, keep your hands off his ears."

Quinn leaned toward Rene and spoke in a low and threatening tone, "Fuck this up one more time, and you'll get my stand-in."

"You wouldn't!" Rene hissed. "He doesn't look anything like you, and his breath stinks."

"I don't give a damn. Keep this up, Rene, and I'll leak it to the press that I refused to kiss you in front of the cameras because you have halitosis."

"Two can play this game, Quinn."

"Try me, Rene, and I guarantee you'll lose."

# two



**"So here's the latest** on your upcoming book launch. I think you'll like the schedule, and we've added some cities you haven't visited in a while."

Davi Thomas looked over the report in front of her. She could have looked at this on her computer screen back at her office. However, it was an invitation to lunch, and Davi wasn't one to pass on a visit to Toronto with the opportunity to mix business with shopping at her favourite boutique. She closed the folder and placed it beside her plate.

"Foxx, why did you call this meeting?"

"I told you, Davi. I thought it was important to go over the schedule in person."

"I've done this before, Foxx. You don't need to guide me through it." Davi took a thoughtful sip from her glass of white wine and gazed at the man sitting across the table. He was in his early forties, tall and lean with a full head of shocking red hair. His green eyes sparkled with mischief. "You do know that I don't like surprises, no matter how good they may be."

"What makes you think I have a surprise for you?" He cocked his head and winked at her.

"Please, Foxx. Just tell me what it is."

Foxx reached for Davi's hand and squeezed it gently. "Davi, how long have we known each other?"

"Two years. You took over from Alice when she retired. Why?"

"Would you say we've grown close in that time?"

She felt a knot form in her stomach. Damn it! Why hadn't she seen this coming? Lunch at the King Edward Hotel—a dead giveaway, and the way he was watching her with eyes no longer belonging to her agent but a hopeful lover. He'd had his thick ginger hair styled in the way she suggested he should wear it. He smelled nice, too, of the cologne they had sampled when they had walked through the Eaton Centre last month after a photo shoot, the one she had said she liked. Davi looked down at his hand. He'd had a manicure and no longer wore his wedding band.

"Foxx, I'm married."

"I'm not. My divorce went through. I'm a free man."

"You're not suggesting—"

"Yes, I am. I want to sleep with you."

Davi pulled her hand from his and shook her head. "No."

"Why not?"

"Why not? Foxx, there are many reasons. The number one being that I'm married, and I don't cheat. I despise cheaters."

"This wouldn't be cheating."

Davi laughed with disbelief. "How can you possibly say that?"

"Your husband's cheating on you. It's not cheating if you are the injured party."

"My husband isn't cheating on me."

"It's in all the celebrity magazines, Davi. How can you deny it?"

"You need a better source than those damned magazines. Haven't you noticed Quinn and I don't grant interviews? We don't trust them to tell the truth. It's all fabricated."

"They say that's why you don't give interviews. Because you've got something to hide."

"Not true."

"What about the word out on the street? I have my sources at the studio, Davi."

"Then get new sources. My husband is not cheating on me, and I am not going to cheat on him because you think I should." Davi stood up from the table and dropped her napkin on her plate. "Thank you for lunch, Foxx. I think our business relationship has come to an end."

Davi didn't stop when he called out to her. The nerve of that man, assuming she'd have sex with him because of rumours that Quinn was sleeping around. She knew who the cause of those rumours was—Rene Adams. Damn that woman. Davi was tired of her games. Two more weeks, and then Rene would be out of their lives for good.

# three

**Quinn pressed speed dial** on his cell phone as he walked toward his RV. He hardened in anticipation of hearing the sinfully sexy voice of the woman who would be answering his call.

"Hello, stud. You're late."

"I'm sorry. I couldn't get away any sooner. Are you alone?"

"I am knee-deep in kiddies, and my husband should be home any moment. We'll have to have our rendezvous another time."

"That's too bad. I was looking forward to having mindless hot sex with you. Guess I'll have to sleep with my wife tonight."

"Your loss."

"Never. My wife's a real livewire in bed." He smiled at the sound of her soft chuckle. "I'm on my way to my RV to clean up. I'll be leaving for home in fifteen minutes at the latest. What's for supper?"

"Your favourite. Lasagna. Did you have a good day? I hope it didn't get too hard for you."

Quinn chuckled at the double entendre. "It wasn't hard until now. You know it only gets hard for you, love."

"You have such a way with words. Drive carefully. I love you."

"I love you, too. Later."

He noticed the absence of the security guard at his RV but didn't give it much thought since he was more concerned with washing off the day's work before he returned home to his wife and family. Quinn opened the door. Once again, the stench of a familiar perfume assaulted him. His shirt and hair reeked of it. Quinn glanced toward the closed bedroom door.

"Damn it, Rene. Not this shit again."

He walked to the bedroom. There was no need to knock. He didn't owe Rene the courtesy of knocking on his bedroom door. Quinn opened the door wide.

"I thought we agreed you wouldn't do this anymore. No more games."

"Quinnie, how can you say that after today? Our love scene got me all hot and bothered. You can't tell me that there's no chemistry between us. We never lost it, lover. You still have the hots for me. Just admit it." Rene Adams winked at him as she pulled the covers off her naked body. "Don't tell me you don't want this."

Quinn would have laughed. Only he knew it would make the situation worse. A drunken Rene didn't take kindly to being laughed at, especially when she was sprawled naked in his bed. The dent in the wall beside him from a poorly aimed bottle of champagne was proof of that. She was a beautiful woman, but not his type. Her bottled blonde hair, overly large breast implants, and a face that had seen the plastic surgeon more than once had never appealed to him.

"You got a tattoo," Quinn said as he noticed the ink on her hairless mons. "Rene! It's my name! What the hell were you thinking?"

"Who else would I have? You're the only one who belongs there."

"Dammit," he cursed as he strode to the bed and yanked the covers over her. Quinn sat down on the bed beside her, exhausted from her endless stunts.

"This has to stop, Rene. These games—there's no winning." He gazed into her eyes, trying desperately to reach her. "I have a wife and family. I'm not leaving them for you or anyone."

"I had you once. I can do it again."

"You didn't have me, Rene. We were just a fling, co-stars getting it on years ago when we were both single. We're not going back there."

"You're wrong, lover."

"It isn't happening."

Drunken anger flared in her eyes. "What does she have that I don't? I'm younger, I'm more beautiful, and I'm great in bed. How could you choose her over me?"

"You promised me that these stunts would stop," he said, ignoring her question. "Ten takes to film a stupid kiss! You are wasting everyone's time."

He'd made her promise before he'd let the studio sign her on as his female lead. No more publicity stunts to make it look like they were having an affair. No more attempts at trying to seduce him. No more drunken calls at two in the morning demanding to know why they weren't still together. Rene and Quinn had the on-screen chemistry that fans wanted to see. They could act, and they could make any love scene look hot and natural, and yet that's all it would ever be. Rene lasted three weeks before she broke every promise.

He had the woman he loved and who loved him in return. Beautiful, intelligent, and sexy, Davina was so confident in their love for each other that she didn't mind sharing him with the world. Quinn couldn't understand how Davi put up with Rene's games. Any other woman would have threatened to kill Rene or had Quinn quit working with her. Not Davi. Rene was an irritation. One that Davi ignored as best she could.

Quinn rose from the bed, walked toward his chest of drawers, and opened the top drawer, pulling out a fresh T-shirt.

"What are you doing?"

"Going home," he answered as he stripped off his Rene-scented shirt and put on a clean one. "It's been a long day, and I want to get home to my family." Quinn picked up his wallet and car keys from the top of the drawer and headed out the door.

"Get back here!"

Quinn pressed speed dial on his cell phone. "Security? It's Quinn Thomas. Guess what? I have a naked woman in my bed, and she's not my wife." He looked back at Rene before he closed the door behind him and then headed toward the exit. "Yes, she's drunk again. Look, will you find someone on her staff and have her escorted out of here? Make sure she leaves my RV without destroying it this time. Thanks. Good night."

Quinn closed his eyes and thought of last night's bath time with Davi. Damn, she was hot. He smiled as he recalled her riding him in the tub, begging for more, tempting him with her breasts, teasing him with her lips. Quinn hardened as he remembered their lovemaking. Why would he ever risk what he had with Davi for any woman? He breathed in the pungent air and scowled. He opened the door and let it slam behind him. It was time to get home.

# four

**Davi made one last inspection** of the homemade lasagna in the oven and then glanced at the clock. Quinn would be home soon. Her heart started to race. She should be used to it by now, but thinking of him got her heart beating faster and brought a blush to her cheeks. Davi pulled out her lipstick from her pocket and applied it expertly to her lips. She checked her reflection in the glass of the microwave oven. Perfect.

She took one last look at the floral arrangement in an expensive crystal vase on her kitchen desk. The handwritten note of apology poked through the fragrant flowers. She'd let Foxx stew overnight while she thought about whether she would forgive him.

Davi entered the family room, looked down at the floor, and made a quick appraisal of the mess. Building blocks, various toys, pillows, and stuffed animals were piled messily in the centre of the room, and the middle of the pile was the reason why her husband was coming home. Not the only reason, but Davi didn't mind coming in second to them, a very close second.

Through the family room window, Davi saw the black Porsche stop in front of the farmhouse.

"Daddy's home," she announced happily.

Immediately, two heads rose above the mess, their bodies scrambling over the toys. "Daddy!" they squealed as they ran to the floor-to-ceiling window to watch Quinn as he made his way to the kitchen door. They slapped their hands against the glass as they called out to him. "Daddy!"

Quinn stopped and looked at his beautiful mop-haired children and then up at his wife. He waved to them and smiled before continuing his walk to the kitchen door. He opened it carefully, making sure a child wasn't on the other side.

"It's clear!" Davi called out to him.

Quinn stepped inside, then bent down and scooped up the brown-haired, blue-eyed twins who had run to him immediately. "How's my gang? Have you been good for Mommy?" The twins giggled in response as Quinn covered them with kisses. "Did you kiss Mommy today? I think Mommy needs a kiss, too."

Davi stepped forward for her kiss. "Daddy," she murmured.

"Mommy," he replied as he leaned down to kiss her on the lips.

Davi wrapped her arms around Quinn's neck and pulled him in close, as close as she could with two squirming four-year-olds between them. Davi released him when she felt the tickles the twins always gave her when they'd had enough of being in the middle of their parents' kisses.

"Rough day?" Davi asked as she took their daughter, Stevie, from Quinn's arm and placed her in her booster seat at the kitchen table. She knew that Quinn hadn't showered. Rene's unmistakable heavy scent still clung to him. "How was Rene today?"

"The usual. I don't know why I signed on for this project," Quinn said wearily. "It's more trouble than it's worth." Quinn placed Jack in the booster seat across from Stevie.

"Don't say that!" Davi protested. "It's a great story. You know it's going to be a wonderful movie, despite your co-star."

"I know," Quinn agreed. "Clint's doing an amazing job. Just working with him is a great privilege. I'm learning so much from him." Quinn walked to the kitchen cupboard and took out a bottle of scotch. "Care to join me?" he asked Davi as he poured himself a drink.

"No thanks."

The twins waited patiently for their supper as Davi served the lasagna, and then Quinn said grace. Quinn sat beside Jack, and Davi sat beside Stevie, across from Quinn. Quinn's long legs stretched out and touched Davi's. After all this time, he still needed to touch her. Davi smiled as she felt the tingle run up her leg.

"So, what did my two favourite kiddies do today?" He looked at Stevie, then Jack.

"Went to the barn," they said together. "A baby girl calf was born today."

"Did you see her being born?"

They smiled at him and nodded their heads in agreement.

"Was she big?"

Stevie nodded her head as Jack stretched his arms out wide to show the size of the calf.

"What else did you do today?"

"Saw Maggie," Stevie answered.

Quinn looked at Davi. "How is our lovely fortune teller today?"

"She's fine. She doesn't like what the press is saying about you and Rene. She says that I should sue the magazine publisher."

"And add more fuel to the fire? I don't think so."

"That's what I told her. This nonsense will pass once the filming wraps up, and you and Rene can go your separate ways." Davi noticed that Quinn had only taken a bite or two of his lasagna. "You don't like it? I know it's not like Rosa's."

"No, it's fine." He smiled at her. "Later?"

Davi knew the code word. They would wait until little ears were fast asleep. Jack and Stevie were sponges for words they shouldn't hear. One day, the twins listened to their half-brother, Rich, talk about stepping in cow manure. It took Davi a week to get them to stop saying the word *shit*.

"Down, please," the twins chorused.

Both had finished their supper. Davi wiped their faces then helped Stevie out of her booster seat. Quinn did the same for Jack.

"Go play until Daddy's finished," Quinn told them. He watched them as they ran back to the family room and buried themselves in their toys. "They're happy," he said somberly.

"Of course, they are. That's the way it should be." Davi looked at Quinn with concern. She noticed the slump in his shoulders and the dark circles under his eyes. "This movie is taking its toll on you. I've never seen you this exhausted before."

"I'm fine. I'll be okay after I have playtime. Don't worry."

"Go play. I'll clean up and put the coffee on." Davi stood then walked over to Quinn. "When you've finished playing with them, perhaps you can play with me." She leaned down and kissed him on his forehead.

Quinn pulled Davi onto his lap and kissed her lustfully. "I'm looking forward to it." He groaned in protest as she pulled away from him.

Davi washed the dishes while Quinn played with the children. She listened to their squeals of laughter. She loved the sound, a sound she never expected to hear almost five years ago. She had never planned to remarry and start a family at her age. However, love had a funny way of changing her plans. Falling madly in love with Quinn was unexpected and so easy, despite their age difference, with Davi being older by fifteen years.

When the coffee maker beeped to announce that the coffee was ready, Davi filled two mugs with the hot brew. She took the steaming cups and entered the family room to find Quinn building a castle with the building blocks while Stevie and Jack sat quietly beside him, handing him blocks as he asked for them. Quinn told them a story as he built the castle. It was his storytelling voice. It mesmerized them, as it did Davi. She sat down on the sofa and listened as he pulled her into his story.

He told Davi's story about the knight and his lady, their castle, and the dragon. Davi wrote stories for Quinn while they were on their honeymoon. In them, Quinn was her knight in shining armour, always rescuing her from some evil fiend. When Davi was in a coma and pregnant with the twins, Quinn read the stories to Davi every day. She remembered hearing his voice calling to her. The twins must have heard him, too, because his voice always calmed them. When he'd tell them a story, everything stopped for them. He had their undivided attention. Quinn would change the endings now and again, play with the adventures, but the knight, his lady, and their love never changed.

Quinn timed the story and the castle building perfectly, finishing both at the same time. Stevie and Jack placed the knight, the lady and the dragon in their usual spots. Then Stevie added a plastic cow, and Jack added a toy pickup truck.

"Is it a farm castle again?" Quinn asked in mock surprise. "Does every story  have a cow and a pickup truck?"

The twins laughed, then knocked the castle down and started to play with the blocks. Quinn got up off the floor and sat down beside Davi. He took the offered coffee.

"It doesn't last for long, does it?"

"What, the castle?"

"No, childhood and its innocence, the joyfulness and simplicity— they don't last for long."

"Oh, that," Davi said as she nodded her head knowingly. "No, but it's all good even when they're in their twenties and getting married. They are still your children. Maybe not so innocent but still giving you joy."

"How are the plans for the wedding? I'm sure you and the wedding planner have everything arranged. And Cat? Has she come to her senses? She can always dump Chas. It's not too late."

"You had to say that, didn't you? It's hard for you to get your head around your stepdaughter slash best friend marrying one of your friends. You've had enough time to get used to the idea."

"I am used to the idea, and they make a great couple. I know Chas loves Cat and will be good to her. It's just that seeing them together is like looking at what you and I should have had—the chance to start early and have a lifetime together. I'm jealous of that, not of them."

"We have what we have, Quinn. Nothing could have brought us together any sooner." Davi nestled into Quinn's chest. "I accept what we have now, and I am thankful for it."

"Oh, I know, and I'm incredibly thankful. It's just that I can't help fantasizing about you and me and kids, lots of kids. I think we would have had six by the time I got snipped."

"Six? And it was all your decision, not mine?"

"Well, I am the lord of the castle, remember, and what I say goes. And you're so great with pregnancy and birthing babies and raising them that you would have kept having them for me."

"Still on that knight's ego trip, I see. I should have given you a different career—maybe a gardener or bus driver."

"It wouldn't have mattered what I did for a living. You would still be mine, having my babies and loving me forever just like I love you forever."

The seriousness in Quinn's voice took Davi by surprise. She gave his words a moment to sink in before she asked, "Are you trying to tell me you want more children?"

"Sometimes, the idea crosses my mind."

"Quinn—"

"We could do it, Davi. You still have regular cycles. My soldiers are in the deep freeze just waiting to get called up for duty."

"My eggs are old. Quinn, I'm almost fifty."

"What if your eggs weren't old? What if we could have them checked out? We could do it, Davi. We could have another child."

Davi sat up and faced Quinn. There was no mistaking the look in his eyes, the excitement and hope of being a father again. She couldn't answer him. Not without hurting him. She turned her attention to the twins.

"Who wants to go to the barn?" she asked with forced enthusiasm.

"Barn!" Jack and Stevie jumped up from their pile of toys. They ran to the kitchen door, eager to go out.

Davi rose from the sofa and offered her hand to Quinn. "Coming? Let's go check on the Ladies."

Quinn took her hand and joined her. He knew this was not the time to push his wife. Just plant the idea and hope it takes root. He'd learned that over the time they'd been together. When they disagreed, Davi would think about his point of view for a while and then talk about it with him later. They always reached a compromise.

The hot July night was quiet except for the crunching of four sets of footsteps along the gravel driveway leading to the barn. Davi and Quinn held hands following the twins, who hurried along in their rubber boots.

"Shhh," Jack whispered as they entered through the main door of the maternity barn. "Baby's sleeping."

Quinn followed as the children led him to the calving stall, where the new mother munched on hay while her newborn calf slept in the clean straw. Stevie and Jack peered through the rails at the sleeping calf as Quinn and Davi stood behind them.

"She's tiny," he remarked.

"She came early. We'll have to keep an eye on her." Davi looked at the cow in the adjoining stall. "This one's due any time, but she's not showing any sign of going into labour."

"I miss this. I was a fool to go back to work."

Davi put her hand on his shoulder and rubbed it gently. "You would not have forgiven yourself if you had passed on working with Clint. This film could be his last. He is eighty-five years old, you know."

"And he has more energy than half the people working for him." Quinn put his hand on Davi's hand. "Don't mind me. I'm tired."

"Later," Davi said softly, knowing that they both had things to discuss. Davi turned her attention to the twins. "It's time to go in now. Say good night to the Ladies."

Stevie and Jack waved to the cows and said good night to them. Then they turned and headed out of the barn.

An hour later found Stevie and Jack freshly bathed and tucked into their beds. Quinn read them a bedtime story, and they were asleep within minutes. Quinn turned off the light and headed to the master bedroom to find Davi waiting for him in the Jacuzzi. Soft music played in the background while tealights flickered along the side of the tub.

Quinn stripped out of his clothes and joined Davi in the tub, facing her. He leaned back and closed his eyes.

Davi stroked his thigh with her foot. She waited for a few moments and then said, "I had lunch with Foxx today."

"How is the wizard of the publishing world?" Quinn drawled.

"He's had a makeover. He looks good. Quite handsome, actually."

"His divorce must be final. Either he's in the market again, or he's found someone."

"Yes to the divorce being final and yes to finding someone."

"Ginger man doesn't waste any time, does he? Maybe he'll have better luck this time around."

"I don't think you'll want to wish him good luck." Davi kept her gaze on Quinn's face as she continued to stroke his thigh. "Foxx's request for a lunch date was actually a let's get naked and have sex proposition. He was quite serious."

Quinn sat up and gazed at his wife with fire in his eyes. "He's dead. I hope you told him to go to hell."

Davi smiled at Quinn, appreciating his reaction. "I fired him, but then he sent me a beautiful floral apology. I might forgive him."

"Why would you forgive him? And what made him think you'd have sex with him?"

"It's that damned rumour that you and Rene are having an affair. He figured I'd be willing to have revenge sex. He said that it's not cheating if your spouse starts cheating first."

"Really? I hadn't heard that one before. Although it sounds like something ginger man would come up with."

"It was news to me, too. Anyway, I told Foxx not to believe everything he heard. He said his source is reliable, and he's confident you're cheating on me, husband."

Quinn opened his arms to Davi. She accepted the invitation and snuggled into his chest as his strong arms held her close.

Quinn's lips grazed the top of her head. "Forgive him if you want to, but don't work with him, love. I don't trust him not to try again."

"I don't think he will. The look on his face when I fired him—I've never seen a man go as white as that."

"Don't risk it, Davi. The man's got no sense of decency."

"That doesn't seem fair. Rene's been after you for weeks, and I haven't asked you to quit."

"That's different. You know I won't do anything."

Davi pushed away from Quinn so she could look at his face. "And I will?"

"You did tell me that you loved his red hair."

"That's no reason to sleep with a man, Quinn."

"I seem to recall your attraction to my hair."

Davi smiled. "I loved your hair before I met you. I still do." She reached out and touched his dark brown shoulder-length strands. "Your hair will always top his."

A wry smile appeared on his handsome face. "I didn't know you kept score unless it's with the Ladies." Quinn knew how much Davi loved her cows and her family. He always joked that all it would take would be one wrong move and he'd be at the bottom of her list, quickly replaced by Davi's bovines.

"And don't you forget it, buster." Davi pulled gently on his hair, guiding him to her lips. She kissed him softly and then released him. "Our love isn't a game. We don't give each other points, and we don't cheat. Ever. I wish others would understand that." Davi stroked her finger down Quinn's chest. "You were going to tell me something."

Quinn's smile turned into a grimace. He leaned back against the tub, pulling Davi back into his embrace.

"Rene's up to something again. We had our big kiss scene today. It took ten damned takes before she would do it right."

"How could that happen? I thought kissing would be the easiest part. She didn't have any lines to remember, did she?"

"She had lines. Reciting them wasn't the problem."

"What was the problem then?"

"She wouldn't stop pulling on my ears."

"She's going for your ears?"

"Only you get to pull on my ears, love. She thought it would be cute. I couldn't let her get away with it. I told Clint under no condition would I allow any pulling of my ears."

"I wonder what he thought about that."

"I have no idea, especially when he heard me tell Rene I'd put up with her ramming her tongue down my throat, but she couldn't touch the ears. Davi, the look on his face was priceless."

Davi reached up for Quinn's earlobe and caressed it lovingly. "Thank you. You didn't have to do that. I'd have survived seeing that on the screen."

"No one gets to touch my ears. You have the magic touch, love. Only you can make me hard by touching them."

"I'm happy to hear that."

"There's more, too."

"Fire away. I'm ready."

"I found her naked in my bed. She's not letting this go. She's determined to win me back."

"That woman is unbelievable."

"Hold on. There's more. Rene has my name tattooed on her mons. She says that I'm the only man who belongs there."

"You saw it?"

"It was hard to miss with her sprawled naked on my bed."

"Quinn, if she shows that to anyone"—Davi's mind raced with the possibilities—"she's advertising your alleged affair. You're going to be guilty regardless."

"Just as long as you know nothing's happening, love. That's all that matters."

"She's fricking crazy."

"One more month then she'll be out of our lives, I promise you."

"Don't make promises where that woman is concerned. I do not trust her."

"I can make you one promise."

"What's that?"

"I'll never ask you to tattoo my name on your beautiful body. Wear my ring. That's all I'll ever ask of you."

Davi left Quinn to finish his bath. She checked on the twins one last time before going to bed, kissing them softly before whispering a prayer over them. When she returned to the master bedroom, she found Quinn talking on his cell phone.

"Hold on, Dad, I'll ask Davi." Quinn turned to face her. "Dad's asking us to come out for a visit this weekend. We've got nothing planned, have we?"

Davi shook her head no.

Quinn resumed talking to his dad. "I've got a full day tomorrow. I'll see what I can do about leaving early. We'll let you know once we know the flight schedules. Kiss Mom for me. 'Night, Dad." Quinn ended the call then put his cell phone down on his bedside table.

"I thought they were going away," Davi mused as she shrugged off her robe and placed it on the foot of their bed.

Quinn eyed her appreciatively. "You've been shopping."

"Do you like it?" She asked as she turned slowly to give him the full view of her baby blue negligee. "I couldn't resist it once I tried it on. The blue reminds me of your eyes."

"That they are always on you?"

Davi laughed. "I was thinking more of sinfully sexy." She slipped into bed. "So, I take it your parents aren't going away."

Quinn turned off the lights then joined her under the covers.

"Change of plan, I guess. Dad insisted that we visit them this weekend."

"Did he say why?"

"No. I guess we'll find out when we get there."

Davi closed her eyes as she made a mental list of what she needed to do to get away. "I'll check the flight schedules and book us a flight. We'll need a car, too. Your folks' car won't hold all of us."

"I'll call you once I get to the set tomorrow. I'll let you know when I can make it home."

Quinn reached for Davi and pulled her close to him. Davi inhaled his scent as she stroked his chest. She loved bedtime with him. He made her feel safe and loved. She thought of him as her very own teddy bear.

"Do you feel like playing? You promised me my turn."

"I can try."

"There is no try. Do or do not," Davi murmured into his chest.

"I don't think my light sabre is up to the challenge tonight, love. Even with that incredible negligee, Yoda's going to have to use a lot of Jedi power to get it up and running."

"I'm Yoda tonight, am I?" Davi chuckled. "Whatever you're into, Skywalker." Davi pulled away from Quinn and slid down his body, leaving kisses along the way.

"It's Sir to you. Luke Skywalker is a Jedi Knight, don't forget."

"Right," she drawled, "And I'm your Master. Got something to confess, Sir?"

She didn't wait for his answer. Quinn breathed in sharply as Davi took him in her mouth. His head wasn't ready for lovemaking, but he knew she'd have his body ready in no time. She had that power over him. Davi worked on Quinn slowly. She was in no rush, and she knew how much he enjoyed her mouth.

He moaned as her soft hands pulled on his shaft while her hot mouth devoured him. Quinn's hands ran through Davi's hair. He loved the feel of the silky strands in his fingers.

Davi looked up at Quinn and saw the lusty sparkle in his eyes. "Your light sabre appears to be fully functional, Sir. Shall I continue?"

Quinn responded by reaching for her and pulling her on top of him. His mouth found Davi's quickly, kissing her hard. His hands slid down the sides of the lacy negligee and then slid back up, pulling the material up above her hips. With one hand, he guided his cock into her. Her moans vibrated in his mouth as he moved in her slowly.

After all this time, she still responded to him as passionately as their first night together. She was always ready for him, ready to love him and let him love her. Holding her close, Quinn rolled over, pressing Davi against the mattress. He knew her legs would instantly wrap around him, pulling him tight to her, and that was what he wanted. His thrusts were hard and deliberate, filling her to her core. His chest pressed against her breasts.

Davi cradled Quinn's head in her hands. Her fingers instinctively went to his ear lobes and pulled them. He thrust harder in response, making her gasp.

"Only you, love," he murmured as he held her gaze with his brilliant blue eyes. "Only you can touch my ears."

Davi knew that Quinn needed her to make love to him. Her hot kisses and soft caresses and her body aroused and ready for him were the perfect remedies for dealing with Rene all day. He needed to forget about Rene and the love scenes that looked convincing in front of the camera but were torture for him every minute. He needed to go to sleep knowing that Davi was the last woman who kissed him, the last woman to touch him and that the sweet scent that filled his dreams would only be hers.

Quinn moaned his release against her neck as Davi climaxed with him. She held on to him as she waited for him to relax in her arms.

"I love you," he murmured. "You will always be the mistress of my heart."

"I love you, too, Sir Knight," she replied, releasing him from her embrace.

Quinn rolled over, pulled her into his chest, and then kissed the top of her head. Davi closed her eyes as she waited for Quinn's soft snore before joining him in dream-filled sleep.

# five

**"I love the way you feel.** Damn, Davi, your skin's so soft." Quinn's hands caressed her legs, finding their way to her sex. His finger rubbed her clitoris as she squirmed from the intense pleasure. "You're so hot and wet."

"Only for you," Davi said softly, unable to open her tired eyes to her early morning lover.

His lips moved to her ear. His hot breath tickled her as he announced, "There's a pile-up on eastbound 401 just past the airport. Authorities report traffic won't be getting through for an hour or two."

Davi reached blindly for her old clock radio and pushed the off button. She lay motionless for a few minutes, letting the warmth from the dream flow through her. She clenched her thighs tight and felt the soft climax ripple through her. Over four years with the man, her body responded to her fantasies of him as strong as ever.

The aroma of freshly brewed coffee made its way into the bedroom —Quinn's personal reminder to her that it was time to get out of bed. She didn't hear him leave their bed. She never did. He woke early, even early for farmers. Before anyone had stepped foot in the barn to start the five o'clock milking, Quinn was already settled in his RV, getting ready for the day's work.

Davi made a mental plan for her morning—pack bags for kids, pack for Quinn and herself, then book a flight once Quinn let her know his schedule. She groaned. Lying in bed thinking about it wasn't getting it done.

"Get your ass out of bed, Davi. The bags won't pack by themselves."

After a rushed cold shower and a quick tidy-up of the bedroom, Davi packed a travel bag for Quinn and herself. The twins would be waking up soon, so she went down to her office to check the weather forecast for Boston. The forecast was good—hot and dry. She wouldn't have to pack a lot for them. Pyjamas, shorts, and T-shirts would do the trick.

Davi's phone rang.

"Hey, lover," she answered cheerfully. "I had a great dream about you. Thanks."

Quinn laughed. "You're welcome. We aim to please."

"You always do. What's the plan?"

"Clint's got the whole day scheduled for us. It's too short notice for him to change. I'm sorry, love, but it looks like I can't get away early."

"Should I call your dad?"

"No. I'll call him. Book the four-thirty flight, and if I don't get out in time, we'll aim for the eight-thirty flight."

"What's Clint got planned for you? Did he say?"

"You know Clint. He likes to surprise us. I've got to go. I love you. Later."

"I love you, too."

Davi ended the call then headed upstairs. She heard Jack and Stevie talking as she neared their room.

"Good morning," she crooned as she walked into the nursery.

The twins greeted her with smiles and outstretched arms for hugs. It didn't take long to dress them. By the time the twins had their breakfast and were playing in the family room, Davi had time to enjoy her morning coffee while solving the morning paper's crossword puzzle.

Her cell phone rang.

"Well, this is a surprise," she said as she recognized the caller's number. "Hello?"

"Davi, it's Foxx. How are you this morning?"

"Foxx, I'm well, thank you."

"Did you receive my flowers?"

"Yes, I did. Thank you. They are lovely."

"Do you have time to talk?"

"Actually, you phoned at the most opportune time. What's a nine-letter word for trickery?"

"Deception."

"No. It doesn't work."

"Philander."

"No. It starts with a C."

"Chicanery."

"Ooh, I like that one," Davi said excitedly. "Hold on." Davi filled in the spaces with the letters. "It works. Thank you."

"You're welcome."

"You think I'd know that word. I know enough people who practice it."

Foxx cleared his throat before replying. "Davi, please accept my apology. I was way out of line."

"Quinn told me to fire you. He's the very jealous type."

"Would it help if I sent him flowers, too?"

Davi chuckled. "You could try, but he can't be bought. Not even a bottle of his favourite scotch would placate him. He's funny that way. He doesn't like being thought of as a man who cheats."

"I'm sorry, Davi. I don't know what got into me. I promise it won't happen again."

"Foxx—"

"No excuses. I shouldn't have done what I did."

"You're right. You shouldn't have. We work together, and I have to be able to trust you. I can't be worried about you making another pass at me. No more stunts. Got it?"

"Loud and clear."

"Good. Now get back to work and sell some manuscripts to those big assed publishers. Goodbye, Foxx."

"Goodbye, Davi, and thank you."

XO XO XO

Foxx ended the call and then placed his cell phone on the bedside table. "Well, she didn't fire me," he said dully.

Arms wrapped around his neck as a woman's lips came to his ear. "I told you she'd forgive you. Flowers always do the trick for women her age." She nipped his ear playfully.

Foxx turned around quickly and pinned the woman to the bed.

"She won't cheat on Quinn. She's made it clear, and I believe her. You're on your own, sweetheart, unless you decide to change your mind and stay with me."

"Just keep an eye on her and feed her what I tell you. She'll start to doubt Quinn's faithfulness. I know it."

Foxx brought his mouth down to hers and kissed her hungrily. "Give him up and take me. We're good together, Rene. You know we are."

Rene smiled up at him, breathless from his kiss. "It doesn't work that way, lover. My heart belongs to only one man, and it has Quinn's name on it."

"I see something else that has his name on it," Foxx said as his gaze took in her tattoo. "There are ways to get rid of it."

"Maybe, but I think I'll keep it just the same."

"I've been there more times than he has."

Rene smiled. "You were both there at the same time, too. Remember?"

Foxx smirked as he thought of their threesome years ago. "He ran afterward. Not the open-minded party boy you thought he was."

"No, but he'll change once I win him back."

Foxx forced her legs apart and thrust into her. He smiled as he heard Rene cry out.

"You're so sure of yourself, babe. You know what you want. That's one of the things I love about you."

"That and how good I am in bed."

"That's a given."

"No more talking. You've got ten minutes. I'm late for work."

# six

**"I was beginning to think** I was doing this scene solo," Quinn complained as Rene slipped into the seat across from him.

"Did you miss me, sweetie?" Rene cooed as she blew him a kiss. "I had business to take care of. You know how it is."

"Leaking more lies to the tabloids?"

"Now, Quinn, you know I don't do that!" Rene smiled as she batted her fake eyelashes at him.

"Here you go," Clint said happily to them as he placed a bottle of tequila and two shot glasses on the table.

"What's this?" Quinn asked. "It's a bit early in the day to start drinking. What are you up to, old man?"

Clint laughed and then winked at Quinn. "I need the two of you drunk for the next scene. Acting drunk, be damned. You two need to get hammered before I start the cameras rolling."

"On tequila?" Rene asked, clearly horrified at drinking the ill-tasting liquor.

"I've seen the two of you toss back booze like it's soda pop. Tequila is the best leveller I know to bring actors down a notch or two." Clint spread out his arms and pointed to the set. "You're in a god damned bar. People come here to get drunk and to get laid. I want that coming across in this scene. I know the last thing you want, Quinn, is to fuck this woman, so maybe with some tequila under your belt, you might be able to act like you want to. Got it? Now start drinking. I want cameras rolling within the hour." Clint turned and walked away.

Quinn stared at the forty-ounce bottle. "I've never had to drink to act. What about you, Rene?"

"Me neither, but if I have to get drunk, I'm glad it's with you, lover." Rene reached for the bottle and poured them both a drink. "What should we toast to?"

"Not getting sick afterward," Quinn answered as he picked up his shot glass and touched it to Rene's.

"Here's to not getting sick," Rene said, smiling.

They took their shots and grimaced as the burning liquid made its way down their throats.

"Damn," Quinn growled.

Rene laughed. "I didn't know you were such a lightweight. I bet I can hold my own against you, tough guy."

"I don't bet, but I doubt you can. Here's to that," Quinn said as he refilled their glasses then tossed back another shot. He grimaced from the burn. "People don't understand how I can drink scotch, and yet they can drink this poison."

Rene matched his shot. "To our friendship."

Quinn hesitated. "We're not friends, Rene."

Rene gave him her best pout. "How can you say that, Quinn? We've been friends for years. We were lovers once, too. You can't tell me you've forgotten that." She held out her shot glass to him, waiting for him to accept the toast.

Quinn grunted, not knowing if he dreaded the toast or the blasted liquor more. "To our friendship."

"That's better," Rene cooed.

"We were never lovers, Rene. We had sex. That's all."

"Ouch! What happened to the gentleman everyone adores?"

"He's trying to keep it real with his new friend."

"Remember when we went to the Golden Globes, or was it the People's Choice Awards? Anyway, we did shots the whole night because we were bored out of our minds. We had so much fun. We had a connection even then."

Quinn smiled as he remembered the night. Having a photographic memory made it impossible to forget the events, good or bad.

"It was the Golden Globes, and we both had nominations for best actor—"

Rene interrupted him, "Actress for me, and I won."

She held up her shot glass for a refill. Quinn poured another shot.

"Best actress," he agreed.

"And we did do shots."

"Yes."

They touched glasses and drank again.

"And then we left and had great sex in your limo. You were unbelievable."

"You gave me a blow job, and then you passed out. I dropped you off at your hotel. The doorman helped you to your room."

"You made love to me. I remember it as if it were yesterday."

"You passed out, Rene, and I did not take advantage of you in your weakened condition. Maybe it was the doorman. You always said you liked a man in uniform."

"Are you sure?"

"About the uniform? Yes."

"No, asshole. That it wasn't you who made love to me?"

"Most definitely. So you got it on with the doorman? Hope you gave him a big tip."

Rene glowered at him. "I didn't have sex with the doorman. I wouldn't degrade myself in that way. What kind of man does that make you if you left me with the doorman?"

Quinn held her gaze then chuckled. "I helped you to your room, tucked you into your bed, kissed you good night, and left. Are you happy now?"

"No sex?"

"I swear it."

"Well then, here's to you being a gentleman."

"To me, the gentleman."

Quinn downed the shot quickly, no longer able to feel the burn.

"Do you think of me when you're in the backseat of that limo? We did have sex in it more than once. You can't deny that."

As much as he would have liked to, Quinn couldn't deny it. It was a time when he was the hot young actor who every female wanted to screw. At first, Quinn liked the excitement and the rush, but the thrill didn't last long. He rarely instigated the sex. The women were always too eager to service him, unzipping his pants and blowing him without one word said. He hated the emptiness he felt afterward.

"I got rid of the limo. Davi and I now have a minivan with car seats for the twins."

"Tell me something," Rene said as she leaned in toward Quinn. "If you're such a true blue family man, why do you still drive your Porsche? Your Porsche doesn't fit the image of a domesticated Quinn Thomas."

Quinn swallowed another shot of tequila and then answered, "I didn't know the type of car I drove was dependent upon my marital status."

"Come on, lover. Your black and shiny Porsche is an advertisement for a big dick and a man who wants to screw around. It doesn't say wife and two kids on board. You're still not as committed to your precious family as you would like everyone to believe. I'm on to you." Rene took another shot of tequila as if to qualify her opinion.

Quinn shook his head and smiled. He sat back, leaning into the plush upholstery of the booth as he crossed his arms across his chest.

"My wife likes my Porsche. We take rides in it all the time."

"She puts up with it. I know her type. She wants you driving that minivan and staying on the farm under her watchful eye. You don't fool me one bit. You're just putting in the time, playing farmer until you can't take the boredom any longer. That Porsche is the only fun she lets you have. Admit it."

Rene filled their glasses then picked hers up, expecting him to accept the toast.

"You don't know anything about Davi."

Quinn held up his glass to Rene. She touched it with hers.

"Enlighten me then."

"You won't want to hear it."

"I'm a big girl, Quinn. Tell me."

They both took their shots. Quinn leaned forward, his elbows resting on the table between them as he rolled the empty shot glass between his fingers. Rene mirrored Quinn, leaning in to meet him. Quinn's gaze held Rene's, and she felt her heart rate quicken. His eyes were sizzling, with a sexual heat he had kept hidden from the camera. She remembered those eyes from a very long time ago, and she wanted them back for her.

"That Porsche is the car I had in California when I first met Davi. We had hot sex in it. She called it fast and furious. She is the only woman I've ever had in that car. Whenever I sit behind the wheel, I remember how she smelled that day, how she tasted, and how she felt when I made love to her. I can still hear her crying out my name as we both climaxed. I'm not driving that car to show off my dick, Rene. I'm driving that car to be in her, only her."

He poured shots again then held up his glass to Rene, challenging her to take the toast.

"You're a prick. You know that?" Rene said as she tipped her glass to his.

"You asked for the truth."

"I still don't know shit about her."

"And yet you hate her."

"She has you, and that's all I need to know."

"Not her fault. Blame me. I'm the one who went after her."

"Don't make me sick. I've read the magazines. That story doesn't fool me. You had a couple of nights with an old lady and managed to get her pregnant. Marrying her was the honourable thing to do, Mr. Do What's Right. I know that's what it was."

Quinn sat back in his seat again.

"And that, my dear Rene, is why we never had a chance. You didn't know me then, and you still don't know shit about me now."

They were too busy staring at each other to notice Clint's arrival.

He picked up the half-empty bottle and chuckled. "It's only been thirty minutes. How are you two feeling?" Clint looked over at Rene and noticed the red glow of inebriation. He smiled with satisfaction. Then his gaze went to Quinn. "You look pissed, and I mean not in the way I was expecting."

"There is no way in hell I'm going to get drunk and fantasize about fucking Rene. Get that into your thick head, old man. But I sure as hell can fake the face you want, so let's get on with this damned scene before I ram this bottle down someone's throat."

Clint smiled. Quinn may not be drunk, but he had the look Clint wanted for this scene. Clint wanted him angry, angry enough to take on Rene. He needed that emotion for the screen, and he knew Quinn was ready to give it to him, whether he realized it or not.

Clint turned and faced the crew waiting on his command. "They're ready! Let's get this scene going!"

"I have to pee first," Rene announced as she pushed away from the table and headed to the ladies' room.

Moments later, Sarah, Quinn's makeup artist, studio companion, and best friend, showed up with makeup tote in hand to get Quinn ready for the cameras.

"How's it going, sexy?" she asked as she appraised Quinn's face. "You've got a bit of red in your eyes. What have you been up to?"

"Clint had this brilliant idea that we'd act better if we got drunk."

"You? Act better?" Sarah snorted. "That's a good one. What's with the Mr. Grumpy look? I haven't seen that face on you in ages. Rene's getting to you again?"

"No. Rene's being Rene. I can deal with her." Quinn gazed at Sarah thoughtfully. "Tell me something. Would I be a fool to ask Davi to give me another child?"

"Give you a child? Is that what you call it?"

"Sarah, I'm serious. I thought I'd be happy with just the twins, but I can't stop thinking that I'd like to add at least one more to our little family."

"I take it you haven't run the idea by your wife."

"I tried, but she managed to change the subject. She's forty-nine, and she's got everything going for her. She's raised five kids, and she's got the farm and her writing career."

"And a sexy movie star husband who she adores and would do anything for, don't forget."

Quinn smiled. "I love her to death. Can I help it if I want another part of her?"

"Honey, I'm sure she'd love to give you another baby if she could, but you've got to be realistic. Time is not on her side." Sarah saw the disappointment in his eyes as she spoke. "But then again, Davi can't say no to you. She never has."

"It wouldn't be that simple. We wouldn't be able to do it the normal way."

Sarah stopped working on his face. "Go on."

"I had a vasectomy when Davi was pregnant with the twins, and she was fighting for her life. I hated deciding who to save—Davi or the twins. I decided I wouldn't put myself through that again, so I got snipped."

"So you can't have kids then."

"I've got some of my soldiers on ice at the New York fertility clinic. The doctor suggested it to me when I asked for the procedure."

"Ah …"

"Davi won't like the idea of artificial insemination. She breeds her cows that way. She won't want to make her baby like that."

"And you know this for a fact?"

Quinn shook his head. "I have no idea."

"Talk to your wife, gorgeous. You won't know what she thinks unless you talk to her."

"What would you say if you were Davi? You two are close in age."

"Oh no, you don't, Quinn. Don't bring me into this. This discussion is for you and Davi only."

Rene stood behind the booth, concealed by the potted plants sitting on top of the divider. Her mind raced as she heard Quinn's confession. He wasn't as happy as he professed to be. He wanted more, and his wife couldn't give it to him. Rene smiled. She'd found the ace to win back Quinn, and it wouldn't take her long to do it. She was sure of it.

Quinn sat at the bar, drumming his fingers on its polished wood surface. He hated waiting while Clint dealt with a telephone call from a concerned producer. Quinn wanted this workday over. He wanted to go home.

Rene took the stool beside him and offered Quinn an opened bottle of water. He eyed her carefully.

"It's water, Quinn, not tequila if that's what you're thinking. Take mine if you don't trust me." She switched bottles and took a sip from his. "I don't care if I ever see another bottle of that shit again."

"Still feeling it?"

"No, I didn't like the conversation that came with it."

"The truth can be a bitch, can't it, Rene?"

"That wasn't the truth, lover. You like to think that everything is great between the two of you, but how do you know it is?"

"I'm not having this conversation with you."

"Humour me. Let me know how it works with the two of you."

"What do you mean?"

"What happens when you want something, and your wife doesn't? Does her vote count more than yours?"

"Her name is Davina."

Rene rolled her eyes. "Who is in charge of the family—you or your lovely wife, Davina?"

"We're equals."

Rene snorted.

"What's your problem?"

"I don't have a problem. I'm just wondering how you know if your wife truly loves you. Saying I love you and giving great sex can only go so far."

"Spoken from the woman who has so much experience in that area," Quinn replied.

"Don't be an ass. How do you know how much your spouse loves you? How do you know who loves the other the most?"

"There's no scorecard in marriage."

"Oh, get off your high horse. Of course, there's a scorecard. Why else do marriages fail? Divorce happens when one spouse believes they aren't getting as good as they are giving. It's simple economics."

"You are so out of your depth. You haven't got a clue about our marriage."

"Prove me wrong then, Mr. Happily Married Man. Ask your wife for something that's not so easy to give to you. See then if you're happy when you're not getting what you want."

"I wouldn't ask anything from Davi. I don't need proof that she loves me, and she knows damned well that she's the only woman I love." Quinn drained his bottle and stood up from the bar. "I need to take a leak."

"Take your time, lover. I'll be right here waiting for you."

# seven

**"You don't have time for a shower!** You're going to miss your flight if you don't get your ass in that Porsche this minute!" Sarah warned Quinn as she hurried behind him as they headed to Quinn's RV.

"I am not sitting beside my wife on a plane, reeking of that woman's god-awful perfume, Sarah. Five minutes. That's all it will take to wash her stink off me."

Quinn was furious. Clint's conversation with the producer took over an hour. Cast and crew alike sat around twiddling their thumbs while they waited for his return. And then Rene decided to let Clint know that she didn't like being kept waiting. There were temper tantrums and then retake after retake as she purposely flubbed her lines. Rene fought with Quinn over the way he delivered his lines. She fought with Clint over his direction of the scene. She fought with any unfortunate member of the crew who happened to be in her sight. Ninety minutes before his flight's departure time, Quinn stormed off the set.

Sarah readied a change of clothes for Quinn while he showered. She chuckled when she heard Quinn howl when the shower's cold water stung his skin. After all this time, he still couldn't handle the cold showers Davi loved. A minute later, he brushed his teeth then ran his hands through his thick mane of wet hair.

"Thanks, Sarah," he said as he donned the black T-shirt, boxer briefs, and jeans.

"Wear your loafers. You won't want to deal with boots when you've got the twins under each arm."

Quinn nodded in agreement and slipped his feet into his leather loafers. Once he pocketed his cell phone, wallet, and keys to his car, he announced, "There. Five minutes. Let's go."

They headed out of the RV and walked quickly to Quinn's Porsche.

"I'm driving," Sarah said as she held out her hand for the keys.

"No way. It's my car. You can have her when we get to the airport."

Quinn opened the passenger door for Sarah and waited for her to get settled in her seat before he closed her door. Despite his rush to get going, he would not cut back on being a gentleman.

Sarah watched Quinn as he walked quickly around the front of the car. She hadn't seen him this tense in years. It figured. Rene always did this to him, keeping him on edge while she pushed all of his buttons. And they weren't the right buttons either. No matter how hard he tried to resist her, Quinn's temper always got the better of him after a few hours in Rene's company. His anger still darkened his baby blue eyes.

Quinn opened his door and slid in behind the steering wheel. He started the ignition, shifted into first gear and then sped out of the parking lot. They drove in silence for the first five minutes as Quinn took his aggression out on the traffic. Sarah held onto the edge of her seat as Quinn moved expertly from lane to lane, merging onto the Gardiner Expressway. She wanted to yell at him to slow down, but she knew he wouldn't. She knew Quinn well enough to let him simmer down on his own.

Finally, unable to keep silent, Sarah asked him, "Why do you let her get under your skin?"

Quinn looked over at Sarah. "She's not under my skin. She's on it—every chance she gets, Rene's touching me, groping me. I can't stand having her hands on me. And that perfume she wears—I can taste it. It's so heavy." Quinn turned his attention back to the traffic. "She promised me no more games."

"Rene? That's all she ever plays. Some women like to play games. They like the chase."

"Davi never played games."

"That's because she didn't want you!" Sarah smiled at the thought. "The only woman in the world who didn't want to fall for you, and you had to pick her."

Quinn returned her smile. "I didn't have much choice. The heart wants what the heart wants."

They sat in silence for a few moments as they let their thoughts wander. Then Sarah noticed Quinn's driving had changed. He was less aggressive, and his gear shifting became smoother, less rushed. His right hand caressed the gearshift instead of squeezing the life out of it. Then she watched his face. The sparkle was back in his eyes, and he was smiling. His features had softened as though he were thoroughly relaxed and sated. Sarah knew that face. It reminded her of when he'd been with Davi.

"Quinn!"

"What?" Quinn asked as Sarah pulled him out of his thoughts.

"You've got that look, kiddo."

"What look?"

"That 'I've-just-had-sex-with-Davi look.' What are you thinking?"

Quinn winked. "Nothing gets by you, does it, Sarah Bear."

"Not when it's that look. Out with it."

"It's the car. It reminds me of Davi. That's all you need to know."

"Some memory," Sarah said, smiling.

"You better believe it."

Quinn stopped the car in front of the entrance to the departure area of Terminal One of Pearson International Airport.

"She's all yours now, Sarah. Look after her," Quinn said as he put the Porsche in park and killed the engine.

He leaned over and kissed Sarah on her cheek before opening the door and stepping out of the Porsche.

"Have a good visit with your folks and say hi to them for me," Sarah said as Quinn opened the passenger door and offered her his hand.

"I will."

"Now get out of here before you miss your flight. Kiss Davi for me!" As he walked away, she shouted out, "And the twins!" Sarah smiled when she saw Quinn's backhanded wave, and then she got in behind the wheel. "Okay, lovely lady," she purred with delight. "Lover boy's gone. It's time for you and me to get to know each other."

Sarah put the car into gear and headed back toward Toronto, taking the longest route possible.

Quinn entered through the sliding doors then stopped as he looked toward the Air Canada kiosks. Then it happened, as it had many times before—the familiar shouting and people rushing toward him as he was recognized.

"Not now," he grumbled as he tried to find his family in the growing crowd.

Davi knew what the fuss was all about without having to see it. She reached for her cell phone and called Quinn.

"Davi," he answered.

"There's a mob scene just outside of our departure area. Any idea who could be causing it? Do you think someone famous is here?"

"Very funny. Where are you? Help me out here."

"Turn left at the newsstand. We're sitting by the windows. Good luck."

"Thanks."

Davi watched as Quinn made his way to his waiting family. He looked his usual Hollywood gorgeous. Jeans and a T-shirt or designer suits, it didn't matter where Quinn was concerned. There was no hiding who he was.

"Daddy," the twins called as they saw him approach.

"Wait for him," Davi cautioned. "Stay here."

They ignored her. It only took Quinn three strides to meet his children and scoop them up in his arms. He kissed both of them. Immediately, Quinn tuned out the rest of the world. Davi, Stevie, and Jack were his only focus.

"Hey," he said after he kissed Davi.

"You're just in time. I was about to call and see if we were getting on this flight."

"No one was going to stop me from getting here. Let's get checked in."

Airport security arrived as the family tried to make its way to the Air Canada counter. Davi had passports and e-tickets in hand as Quinn carried the twins. Quinn appreciated the efficiency in processing their tickets and boarding passes.

"Stay with the twins while I pick up some treats," Davi whispered in his ear once they made it through security.

Quinn smiled. She couldn't fly without her junk. Licorice and chocolates were her standard fare, but now, Davi focused on more healthy treats with the kids in tow. Although she always managed to stash a few goodies for herself on the bottom of her travel bag.

The twins were easy travellers since Quinn and Davi didn't go anywhere without them. Cars, planes, trains—it didn't matter. As long as they had their comforts, they would go anywhere—teddy bears, books, and tablets with their favourite children's songs and stories.

Once the plane was in the air, Stevie and Jack settled in with their teddy bear tucked under one arm as Quinn read to them in his storytelling voice. It didn't take long before the mop-headed twins were fast asleep and tucked in under a blanket in their seats. Quinn moved over and sat beside Davi. He took her hand and squeezed it gently.

"They don't make it hard at all, do they?"

"They are pros, Quinn. Besides, they're exhausted. They didn't get much of a nap today." She gazed at Quinn and touched his face. "You should take a nap while you can. You look tired."

He sighed heavily. "I know. I'll sleep tonight."

"It will be nice to see your parents. It's been a long time since we last had a visit with them."

"We saw them on my birthday when they stopped by on their way to London."

Davi smiled as she remembered their visit. "I wished they lived closer. The twins love spending time with them."

"I can't see them leaving their posts at Harvard, love. They both enjoy teaching too much."

"We should try to visit them more. Time has a way of passing too quickly."

"Maybe when this project ends, we can go on holiday with them."

Davi chuckled. "What about Cat's wedding? You're not planning on skipping it, are you?"

"The thought had crossed my mind." Quinn still couldn't get his head around the idea that Cat was marrying Chas Elliot, a long-time friend of his.

"You are so bad!"

Quinn leaned over and kissed Davi. "Is this bad?"

"*Mmm,* I've missed that," Davi said dreamily.

"I kiss you all the time."

"I know, but I miss your kisses when you are away, even if it's for just a few hours." She nestled into his shoulder. "So, have you decided on your next project? Another movie or have you found a charity you want to sponsor?"

"Do I have to have something planned? Can't I just go back to being the farmer's husband and play at being a farmer?"

"Where did that come from? You never played at being a farmer."

"Rene. Something she said. It doesn't matter."

"Clint's offer came at the right time. You were getting restless."

"I managed for four years."

"Yes, you did. You wanted to be at home with the twins. It's time you'll always treasure, and I know they are better off for having you around. But—"

"But what?" Quinn interrupted her.

"They start preschool in the fall. You may want to find something else to occupy your time."

Quinn didn't have to farm. The farm was Davi's family business started by her and her late husband, Ross, almost thirty years ago. The couple was well known in the agricultural community for their farming practices. When Ross died suddenly six years ago, Davi continued to run the farm. Quinn joined her and learned all about cows and crops. He loved farm life, and he loved his farm wife. For four years, he stayed away from Hollywood, turning down countless movie offers. Now Davi was handing the farm over to her son, Rich, who had proved himself capable of keeping the family farm going. Davi wanted to concentrate on her husband, the twins, and her writing career.

"Now that you mention it, there is a project I'd like to start."

"Tell me what it is."

"I want to make another baby."

His words were like a vice across her chest, tightening as it squeezed her heart. Her hand went to her chest as if it could ease the pain. Davi sat up and faced Quinn.

"This isn't the place to have this discussion."

"Why? No one can overhear us. Let's talk about this, Davi. I want another child with you. It's that simple. Say yes."

"It's not that simple. I'm forty-nine years old, Quinn."

"I don't see you that way."

"Well, maybe it's time that you did."

"Why?"

"My eggs are old. I don't want to risk the baby's health, and it would be a high-risk pregnancy for me."

"You'd have the best medical care. We'd make sure that you and the baby would be fine."

"Have you looked into this, or do you imagine it?" Davi's gaze searched his face for a sign that he was playing with her. Anything that would put her mind at ease, but his gaze was serious. She knew that look. "Who did you talk to?"

"I called Dr. Marsh, and I called the specialists who looked after you when you were in your coma, and I called the sperm bank where my soldiers are on ice. They're good to go anytime."

"Everyone's good to go but the mother, Quinn. I'm not good to go."

"Why not?"

"Don't you think that five kids are enough for me? Cat's getting married in a few weeks. She and Chas will be starting a family soon. Rich and Beth are working on it already. I won't add to my family when my kids are starting their own." Davi shook her head. "I couldn't do that."

"What about our family, yours, and mine? Forget about your first family. Think about the family you have with me. Why won't you give us another child?"

"Why is this so important to you?"

"I want more of us, Davi. Is that so wrong? I want to have more of you around me. I want to be surrounded by more little Davinas and Quinns."

Davi felt tears start to form. "I thought we were enough for you."

"You are, but am I wrong to want more?"

"Why now?"

"Why not now?"

"You've had almost four years to broach the subject. Not once did you mention having another child. Maybe we could have done something then. Not now, Quinn. It's too late."

"It's never too late. You of all people should know that."

Davi laughed bitterly. "My being so much older, you mean."

"I didn't mean it that way."

"It doesn't matter. I love the twins, but I won't have another child, Quinn. I won't."

"If you could, though, would you have another child? For me?"

Davi gazed into his eyes. She could see the desire that burned for her to say yes.

"Excuse me, I hate to interrupt you, but we're going to be landing in a few minutes. We'll need you to sit with your children."

The voice of the flight attendant was a welcome interruption. Davi smiled up at her and nodded.

Quinn took hold of Davi's wrist. "Answer me. Yes or no. Will you have another child?"

"No," Davi said as she forced back the tears threatening to fall. "I can't."

# eight

**Davi sat with the twins** as she waited for Quinn to deal with their rental car reservation. She tried to keep the twins interested in a car magazine while she heard Quinn's temper getting the better of him.

"What the hell do you mean that you don't have a car for me? We booked it this morning. Look. Here's the confirmation number with the payment details. We've always booked through your company. How can you say there's nothing for us?"

Davi listened intently as the customer service agent tried to explain with great patience and politeness that their computers were down and they had no way of verifying Quinn's rental.

"This makes no sense. Just fill out something on paper the way you used to do it, and I'll sign for it. I want my car."

Again, the customer service agent tried to plead with Quinn to be understanding. "Mr. Thomas, if you don't mind waiting for a moment, I'm sure we'll be able to sort things out."

"How long is a moment in car rental time?"

"I can't say for sure. Fifteen minutes. Maybe more?"

"Fuck it. I'll use another company. Your customer service is unacceptable."

Quinn scrunched his papers into a ball and threw them at the sign hanging behind the counter. He turned and walked back to his waiting family.

"Can you believe it? They don't have a fucking car for us."

"Quinn, your language," Davi said softly to him.

His blue eyes darkened. He was angry and had every reason to be, but this wasn't the Quinn she knew. He was always polite, always in control, especially when there was a chance of someone recording him to post on social media.

"Sit with the twins. I'll see what I can do," Davi said as she stood up and put her hand on his arm. "Try to calm down."

"No. I'll do it. It's time this face got me something I want," Quinn said before he headed off to the next car rental kiosk.

He had a car rented in less than fifteen minutes, and they were on the road headed to his parents' home. The twins sat in their car seats, talking away in their unique twin talk as they played with their teddy bears. Quinn and Davi hadn't spoken a word to each other since leaving the airport.

Then out of the blue, they heard that one word, "Fuck!"

Davi's head turned around immediately to look at the culprit. Jack sat looking down at the car floor where his teddy had fallen.

"Fuck. Fuck. Fuck."

Stevie decided to join him in his lament.

"Jack! Stevie! We don't say that word. It's not a nice word. Daddy said it when he was mad. Daddy shouldn't have said that word."

"Is Daddy bad?" asked Stevie.

"Yes, Daddy was bad to say that word."

Davi looked over at Quinn. "I told you to watch your language. They repeat everything they hear. I'm sure your parents will love it when they hear them say that word. You can tell them how they learned it."

"I'm sure they've said worse when dealing with customer service reps. I wasn't that bad," Quinn grumbled.

"You lost your cool. You never do that."

"Maybe someone pissed me off."

"Me or the service rep?"

Quinn looked at Davi and didn't answer. Davi looked away, unable to bear his gaze.

XO XO XO

"We're at Grandma and Grandpa's," Davi announced as Quinn turned up the driveway.

It was a large two-storey red brick house with a manicured lawn and beautiful gardens. The house was Quinn's present to his parents when he received his first cheque from his first blockbuster movie. It was close to the university, so his parents could walk to the campus. They didn't want to accept the gift, but they couldn't say no when he agreed to keep his name on the deed. The house was well lit, giving a warm and inviting welcome.

Quinn stopped the car and turned off the engine. He gazed at the house, wondering what was waiting for him inside and what made his father's invitation seem so urgent.

Davi touched his arm. "Coming?"

Quinn got out of the car and opened the door to get the twins. Davi got out and gathered their backpacks and their carry-on luggage. Quinn hugged the twins close to his chest, careful as he walked up the stairs to the front door.

The door opened. Quinn's father stood in the doorway smiling at them. John Thomas reached for Jack, hoping for a hug of recognition. Jack didn't disappoint him.

"Poppa," he cried out excitedly.

Immediately, Stevie squirmed to get her hug. Quinn's father offered his free arm, took his granddaughter, and hugged her close. Davi could see the pure joy on his face.

"John," she said warmly. "It's good to see you."

"Davi, please come in. Margaret's been looking forward to seeing you all day. I think it has made her feel better knowing you were coming."

"Dad," Quinn said as he entered the house. He looked into the living room, hoping to find his mother. "Where's Mom?"

"She's upstairs resting. She'll be down shortly. I told her to wait until you arrived and supper was ready. I didn't want her to tire herself out." John turned and walked toward the kitchen. "Come see what your old man has made for supper. I'm getting to be pretty handy in the kitchen if I say so myself."

Quinn and Davi followed them into the kitchen. John had set the table for six, with booster seats and Sesame Street placemats for the twins. Davi smiled when she saw them. They had been Quinn's when he was a toddler. His mother had kept everything of his.

"There's wine in the fridge, Quinn. Help yourself. I know Davi likes the Riesling. You can have a beer if you want, or there's scotch. You know where to find it." Quinn's dad put the twins down on the floor. "Grandpa has to get supper out. Are you hungry?"

The twins nodded their heads and ran to Davi, who was already seated at the table. She let them climb onto her lap and watch as the men prepared drinks and dinner.

"How is Mom?" Quinn asked warily. It wasn't like his mom not to greet him at the door. He didn't like the feeling of uneasiness creeping over him.

"She wants to tell you herself. Let her do it in her own time. Don't push her."

"This is killing me, you realize," Quinn grumbled.

"No. What she has is killing her," Quinn's father said tersely. He stopped what he was doing and looked at his son. "I'm sorry, but you have no idea what's been going on." He continued in a calm voice.

"You're not the lead character in this story, Quinn. You have to wait it out, just like the rest of us."

"Damn it, Dad, tell me what's going on," he pounded his fist against the countertop.

"Son. It's her story to tell. You know better than anyone that your mother has control over her story and no one else."

A silence fell over them. Even the twins knew that something was wrong. The tone of the conversation was unfamiliar to them. The laughter and the gentle cooing of their parents and the loud happy voice of their grandfather were missing. Jack and Stevie looked at each other. In a split second, they voiced their feelings.

"Fuck."

"Excuse me?" John asked. "Did they just say the F word?"

"I'm sorry, John. They heard Quinn say it earlier. I think they've figured out that it fits situations like this."

"Why would you ever swear in front of your children?" John looked at Quinn. "You should know better, Quinn."

Davi gave the twins a loving hug, silently thanking them for interrupting the conversation.

"It's been a rough day." Quinn looked toward Davi. "And I have no excuse. Sorry, Dad."

"What are you apologizing for now?" Margaret Thomas asked as she walked slowly into the kitchen. "Have you been caught by the tabloids being naughty with that co-star of yours?"

Margaret had aged a great deal in two months since Davi and Quinn had last seen her. Her face was thin and ashen. The strain in her face showed her determination to walk into the room. John moved quickly to put his arm around her waist and guide her to a chair.

"You should have called me," he said softly with genuine concern. "You know you shouldn't come down the stairs alone."

"I'm fine," Margaret said as she adjusted the wrap around her shoulders. "I held on to the banister with both hands, and I took my time." She looked up at Quinn, who hadn't moved since she walked into the room. "So? What are you apologizing for, and why that gloomy Gus look on your face? Has someone died?"

Davi recognized the mother's love in Margaret's eyes. Quinn was her pride and joy, and she still worried about him. Quinn called her almost daily to tell her how his day was going and to give her a bit of Hollywood gossip if he had any to share. Davi looked up at Quinn. He couldn't mask his shock at seeing the drastic change in his mother.

"Mom, what's wrong?"

"Have you poured me a glass of wine?" John handed her a drink. "Thank you," she said, then looked at her son lovingly. "Here's to my family. May your children give you as much pride and joy as you have given me—a lifetime's worth and more." Margaret took a sip of her wine. She noticed that Quinn did not take a drink from his glass. "Take a sip, Quinn. It's rude not to accept a toast when given in your honour."

Quinn took a sip from his glass then asked, "What's going on?"

"We'll talk later. Right now, I want to have a nice family dinner and visit with my grandchildren. My story can wait."

Davi and Margaret did their best to keep the conversation flowing through the meal. Quinn kept to himself, only giving one-word answers to questions his mother asked of him. Davi knew he was lost in his thoughts, trying to deal with what he knew was not good news. John chatted with the twins, asking Davi to interpret what they were saying most of the time. Most of it had to do with cows and the farm.

"They look so much like Quinn," Margaret remarked. "Jack's got Quinn's personality. You can see it in his eyes. He's a thinker, isn't he?"

"He's a thinker, and he's a watcher, too. He takes in everything he sees. Stevie's more like me. She takes things as they come. It takes a lot to get her upset. She's the calming influence on Jack."

"Just like her mother," John remarked. "I can see your influence on Quinn. Normally he'd have kicked up a storm to have things done his way."

"My mother told me to wait, and I'm waiting. The storm could still come," Quinn said quietly. His stony expression hid the smouldering anger deep inside him.

"I think I'll take the twins up for a bath and put them to bed. It's late. You can tell your story to Quinn, Margaret. I think he's been very patient to wait this long." Davi got up and helped the twins out of their seats. "Come with Mommy. It's time for a bath."

"I'll join you," Quinn's father offered. "Don't worry about the dishes, Margaret. I'll see to them later." John kissed his wife on the forehead as he left with Davi and the twins.

XO XO XO

The twins splashed in the warm bathwater. Davi leaned against the bathroom counter as John sat on the edge of the tub watching them.

"She has an inoperable brain tumour," John said softly. "She's had it for quite some time. Margaret didn't want Quinn to know while she was still feeling well. She wanted to focus on teaching and finishing her book. And she wanted Quinn to focus on his family. She didn't want him to feel torn between the two of you."

"I would have understood," Davi said.

"Oh, I know. But you know how Quinn handles things like this. It was hard on him when you were in the hospital. He put on a brave front, but we knew it was torture for him. Margaret didn't want him to go through that with her."

"How much time does she have?"

"The pain is quite bad now. She's increasing her pain meds constantly. The doctor said that it doesn't matter at this point. Whatever gets her through the pain is okay. It won't be long. She won't go to the hospital. She wants to die at home."

"I'm so sorry, John."

"Don't be. We've had a great marriage. We've said our goodbyes, Davi."

"You're lucky."

"I know. You didn't get that with Ross. I still don't know which way I would have preferred, though. Having the chance to say goodbye while your loved one suffers or having them taken from you suddenly with no goodbyes but without suffering."

"Having the chance to say goodbye would be my choice."

"Perhaps."

John Thomas was ten years older than Davi. His dark hair had become a beautiful silver grey. He was handsome and charismatic, and he had the sizzling blue bedroom eyes and the irresistible smile, all of which he passed on to his son, except for Quinn's temper. It was Margaret who had that trait.

John turned his attention to the twins. There wasn't anything left to discuss. He and Davi both knew that the most difficult conversation was happening right now, one floor below them.

# nine

**The twins were tucked into bed** and fast asleep. John marvelled at how they clutched their teddy bears, closed their eyes, and fell asleep in seconds.

"They're exhausted," Davi said as she closed the door behind them. "I hope they sleep in tomorrow. I could do with some extra sleep, too."

They made their way downstairs to the living room. Margaret and Quinn sat beside each other on the sofa. Margaret had her arm around her son as his head rested on her breast. Tears streaked down their cheeks.

"Are my grandchildren asleep?" she asked quietly.

"Tucked in and out in seconds," John said proudly.

"They're growing so fast, Davi. Quinn looked just like Jack when he was that age."

"He's his father's son," Davi said, nodding in agreement. "I wonder if he has a photographic memory, too. Did anyone else in the family have the gift?"

"Not that I'm aware of," Margaret answered thoughtfully. "Although, my father was proud of the fact that he could recite *The Mighty Casey at Bat*."

"Only when he had a few drinks under his belt," John reminded her.

"True. And no one dared to correct my father when he made a mistake."

Quinn looked up at his mother. "How can you be so calm about this? You're dying, and you're talking about a fucking baseball poem?"

"Quinn!" Davi gasped.

"What else should I be doing? Wringing my hands and wailing about the unfairness of life?"

Quinn rose to his feet. "I have to leave," he retorted as he stormed out of the room.

They heard the front door slam.

"Go after him, John. He shouldn't be alone."

John nodded in agreement then headed after Quinn.

"Quinn's exhausted. The film he's working on is taking its toll on him. He's—"

"He's my son, Davi. I understand why. I'm always supposed to be here for him. It's why I didn't tell him earlier. I couldn't put him through this."

"I don't think it would have mattered when you told him."

"I think you're right."

"Mothers and sons have a unique relationship."

"I know. I remember your son, Rich, when you were comatose. Everyone tried their best to comfort him, but we just couldn't."

"He still won't talk about that time. Would you like some tea or a cold drink? I could do with something."

"Tea would be lovely, thank you. I feel chilled." Margaret pulled her wrap around her shoulders. "Let's go into the kitchen. It's warmer in there."

Davi brewed a pot of herbal tea while Margaret sat at the kitchen table. Her fingers played with the fringe of the tablecloth.

"I've always admired you, Davi."

"Me? Why?"

"The way you've handled yourself, the way you seem to handle your life with your family, your farm, your writing, and Quinn—you've been a godsend for him."

"I love him."

Margaret closed her eyes and sighed. "When you got shot, I prayed that you would survive so that I wouldn't lose my son. I was sure he'd go mad if you had died."

"Margaret—"

Margaret held up her hand. "I'm not saying he'll go mad when I die. Quinn has you and the children. Be there for him. Keep him strong. That's all I ask of you."

Davi poured two cups of tea and brought them to the table.

"What about John?"

"John will be fine. There's a long list of widows and divorcees waiting for him. He won't be left alone."

"Did you make that list for him?" Davi teased, knowing Margaret's penchant for making to-do lists for her husband.

Margaret smiled. "Yes and no. John's still a catch at his age, Davi, very much like you. He won't have trouble finding someone to keep him company." Margaret reached for Davi's hand. "Do you remember when we first met?"

"How could I forget it? I don't think I had ever been so nervous."

"I could tell how much Quinn loved you, and I knew right away that it didn't matter what I said or thought about you. Quinn was determined to marry you."

"You hid it well, Margaret. You were so protective of Quinn. You didn't like that I was older, and when we said that we weren't sure about going through with the pregnancy, I thought you were going to stab me with your steak knife."

"I wasn't that bad."

"Pretty damned close," Davi chuckled.

"I had to test you."

"I wouldn't have expected anything else from you."

"Look after him for me."

Davi squeezed Margaret's hand and said, "Always."

Margaret got up slowly from her chair. "I need to go back to bed now. Will you help me up to my room?"

Davi assisted Margaret up the stairs to the master bedroom. She waited for Margaret to use the bathroom and then helped her get settled in her bed.

"Sit with me, Davi." Margaret patted the space beside her on the bed then closed her eyes.

Davi took Margaret's hand in hers. "You're in pain," Davi said softly. "Is there anything I can do for you?"

"It will pass." Margaret opened her eyes. "There. It's gone." Margaret pointed to her bedside table. "I have all of my instructions written in a book there. John has read it. He knows my wishes for my funeral. I've listed what I want you to have and what I've left to Stevie and Jack. Quinn can take whatever is his. There's a box of his things in the guest bedroom that I thought he'd want to have. If not, he can ask John for anything."

"You're too organized, Margaret."

"I'm ready." Margaret gazed lovingly at Davi. "I told my son I loved him and that I am so proud to be his mother. He knows how much I love him and you and my grandchildren."

Davi wiped away a tear. "I love you, Margaret."

Margaret motioned for Davi to hand her the bottle of painkillers.

"Here you go," Davi said as she opened it for her.

"I'll only take three. Three should knock me out for the rest of the night." Margaret washed down the pills with a sip of water. "Good night, Davi. Thank you for the company. I've enjoyed our chat."

Davi leaned over and kissed Margaret on the forehead. "Good night, Margaret. Sleep well."

Davi turned out the light then closed the door behind her. Davi checked on the twins who were sleeping soundly, and then she closed the door quietly and walked downstairs to the kitchen. She sat at the table and had a good cry. Davi would cry for Margaret now while she could. She'd have no time for tears when Quinn would need her, and that time would be soon.

It was late, and she craved sleep, but her mind wouldn't shut off. The hot scented bathwater soothed Davi's tired body. A hot soak usually did the trick or lovemaking with Quinn, but he hadn't returned home with his father, so the bath would have to suffice. Davi rested her head against the cool porcelain of the tub and closed her eyes.

Margaret was ready to die. Davi sighed as she thought of Quinn. She knew he'd take his mother's death hard. The two of them were close. Davi understood their bond. She shared one with her eldest son. Why was it that sons were so different? She spent plenty of time with her two adult daughters and had a close bond with them, but it was her son, Rich, who she was closest to. Was it because he was so much like his father? Was it because he seemed to need more guidance from her than the girls did? Davi could never quite figure out the reason why, but she knew that it was true. Davi prayed that she could help Quinn through this.

XO XO XO

She felt his breath on her neck. His kisses were hot and wet. He smelled of scotch.

"Davi," he moaned as his hand slipped between her legs.

"Quinn—"

"Don't say anything. Just let me love you. I need to love you."

She relaxed beneath him, opening her legs to him. His cock pressed against her.

"God, you're so tight," he bit out as he pushed slowly into her.

Davi's hands instinctively went to Quinn's head. She ran her fingers through his hair then found his ears. Only Davi knew how to touch him there.

"Yes, baby, just like that."

Quinn kissed her hard. His tongue stroked the inside of her mouth then mated with her tongue. Davi liked the taste of scotch on Quinn. The smell and the taste of it filled her senses. She kissed him in return, hungry for the taste of her favourite aphrodisiac.

She was doing it to him again. Even in his drunken state, Quinn knew that Davi was pulling him into her. She was never one to lie back and take it. He tensed as he felt the scrape of her nails along his back and the pressure from her legs as she wrapped them around his waist, holding him tight. It turned him on. He swore his cock thickened with every squeeze she gave him.

Quinn broke away from her kiss. He heard her whimper then gasp when his hot mouth found her nipple—biting it, pulling on it with his teeth, then suckling the sensitive tissue. He knew she liked what he was doing to her by how her nails dug into his shoulders. Quinn reached for her hand and brought it to his ear.

"Don't stop."

Her fingers played with his lobe, pulling on it. Quinn lowered his head to her, turning his face so that his ear touched her lips. Her breath was hot against it as her tongue traced along the inside. Davi's lips surrounded the lobe and suckled it.

"Ah fuck," Quinn growled as he felt her tighten around him.

"Love me, Quinn," Davi whispered in his ear. "Harder."

Davi's commands stroked and excited him. He thrust into her, giving her what she wanted.

"Ah, Davi!"

Davi cried out with him, holding him tight as he finished his release. Quinn lay down beside Davi and nestled into her breasts.

"Do you want to talk?"

"No. I just want to hold you. I need to hold you, Davi."

Davi closed her eyes. She let the silence comfort them, and then she soothed him when she felt his hot tears on her breast as he grieved for his mother.

# ten

**Davi woke** with a heavy weight across her chest, Quinn's arm draped protectively over her breasts. He slept soundly while a soft snore escaped from where his face burrowed into his pillow. Davi looked at the bedside clock. She knew she wouldn't be able to fall back to sleep, so she carefully slipped out from underneath Quinn's arm then dressed quietly.

Davi checked on the twins to find them sleeping soundly. She blew a kiss to both of them from the doorway, then headed downstairs to the kitchen.

She found John sitting at the kitchen table drinking his morning coffee and his Saturday morning paper spread out in front of him as the radio played quietly in the background. It looked like a typical morning in the Thomas household except that Margaret wasn't with him.

"Good morning," Davi said as she put her hand on his shoulder. "You're up early. How did it go with Quinn last night?" Davi helped herself to a cup of coffee and joined John at the table.

"We went to my office. I had an unopened bottle of scotch Quinn gave me last time he visited. I had one drink. Quinn drained the bottle. I don't know how my son can stomach an entire bottle and still manage to walk home. I could never drink like that."

"Never?" Davi teased him as she recalled Margaret's stories about John when he was younger.

"Maybe once or twice," he relented. "But I grew out of it."

"He likes his scotch, although he hasn't drunk that much in ages. I hope he can sleep it off this morning." Davi put her hand on John's. "How's Margaret?"

"She had a good sleep, but she woke up a couple of hours ago in a lot of pain. She doubled her pain meds again, and it didn't seem to help much. I told her to take more, to do whatever helped her. She's resting now. I think it won't be long now before—" John didn't finish. The words were too hard to say.

"What would you like to do today? The weather forecast is hot and sunny. Should we spend the day in the backyard out by the pool? We can keep the twins busy, and Margaret can rest out on the patio and watch them. We'll keep her comfortable and enjoy her company."

John smiled, his eyes sparkling. "Margaret would love that, Davi. She wants to spend time with you and the twins. We can barbeque and have a real family day. We've got everything we need."

Davi heard laughter coming down the hallway toward the kitchen. Her heart skipped a beat as she watched Quinn enter the kitchen with the twins in his arms. His shaggy brown hair looked just fucked perfect. He wore no shirt, showing off his perfect abs that invited her gaze down to his jeans resting low on his hips.

"Good morning, Mommy," Quinn growled happily. "These two decided it would be fun to jump on Daddy while he was sleeping."

Jack and Stevie's smiles touched their eyes, just like Quinn's smile touched his.

"I'm sorry," Davi said as she got up and took Stevie from him. "I thought they'd sleep for at least another hour." Davi kissed Stevie and put her in her booster seat. "Do you want to go back to bed?" she asked Quinn.

"No. I'm up now. No sense in wasting the day," he answered as he placed Jack in his booster seat. He leaned toward Davi and kissed her. "I'm sorry for yesterday."

"It's forgotten," she answered softly.

"Right then!" Quinn said as he clapped his hands. "Who wants pancakes?"

"Me!" the twins chorused.

"We've decided to spend the day out by the pool," Quinn's father said happily. "Your mother will love it."

"How is she?" Quinn asked cautiously.

"She had a good night. She was awake earlier but is resting now. I'll go check on her later."

"I'm sorry for how I behaved last night. I shouldn't have."

"Don't, Quinn. You did nothing wrong," John said as he made a funny face at the twins. "I thought you said you were going to make pancakes. I think there are two little people here waiting for their breakfast."

"And me," Davi added. "I'm starved. Pancakes are the one thing I cannot make," Davi said with regret. "It doesn't matter what I do. They never turn out right. Quinn is our official pancake maker."

"And egg cooker, and bottle washer and all-round cook," Quinn added happily.

"I can cook," Davi protested. "It's just that it's such a treat when someone else does it. And Quinn does it so well."

"You can thank my mother for that," Quinn said proudly.

"I have thanked her many times for that and other things about you."

"Do I get any thanks?" John asked with feigned indignation.

"Of course you do! You gave Quinn his amazing good looks, his sparkling eyes, and his sex appeal."

"Sex appeal?" Quinn asked.

"Of course, Quinn, your dad is extremely sexy. You didn't come by it all on your own, you know. You have him to thank for it."

"You know, my son has never thanked us for anything we passed on to him, Davi. He assumes everything he is has nothing to do with us. He's very conceited," John teased.

"Well, he's an actor, John. Quinn has to be conceited." Davi winked at him. "Ego's what got him on the silver screen."

"I don't have an ego, Davi. You of all people should know that."

Davi watched Quinn as he made breakfast. He was a natural in the kitchen, relaxed and confident in what he was doing. Quinn was right. He didn't have much of an ego, at least a Hollywood ego. Quinn was comfortable in his skin, not caring what he looked like as long as Davi liked what she saw. He was only for her—a promise he made often.

Quinn caught her watching him. He winked at her, knowing that look and loving it. She was the only woman he ever wanted to look at him that way. She blew him a kiss in response.

Breakfast was delicious and messy. The twins ended up with syrup in their hair, on their hands and all over their pyjamas. Davi didn't know where to start to clean them up.

"Take them into the pool," John suggested. "It's warm, just like a bath. Strip them down to their birthday suits. They'll be fine."

"Are you sure?" Davi asked. "They're pretty sticky."

"Don't worry about it. Enjoy it. That's why we have the pool."

Quinn didn't need convincing. His blue eyes sparkled with mischief, showing everyone that he was about to have fun.

"Come on, kiddies, let's go for a swim." He laughed as he scooped them out of their booster seats and headed outside toward the pool.

Davi got up and followed close behind. Both children stood still while their parents peeled off their sticky clothes. Quinn began unzipping his jeans.

"You're going to swim in your birthday suit, too?"

"Of course! You've seen me naked before, and so have the kids. I don't think my dad will care, and there aren't any neighbours who can look in over the fence." Quinn grabbed Davi and pulled her in close. "Why don't you join us? I know you like to skinny dip." His breath was hot against her ear.

"Maybe another time, stud. I'll get some towels while you're having fun."

Quinn dove into the pool then swam back to the side to gather his children. Neither child had a fear of the water. They eagerly jumped into Quinn's muscled arms and laughed before he dunked them under the water.

John met Davi at the kitchen door with an armload of towels.

"Here you go. I'm going to bring Margaret out here. She'll want to see this."

Davi took the towels and sat in a chair. She smiled and laughed along with the three in the pool.

"You really should come in," Quinn teased her. "We could have some fun, just the two of us."

"Who'll watch these two while we're having fun?" Davi shook her head. "I don't think so, but thank you for the offer."

"Hear that, kiddies? Mommy doesn't want to come in and have fun with us. We'll just have to show her how much fun she's missing."

Quinn whispered in their ears. Davi saw their faces light up with mischief, and their sparkling eyes matched their father's.

"No, Quinn, don't you dare."

She was too late. Immediately, the twins started splashing her. Davi scrambled out of her chair before she was soaked right through.

"I'll have to remember to thank you for this later, Daddy," Davi said, trying to feign anger.

"I'm looking forward to it, Mommy." Quinn laughed, then took the twins further out into the pool.

Davi moved her chair far enough away to be safe from any more splashing. She chuckled as she dabbed at the wet spots on her T-shirt.

"Has my son been up to his usual antics?" Margaret asked as John led her to the chaise lounge.

"Good morning, Margaret," Davi said as she got up to help Margaret get comfortable. "He's full of mischief this morning. I'm staying away from the water while he's in there. It's not safe."

Margaret laughed as she waved to her son and grandchildren in the swimming pool. "Good morning," she called out.

Davi heard the strain in Margaret's voice. She knew that it took every ounce of strength she had to raise her voice.

"What can I do for you, Margaret?"

"Enjoy the day with me, Davi. Just enjoy the day."

The morning turned quickly into the afternoon. The twins played, and the adults focused on them, trying to block out the inevitable hovering so close around them. Margaret smiled and laughed at the twins as they played with their father and grandfather.

"They're so alike, aren't they? That Thomas gene is pretty strong."

"Oh, there are some of your genes in there, too, Margaret. You left your mark."

"Yes, I did, but it's the temperament. Sometimes that isn't such an admirable trait to pass on to one's child."

"You passed on the right parts, Margaret. You can be proud of that." Davi squeezed Margaret's cold hand.

"I'd like to go for a swim," Margaret announced. "John," she called out. "Let's go for a swim, shall we?"

"I'll go get your swimsuit," Davi offered.

"No." Margaret raised her hand in protest. "I'll go in my underwear. That's all a swimsuit is anyway. Just help me out of my clothes, will you, Davi?"

Davi helped Margaret undress as she peeled off the heavy sweater, the loose T-shirt, and the baggy sweat pants.

Davi smiled as Margaret's underwear became visible. "Very nice, Margaret. I like your style."

"Just because I'm old doesn't mean I have to wear granny pants in beige, Davi. My husband bought these for me. Aren't they beautiful?"

Margaret stood up, showing off her bright pink lingerie. They were her colours, and they suited her beautifully. John came up to Margaret and took her in his arms. He hugged her close.

"Isn't she the most beautiful woman in the world?"

"Yes, she is," Davi answered. She felt Quinn behind her, his hand on her waist.

"Always has been," Quinn added.

"Thank you. Now take me swimming." Margaret held out her hand to John, who then led her slowly to the swimming pool stairs.

The twins sat on the edge of the pool and watched their grandparents. They waved to them as they splashed their feet in the water. Davi sat beside them and tried not to watch. She felt like a voyeur as John held Margaret in his arms and walked with her in the pool. Margaret's thin arms wrapped around his neck as her head rested against his chest.

Davi remembered when Quinn carried her in the sea in Aruba. She remembered the sound of his heart beating when she rested her head against his chest and the waves splashing against them. How easily Quinn moved through the water with her in his arms. Davi remembered how safe and loved Quinn's embrace made her feel. She gazed at Quinn and wondered where his thoughts were taking him.

Time seemed to stand still. Everyone was quiet as the couple moved through the water. It was as though everyone knew that this was the last dance before Margaret would be leaving the party.

"I can't watch this," Quinn whispered roughly in Davi's ear. "I'm going for a walk. I'll be back."

Davi nodded. She didn't want Quinn to see her tears, and she knew he didn't want her to see his.

It wasn't long before Margaret cupped John's face with the palm of her hand. She gazed into his eyes and smiled at him. "It's time."

John carried Margaret out of the pool, and Davi met them with dry towels. She wrapped a towel around Margaret while John dried himself.

Davi kissed Margaret on her forehead. "I love you, Margaret."

Margaret smiled back at her. "Take care of him, Davi. I trust you to love him always."

"Always."

The twins ran to Margaret and hugged her legs. She bent down as best she could and kissed them.

"Grandma loves you."

John picked Margaret up and cradled her in his arms before heading into the house. Davi picked up her phone and called Quinn. It went directly to his voicemail.

"Come home, Quinn. It's time." Davi ended the call.

She stayed behind with the twins and read them a story, hoping to give John and Margaret quiet and private time. When the twins became restless, Davi took them upstairs for their nap. Before she could stop them, the twins ran off to their grandparents' bedroom. She called out to them, but it was too late. Jack and Stevie pushed the door open and ran to the bed.

Margaret wore her satin nightgown. Her hair was dried and brushed. John sat beside her on the bed, holding her hand and talking to her. Davi heard his quiet words. They were the words of a lover's final goodbye.

John turned to look at them. "She went quickly, just like she wanted. Doesn't she look beautiful?"

"Is Grandma sleeping?" Stevie asked in her quiet voice.

Davi knelt beside them by the bed. "Grandma's dead, Stevie. She died."

"Oh," the twins answered together. "Grandma's dead."

"Like the baby calf?"

Stevie and Jack had witnessed the death of a premature calf. Davi worked tirelessly to keep the calf alive without success. Davi tried her best to explain death to her children.

"Yes, Stevie, just like the baby calf. Grandma was sick, and she died."

Stevie reached out to touch her grandmother and stroked her arm. Jack followed soon after, gently stroking his grandmother's hand.

"Bye-bye, Grandma," they said softly.

"Do they truly know that she's dead?" John asked quietly.

"As much as a four-year-old can comprehend it, John. They've seen dead animals on the farm and have touched them. They know they don't wake up, that they're dead. Jack and Stevie know that Margaret's gone, and they accept it."

"I wouldn't mind being four years old right now."

"Neither would I."

Stevie put her hand on Davi's shoulder.

"They're ready for their nap. I'll put them to bed then come back. I called Quinn and left a message on his voicemail."

"Thank you."

Davi left with her children and closed the door behind her.

"Come home, Quinn," she whispered. "Your family needs you."

Davi was thankful that the twins accepted what had happened. They clutched their teddy bears and fell asleep soon after their heads touched their pillows. She met Quinn at the top of the stairs as she came out of the twins' room. She held out her arms to him.

"She went peacefully, Quinn. Just the way she wanted."

Quinn hugged Davi close. "I couldn't be here and watch. I'm sorry. It brought back the memories of when I almost lost you. I just couldn't—"

"Don't apologize. You did nothing wrong." Davi pulled away and looked up at him. "Your dad is sitting with her. Do you want to go in?"

"Yes. Come with me."

Quinn took Davi's hand and walked with her to his parents' bedroom. His father sat in the armchair beside the bed, reading Margaret's journal. He looked up as Quinn and Davi entered the room then rose to greet his son. Quinn accepted his father's embrace and hugged him back.

Quinn released his dad then knelt beside the bed. He gazed at his mother. He thought he had no more tears to shed for her, but he was wrong. The tears flowed as he rested his head against her hand.

John left the room and let Quinn be with his mother one last time. Davi sat in the armchair, waiting to comfort her husband.

There was a light knock on the door before the family doctor and John entered the room. Quinn stood up, his back to them. Quinn ran his hands through his hair and straightened his shoulders before facing the others in the room.

"Hello, Doctor," he said as he extended his hand to him. "I wish it were under better circumstances to see you again."

"Quinn, your mother was a wonderful woman. I'm so sorry for your loss."

"Doctor," Davi greeted him. "We'll leave you alone." Davi put her hand on Quinn's arm. "Let's go, Quinn."

"Take this," John said, handing her Margaret's journal. "She's written her instructions inside."

Davi pressed the journal to her chest as she walked with Quinn to the kitchen.

"I'll make coffee," she offered. "Do you want something to eat?"

"Just coffee," Quinn answered. He sat down at the kitchen table and pulled out his cell phone from his jeans pocket. "I don't know if I can do this, Davi. I don't know if I can phone the gang."

"There's no rush. Let's read through her journal first. Maybe she doesn't want a funeral. We need to know your mom's wishes before we phone everyone. They're bound to have questions."

Davi sat at the table and opened the journal. She read the first sentence aloud, "Quinn, don't be sad for me. I lived a full life. Always remember that I love you." Davi wiped away her tears.

"She always had to have the last word."

"Just like her son."

"That's not true."

Davi rolled her eyes and then continued to read through the first few pages.

"She has everything she wants right down to the smallest detail. Amazing." She smiled.

"What?"

"Margaret wants cremation, and she's picked out the urn. She wants the funeral service to be on Wednesday because it's the same day of the week that she was born. She has a guest list made up of family and a few close friends. The reception afterward will be here, and she's made a list of the food and wine, and the caterer is on standby." Davi shook her head. "Quinn, she didn't miss a thing. Even her favourite flowers are listed and the music she wants to have played."

"Did she mention what she wants me to wear?"

"Let's see." Davi scanned the next page. She chuckled. "Margaret writes that she knows that you'll dress appropriately. However, she wants you to wear underwear. She doesn't care what colour."

"She didn't!"

"It's right here, love. Your mother knew everything about you. What a wicked sense of humour."

Quinn took the book from Davi and scanned the page. A sparkle came to his eyes.

"She did write that!"

"Remember when the paparazzi published that picture of you? Margaret called to tell you that going commando was only for men not as endowed as yourself. What did she say?"

"There are only two women who should ever see your penis—your mother and your wife. Let the rest fantasize about the gift your mother gave you and the gift you give your wife every day."

"Quinn, this is so your mother. I'll bet she's got some other requests in here for you." Davi snatched the book from Quinn. "I guess we've got our homework cut out for us."

# eleven

**Davi sat out by the pool,** stealing a brief moment of quiet. She savoured the steaming cup of coffee and the cookie the caterer had placed in her hands. They hadn't spoken, but the woman who Davi had just met knew that Davi was running on empty. She hadn't slept well since Margaret had passed away a few days ago.

Quinn wasn't coming to bed, or if he did, it wasn't until early morning just before Davi rose to look after the twins. He wouldn't talk to her. It was as though something switched off in him a few hours after his mother died. No matter how hard she tried, Davi couldn't reach him. A simple yes or no was all she would get in answer to her questions. Quinn remained silent. It wasn't only Davi he ignored. He barely acknowledged his father or the twins.

It was exhausting keeping Jack and Stevie away from their father. The four-year-olds didn't understand why Daddy couldn't play or read them a bedtime story. They didn't understand why Mommy would take them for a walk without Daddy. Daddy had always gone on walks with them and played with them.

Margaret's funeral would be in an hour. Davi's adult children had flown in from Toronto the previous night. They were somewhere in the house, keeping their half-siblings busy. Quinn had made himself scarce this morning. Davi hadn't seen him since he locked himself in his father's study under the pretence of preparing his mother's eulogy.

Cat's voice interrupted Davi from her thoughts. "Mom, you have to come inside. I think Quinn's lost it. He's arguing with Jack, and he's losing."

"Why is he arguing with Jack?" Davi asked as she put down her mug of coffee and headed to where Cat was standing.

"It's over a truck. I can't quite figure out Jack, and Quinn definitely can't. You've got to get in there. I've never seen Quinn like this."

Davi entered the living room to find Quinn sitting in an armchair holding a tiny toy truck while Jack stood in front of him. Jack's eyes were tearing as he stared up at his father. As always, Jack's wingman, Stevie, held onto Jack's hand and stared at her father in united defiance.

"No, Jack, Grandma is not a truck."

"Truck," Jack said with more determination as though saying it louder would make Quinn understand.

"What's the problem here?" Davi asked as she kneeled beside her little ones.

"Jack's telling me my mother's a truck. I don't know where he got that idea, but I can't get him to shut up about it. Will you deal with him?"

Davi looked at Quinn, swallowing the urge to yell at him. Jack was four years old. He didn't deserve that tone of voice. Ever. "Quinn, calm down. Please."

She then looked at the truck Jack held in his tiny hand and then at the assortment of cars and trucks on the floor—old toys of Quinn's from when he was a young boy. Davi picked up an old station wagon and showed it to Jack.

"Jack, honey, Grandma isn't in the truck. She went in a car that looks like this."

"Car?" Jack repeated.

"Yep, car," Stevie said in agreement.

"Yes, it's called a hearse, but you can call it a car. When Grandma died, she went away in this, a hearse, not a truck."

Jack took the car from Davi and faced his father. "Grandma died, and she went in a car." He nodded his head to emphasize what he was saying.

"I still don't understand him at all."

"If you'd only stop to think about it, he's making perfect sense. When an animal dies, we call in the dead wagon to take the body away. You know that. It's a truck that looks very similar to this one Jack was showing you. Jack knows that your mother died. He just assumed that the dead wagon came and got her. He was telling you that he knew what happened to her body."

"What the hell, Davi! Why would you let them know about things like that? They shouldn't know about dead animals and dying. My God, what were you thinking?"

"I'm teaching my children about the cycle of life on the farm. Cows are born, grow up, and sometimes they get sick and die. Sometimes they don't have the chance to grow up. They die. All of my children have seen a calf's birth, and they've touched a dead animal. They've seen the body loaded onto the dead wagon and taken away. They know that it's all part of life."

"Those were animals."

"I know your mother wasn't an animal, but it doesn't make death any different. Jack and Stevie both touched her and said goodbye to her when she died. They weren't afraid of death and accepted it. When Jack saw your mother's body taken from the house, he didn't know any different. He thought it was a truck taking her away. He was only trying to tell you what you weren't around to witness for yourself."

Davi was right. Quinn couldn't stay in the house when the hearse arrived. He walked around the neighbourhood until he was sure it had left. He didn't know that Jack had witnessed his mother's body leave the house.

"Please apologize to Jack. You've upset him and everyone else in this room."

Quinn's shoulders dropped as he exhaled heavily. "I'm sorry. I'm an idiot." He opened his arms to Jack and Stevie. "Daddy's sorry. Daddy didn't understand you, Jack. You are right. Grandma died, then she went away in a car."

The twins fell into Quinn's arms. His soft voice reassured them that everything was right with their world again. Quinn held them close until they squirmed free.

"Idiot," they chirped as they went back to play with the toy trucks.

Davi stood up and offered her hand to Quinn. "Come with me. We need to talk."

Davi led Quinn out of the living room into his father's study. She closed the door behind them.

Davi pointed to a chair. "Sit."

Quinn sat in the chair. "I'm sorry."

"For what? Taking your temper out on Jack or being an ass for the past few days? Taking your temper out on the twins is not acceptable. Ignoring the rest of us is just plain rude."

Quinn shoved his hands through his hair. "I had no idea what he was talking about."

"No excuses. You weren't listening to Jack. If you had, you would have figured it out. You've seen the dead wagon before. You knew it was a truck that looked just like the one Jack was showing you. He's a smart little boy, smarter than his father at times."

"Way smarter," Quinn agreed. "He gets it from his mother. No argument there."

"I don't want there to be any arguments, Quinn. Can't you see? You've been short with everyone the past few days. No one has the nerve to say anything to you. I'm tired of being the go-between. I can't do it all the time."

"I'm sorry."

"I don't want your apologies. I want you to pull yourself together. Man up."

Quinn looked up at his wife. "Man up?" His arched brow emphasized the surprise in his tone.

"Yes. Be the man that we all know you are. Quinn, you're not the only person to mourn your mother. Be supportive of your dad. Be supportive of your friends and family who are grieving. Believe it or not, we all need a hug, too. Margaret was special to all of us."

"I know."

Davi knelt beside Quinn. "I know it hurts, but you've got to move on. Your mom had a great life. She loved you and your father, and she was so proud of you. Let her be proud of you today. Pull yourself together for today."

"Man up?" Quinn couldn't let it go. "Aren't men allowed to grieve?"

"Everyone is allowed to grieve. You can find your time to grieve later when your family doesn't depend on you to help them through this difficult time. Man up, put on your best Hollywood, Quinn. It doesn't matter to me right now. Just help your family get through this day. I can't do it all by myself. I need you."

Quinn shook his head. "God, I can be such an ass, can't I? I'm feeling so sorry for myself that I can't see that my family needs me. You deserve better from me."

"Let's try to manage today. I'll be right beside you."

Quinn kissed Davi tenderly. "Thank you."

"You're welcome."

There was a rap at the door. "The limos are here. It's time to go."

Davi stood up with Quinn. She adjusted his tie and ran her hand through his perfectly mussed hair, then kissed him once more.

"I love you."

"I love you, too. Come on, let's go."

Quinn and Davi walked out to the living room to find their family waiting for them.

"I'm sorry for being so caught up in my grief that I couldn't see anyone else's." Quinn bent down and picked up Jack and Stevie. "I need to be more like these two and their mom. Is everyone ready? We don't want to keep Margaret waiting."

XO XO XO

"What is she doing here?" Cat hissed in Davi's ear when she saw Rene Adams taking a seat in a nearby pew.

"She's allowed to come and pay her respects, Cat. Don't make it into something it isn't."

"Tell her that." Cat hated how Rene played the press, making it look like something was going on between Quinn and her. She never missed an opportunity to have her hands on Quinn and to have that opportunity photographed. "I don't trust her. She'll turn this into a media circus."

"It already is."

Davi was thankful that Jake, Quinn's long-time head of security, had been ready for the onslaught of paparazzi and news reporters. The parking lot to the church had been cordoned off for guests only. From across the street, cameras and news reporters focused on the church, the grieving family, and guests.

The funeral service was as Margaret had planned. The minister, a family friend, read one passage from the Bible then read one of Margaret's favourite poems. He spoke of Margaret with affection and respect.

When it was time for Quinn to give the eulogy, Davi asked him, "Would you like me to stand with you?"

"No. Just keep your eyes on me. I need to see your face," Quinn whispered back to her.

Quinn didn't have any papers with him. He stood at the podium and gazed at his family and friends.

"My mother's life focused on stories. She loved to read stories and talk about them—what the stories meant, what the authors were experiencing when they wrote their story, and how our own life's story was affected by what we read. Her class was one of the most popular English Literature courses on campus. I audited her class when I could, and I left thoroughly awed and amazed every time.

Mom believed that our life was our story. We owned it, and no one else had the right to impose their own beliefs or standards on it. She taught me to take ownership of my life. She supported every choice I made, regardless of her agreeing or disagreeing with me. It was my story to be lived the way I chose."

Quinn chuckled. "However, my mother believed that it was perfectly acceptable to tell me when my choices weren't the best. Every once in a while, when she didn't like what she read in the tabloids, she would text me with the words, "plot twist." I knew then that it was time to smarten up. You see, with having ownership of your life, there comes a great deal of responsibility. Responsibility to yourself to be the best person you can be, responsibility to those who you love and who love you, and responsibility to those who depend on you—whether it's your family, your co-workers or your fans.

Mom was very open about her own story. She had no secrets. She told me once that she had spent her life researching others' stories and didn't want anyone to misinterpret hers. It was what it was. No reading between the lines, no asking what if? Mom had no regrets. She did everything she wanted to do and then died as she had planned, with all the goodbyes said, and no page left unturned.

I must admit that this wasn't a plot twist I was expecting. My mother's story ended much too soon." Quinn paused and took a deep breath. "I am so grateful to have been a part of Margaret's story. I love you, Mom. Forever."

Quinn returned to the pew and sat beside Davi. Jack and Stevie both reached for him to hug him.

**XO XO XO**

"She is so dead," Cat snarled under her breath, glowering at Rene Adams as she watched her from the kitchen window.

Rene had managed to get Quinn alone by the pool. Her hand rested on his arm as she spoke to him.

"Cat, leave it alone," her fiancé Chas Elliot warned her. "Your mom is fine with her being here. You should do the same."

"She's after him, always after him." Cat couldn't believe the audacity of that woman—wearing killer heels and dressed in a short black dress that showed off every fake oversized curve. "The woman isn't in mourning. She's in heat."

"He hasn't taken the bait. Quinn's with your mom. Believe me, babe, that man is devoted to your mom." Chas hugged Cat from behind and kissed the top of her head. "I hope you're that protective over me."

"Don't ever test me to find out, cowboy."

"Come on. Let's give Quinn some privacy. Your mom asked that we mingle with the guests while she puts the twins down for their nap."

"Fine, but if they are still out there in ten minutes, I'm going out there and pushing that tramp into the pool."

## XO XO XO

"Your step-daughter is watching us, Quinn. Do you think she's going to tell her mommy?"

"Don't, Rene. Be a bitch another time, but not today, okay? It's my mother's funeral."

Rene grimaced. "I'm sorry, Quinn. You're right. No more Rene the bitch today. Truce, okay?"

"Fine." Quinn led Rene to the patio's sitting area and offered her a seat. "Thanks for coming. I appreciate it."

"Quinn, you don't have to thank me. I know what it's like to lose a parent. I lost my mom too soon. One of my biggest regrets is that she didn't see me make it in the movies."

"I didn't know that."

"There's a lot that you don't know about me. You and I are now members of the same club. We're both motherless children now."

"Not quite children, Rene."

"You know what I mean. We don't have moms to call whenever we need someone to listen to our complaints or just chat with." Rene sensed that she was reaching him. "There's nothing that can make us feel as good as a mother's kind words."

"I have Davi."

Rene bit down on her lip, trying desperately to bite back the smart assed remark about Davi's age. "You're lucky. I don't have anyone."

"Maybe if you stopped focusing on me, you'd have someone in your life."

"Maybe, but I'm not in any hurry." Rene hooked her arm through Quinn's and leaned against him. "Have you ever thought about why we have kids?"

"The condom broke?"

"So that's what happened with you and Davina. I knew it had to be an accident."

Quinn grimaced. "I was joking, and that's not what happened." He picked at an imaginary piece of lint on his pant leg as he pondered the question. "We have kids to complete our life. There is no greater gift than a child."

"Wow. Aren't you deep today?"

"It's my mother's funeral, Rene."

"Sorry. Geez." Rene pouted. "I think we're more selfish than that. We want a part of ourselves to go on for generations. It's something like living vicariously through our offspring and theirs and so on."

Quinn gazed down at Rene. A bemused smile touched his face. "What the hell are you talking about?"

"You are all that remains of your mother, and your twins will be all that remains of you. You are the perfect father. The world needs more Quinns."

"You think so?"

"I saw how your two clung to you at the funeral. Jack and Stevie adore you. You should have more kids."

"Thanks for the vote of confidence, but I don't think it's going to happen."

"So, the two of you have decided on not having any more?"

"Let's just say that there hasn't been the opportunity to discuss it since we got here."

"Then you still want them. You haven't changed your mind."

"Rene, I'm not comfortable talking about this with you."

"Why?"

"Because I should be talking to Davi about having kids, not you."

"I'll give you children. It doesn't matter how many. I'll give you ten if you want."

"Rene—"

"Quinn, I'm thirty years old. I love you, and deep down, I know that you love me. You're just so caught up in this mess with Davi that you can't see your way out of it. I'm offering you a lifeline. I'll give you as many babies as you want."

"Christ," Quinn said as he pulled away from her. "Are you crazy?"

"I assure you, Quinn, that I am not crazy. All you have to do is say yes."

"I had a vasectomy. I can't give you what you want."

"Have a reversal. I read that men can have their vasectomy reversed now with great success. A lot of the old-timers do it when they find themselves a twenty-something wife."

"Stop it, Rene. Please just stop it."

"I know you want more children, Quinn. Think about what I said. I'll give you what you want."

"Is everything okay here?" Jake Goodman asked as he approached the couple.

Rene turned to him and gave him her best sex kitten smile. "Well, hello there, big guy, how are you?" she purred as she rose to her feet.

"Rene," Jake said, giving her a polite smile. "You are looking well."

"Thank you. You don't look so bad yourself. Still married?" Rene asked while patting his lapel and eying him appreciatively.

Jake stood about six feet five inches tall, with a body builder's physique. He kept his hair cropped short, military-style.

"Yes."

"Why is it that all the handsome ones are taken?" She turned to Quinn. "Think about my offer, Quinn. Don't take too long." She turned and walked toward the house.

Jake shook his head in bemusement. "That woman—"

Quinn's gaze went to the plate of sandwiches Jake held in his hands. "Are those for me by any chance?"

Jake handed Quinn the plate then sat beside him. "Cat wanted to come out here and tear Rene's hair out. I thought it best that I come out here instead."

"She's very protective of me," Quinn said before he took a bite of his roast beef sandwich.

"We all are, especially when that blonde hellion is around you." Jake took a sandwich from the plate and finished it in two bites. "We're going to miss your mom, Quinn. She was quite the lady."

"Thanks, man." Quinn reached for another sandwich and stared toward the swimming pool. "Are you and Sue going to have more kids? Do you talk about it?"

"We did talk about it shortly after Connor was born."

"And?"

"And I love the two we have, and if we have one or two more, I'll be just as happy."

"So when will you decide to have more?"

"It's Sue's decision. Rachel is seven, and Connor is five now. If Sue wants more children, she'll go off the pill, and if she doesn't, then one day she'll tell me it's time to get snipped."

"Just like that? You're leaving it up to her?"

"Happy wife means a happy life, man." Jake chuckled. "I want Sue to be happy. If two kids are all she wants, I'm happy with that. If she wants more, I'll arrive home one day, and she'll show me the pregnancy stick. That's the deal." Jake looked at Quinn with concern. "Why the sudden interest in kids?"

"Just thinking."

"About?"

"I'm just thinking, Jake. Funerals have a way of making you think of all kinds of things."

# twelve

**Davi awoke shortly after midnight** to find that she was alone. Quinn hadn't slept with her since Margaret's funeral two days ago. Friends and family were long gone, leaving Davi to deal with a grieving father-in-law, a grieving husband and two busy four-year-olds.

She found Quinn in John's study with his attention focused on the laptop screen in front of him.

"Quinn," she said as she watched him from the doorway. "Come to bed. It's late."

He didn't look away from the screen. "I can't."

"What are you looking at?" Davi asked as she made her way to the desk. She stopped behind him and gripped his shoulders as she leaned closer to read the laptop screen. "Pregnancy in older women? Quinn—"

"There's no reason why older women can't bear children, Davi. It says here that if the woman conceived easily in her twenties and had easy pregnancies, the odds are in her favour to have a non-risk pregnancy later in life."

"What about the state of her eggs? Does it mention anything about her having healthy eggs?"

"You'll be fine."

"Is this what you've been doing instead of sleeping? Researching pregnancy?" Davi reached over and closed the laptop. "Quinn, this has to stop."

Quinn turned around and pulled Davi onto his lap. She wrapped her arms around his neck and kissed him softly on the lips.

"Why?"

"Because I don't want to have another child. My child-bearing years are over."

He struggled to keep his voice calm. "So you can say no, but I can't say yes? What about what I want, Davi?"

"If you had asked a year or two ago, I might have considered it, but now when I'm almost fifty? Quinn, you're asking the impossible."

"It's not impossible. There are women in their late fifties and sixties who have given birth to healthy children. Some have conceived through in-vitro fertilization and others the natural way. There is no reason for us not to try."

"There is every reason for us not to try. I don't want another child. I'm sorry, but I just don't." She saw the disappointment in his eyes. She was saying no to him, and she had never denied him anything. "Let me enjoy the twins while I have the time and the energy. Don't ask me to bring another child into the family that will take away from them."

He wouldn't give in. He couldn't.

"She'll add to the family, not take away from it."

"She? Do you have this all figured out? We can't replace your mother, Quinn."

"I'm not trying to replace my mother! Damn it, Davi, I'm trying to add to us. Is it so wrong to want to have more of us, more of our family, yours and mine?"

"We have a family, Quinn—a large family, or do you not consider Cat, Rich, and Tigger to be a part of our family." Davi let go of Quinn and ran her hand through his hair. "Quinn, you're breaking my heart. I'm asking you. Please stop asking for something I can't give you."

Quinn closed his eyes and sighed heavily. "I wish I could, but I can't. I want this. If you loved me, you'd say yes."

"You know that I love you. Saying no has nothing to do with my love for you." Davi got up from Quinn's lap and headed to the door. She turned to face him. "Does Rene have anything to do with this?"

"Why do you ask?"

"You spent time alone with her after your mom's funeral. Cat said that you looked like you were having a very intense conversation. I didn't think much about it. Now I'm starting to wonder if something's going on." Quinn looked away from Davi, unable to meet her gaze. "Quinn? What is it? What's going on between you and Rene?"

He looked back at her with serious eyes. His voice was low and distant. "Rene's offered to have my babies. She wants to start a family, and she'd like me to be the father."

"You aren't considering her offer, are you? You'd walk away from our family to start a new one with her, just to have more kids?"

"I want more children, Davi. You're forcing my hand."

Davi felt the blood drain from her face. She stepped back into the doorway, thankful to have the door jamb to support her.

"I can't believe you're saying this. Quinn, your mother's death— it's hit you hard."

"It has nothing to do with my mother dying. I've wanted more children for a while, Davi. You just haven't been listening."

This conversation wasn't happening. It couldn't be. Davi rubbed her forehead, trying to think of what to say to get through to Quinn. She searched his face for understanding and saw nothing but cold eyes set in an emotionless face.

"I'm sorry," she said. "But I won't change my mind."

"Then I guess that's it. At least we know where we both stand."

She felt the pain in her chest as his words cut through to her heart. She pulled her robe tight around her, fearing her heart would burst out of her chest and explode on the floor.

"For the first time, I feel my age. I look at you, and I feel old, incredibly and painfully old."

Davi turned and headed back to their bedroom. She closed the door behind her and crumpled to the floor as her legs gave way to her overwhelming grief. She was losing him, and there wasn't a damned thing she could do about it.

XO XO XO

The mouth-watering aroma of freshly brewed coffee wafted into Davi's bedroom. She stretched and once again felt the cold space beside her. The memory of last night still stabbed at her heart.

"Quinn," Davi whispered.

She struggled out of bed and then shrugged on her bathrobe as she opened the door and headed down the stairs. Davi heard the twins chatting happily with their grandfather. Surely, Quinn would be there, too, making breakfast for them.

"Good morning," John said, giving her a sad smile. "We've just made some toaster waffles. Would you like one?"

"Yes, please." Davi bent down and kissed the twins sitting at the kitchen table. "Good morning." Straightening, she looked around the kitchen. "Where's Quinn?"

John reached for an envelope on the counter and handed it to her. "I found this when I came down this morning."

Davi took the envelope and then sat down at the table. She hesitated before she tore it open.

She read the handwritten note attached to an official-looking form. "I'm sorry, Quinn."

Davi read the form. It was a signed travel document allowing her to leave the country with the twins.

Davi looked up at John. "He's gone."

# thirteen

**"Hey, lover,** this is a pleasant surprise," Rene Adams purred into her cell phone.

"Rene, we need to talk. Dinner. Tonight. I'll pick you up." Quinn was gruff and to the point.

"Does that mean you're taking me up on my offer?"

"Eight o'clock. Don't keep me waiting."

The call went dead. Rene smiled then placed her cell phone on the bedside table. Foxx took a long drag from the joint he was smoking, then offered it to Rene, nestled beside him in her king-sized bed. She accepted it and inhaled deeply.

"Quinnie wants to meet for dinner. It sounds like he's ready to play."

She handed the joint back to Foxx before getting out of bed. Foxx ground the finished joint into an ashtray. He followed Rene to the bathroom and stood in the doorway, watching her prepare her bath.

"So, what's next?"

Rene moved toward him, giving him her best starlet smile. She caressed his face as she crooned, "You, dear Foxx, will put the moves on Davi. Try to be subtle. Give her a call and ask her how she's doing. If she happens to tell you that Quinn has left her, be supportive. Give her a shoulder to cry on, then do your damnedest to get her into bed. I want that woman out of Quinn's life sooner than later. Got it?"

"And what about you?"

"If things go according to plan, I'll be in his life and his bed by tonight."

XO XO XO

Quinn ended his call to Rene and then turned off his phone before tossing it onto the bed in his hotel suite. He poured the last of the bottle of scotch into his glass then drank it in one swallow. Quinn knew full well that there was not enough alcohol on this planet that would make him forget last night. He closed his eyes, replaying the last few words Davina said to him. *I look at you, and I feel old, incredibly and painfully old.*

He'd hurt her. He'd never seen her in so much pain before, and he was the cause of it. He knew what he was doing, and yet he couldn't stop himself. Quinn toed off his shoes and lay on top of his bed. He closed his eyes. He hadn't slept in days, and he needed to rest before his date with Rene. Quinn needed to be in top form to play the next round.

XO XO XO

Davi closed the door behind her when she entered John's study. She'd gone into autopilot with her emotions numbed while she dealt with the immediacy of the situation. It happened once before when she found her first husband, Ross, dead in their bed. This time, instead of calling an ambulance, Davi called the direct line to Air Canada reservations and booked the first available flight back to Toronto. Then she called Jake.

"Lovely lady," he answered happily. "What can I do for you today?"

"I need security to escort the twins and me to the airport. I have a flight in four hours. Then I want security to meet me at Pearson to take us home. I'm assuming the news will be out by then."

"Talk to me, Davi." His cheerful tone changed suddenly to one of professionalism.

"Quinn's left me, and I want to fly home today. Can I count on you to help me?"

"There will be an army of my men to escort you and your little ones home. No one will get near any one of you. You have my word."

"Thank you."

"Davi?"

"He's left me for Rene. That's all I know."

"No! That can't be right. He can barely stand the woman."

"That's what I thought, too. I'm sorry, Jake. I have to go." Davi ended the call, unable to say another word.

She opened the browser on the computer and clicked on her email account. There was nothing from Quinn. She decided to send him an email. She couldn't call him. Not right now. She was too raw and needed to have control over what she said to him. She typed:

*Quinn—*
*If it's Rene you've run to, you know the rules. No cheating.*
*There's no coming back. Think of what you'll lose, what all of us will lose.*

*You said that you were sorry. I'm sorry, too. I'm sorry that my love isn't enough for you anymore. —D*

She sent the email and then decided to send another. Davi typed the word family into the address box and then typed her message:

*Thank you so much for being so supportive over the past week. Quinn and I appreciate the love you've given us over this difficult time. I am asking that you continue your support in the next while. Hollywood is at it again. That's all I can say for now.*

*See you at the wedding.*

*Love always —D*

Davi clicked send. Her family was all too familiar with what the word Hollywood meant when she used it. All the bad stuff—the rumours that plagued them from the moment they became a couple, the speculation behind Guy Tremblant's attack on Quinn and then Davi, and then the gossip behind Quinn's retirement from the business. Although lauded as one of Hollywood's favourite couples, Quinn and Davi were always in the media's crosshairs as they eagerly waited for more trouble to befall them.

"Davi?" John called out from behind the door.

"Come in," she answered, standing up from the desk. "I booked our flight home, John. We leave this afternoon. Jake is sending security to get us to the airport. I'm sorry for leaving you like this."

"No, it's fine. I'm sorry about what happened. I know Quinn was having difficulty dealing with Margaret's death, but to take it out on you is so wrong, Davi."

"Thank you." She couldn't talk about Quinn. Not now while she was still struggling to make sense of it.

"Chas seems like a nice fellow," John said, realizing the need to change the subject.

"He is. He's perfect for Cat." Davi picked up her e-tickets from the printer then looked at John.

"Cat told me her wedding's going to be epic. That's a new term for me."

A smile came to Davi's face. "I hope it will be for her sake." Davi walked around the desk and stopped in front of John. She took his hand and held it. "I feel as though someone should be here with you. You shouldn't be left alone."

It was John's turn to smile. "Don't worry about me. Once my female neighbours know that you've left, they'll be lining up along the street to check up on me. Margaret made sure of it."

"I hope it's not too much for you."

John chuckled. "I'll be fine, Davi. I'm in no rush to have Margaret's place filled. She left quite the mark on my heart."

"She loved you, John. I saw it in her eyes, just like I can see it in yours."

"It's in your eyes and Quinn's, too, the love you have for each other. Don't give up on him, Davi. He'll come back."

"I don't know, John. I honestly don't know."

Xo Xo Xo

When the black security van pulled into his driveway, and eight burly men got out and made their way to the front door, John Thomas thought that his home was under attack. He thought it was a bit much and that certainly Quinn's family wouldn't need that kind of security to catch a flight to Toronto. John didn't know what it was like to be married to one of Hollywood's top ten sexiest men alive. He'd never experienced the crush of fans as Quinn and his family tried to make their way through an airport.

Davi had her fears realized when the van and the rental car arrived at the airport. Somehow, word got out that Quinn had left his wife and family in Boston and that Davi was flying home with the twins. One guard held both children; their faces tucked protectively into his chest. Seven security guards acted as a shield around Davi and him as they made their way to the Air Canada check-in.

Airport security then took over and escorted Davi through the security and customs. Two guards stayed with her and the twins until their flight boarded. Once on the plane, the twins had their snack then fell asleep. Davi was thankful that she had a moment to herself. Quinn. She couldn't help but think of him and his promises of undying love and how he made love to her as though she were the only woman in the world for him. She believed him. Everything was perfect until when? That damned movie and Rene Adams. Davi blamed herself for encouraging Quinn to take the role despite his reluctance.

*"I don't have to act. I can stay home. I'm happy here with you."*

*"You don't want me to work with Rene again, do you?"*

*"She's at it again. She lasted three weeks before she started her games. I told you this would happen, Davi. The woman can't be trusted."*

*"And what about you, Quinn,"* Davi thought to herself. *"Will I ever be able to trust you again?"*

# fourteen

**"I hate him!"** Cat screamed as she slammed the kitchen door behind her.

Davi followed her eldest daughter onto the kitchen porch. She sat beside Cat on the steps and wrapped her arm around her shoulders.

"I won't make excuses for him. I can't do that right now. I don't even understand him. You have to know that this isn't about you. He's not abandoning you."

"I'm getting married to Chas in two weeks. I asked Quinn to walk me down the aisle. Quinn's my best friend. How can you say he's not abandoning me?"

"I don't think he thought that far ahead, sweetheart."

"No, Mom, don't. He abandoned all of us. You're supposed to be the love of his life, his soul mate, and he can't even tell you to your face that he's leaving you. He's lower than dirt." Cat got up off the step. She kicked at a stone with the toe of her boot. "Fuck him."

"Cat—" Davi ached for her daughter. She was the one who was closest to Quinn out of her three kids. "I'm sorry."

"It's not your fault, Mom. Husbands can be such bastards. I don't know if I want one anymore."

"Don't say that! Don't judge Chas by what Quinn is doing. Quinn lost his mother. He's going through hell."

"And what about Dad? Who did he lose when he fooled around on you?" Cat saw the shock on her mother's face. "He told me all about it, Mom. When I wanted to get back with Mark, Dad told me what he had done to you. Dad warned me not to take back a cheater because he'd do it again. Dad broke your heart, Mom, and now Quinn's done it. I hate them. I hate both of them."

"You weren't supposed to know about the affairs. Your dad was a good man, Cat. He was a great father to the three of you. I didn't want his affairs to spoil your relationship with him."

"They didn't. But, Dad was a lousy husband, Mom."

"He wasn't lousy in everything. He just couldn't keep a promise."

"You deserved better."

"Yes, I did." Davi wanted to say that Quinn was better, but he hadn't kept his promise either, for whatever his reason. "You'll get that with Chas. Chas won't let you down."

"Can you promise me that?"

"No, I can't, but I know Chas will do the best he can, and he'll give you all that he has. You can't ask for more, love."

"I want forever."

"We all do, Cat, but forever is too much to promise and way too much to expect."

Cat started down the steps. "I have to go."

"Where are you going?"

"I'm going for a walk. I'll take the twins out for ice cream when they wake up from their nap. Tell them I haven't forgotten."

Davi watched Cat as she walked. She saw Cat's father in her. The way she held her head up high as if she were challenging the world to throw another curveball at her, the deliberate steps and fast pace in her walk, and the small curved bum.

The temper was all Cat's. Neither parent could take credit for that. Davi hoped Chas would never have to feel the full force of Cat's temper.

Davi heard her cell phone ring. She got up and went inside to answer it.

"Hello?"

"Davi? Hi, it's John. How are you? I saw you on television. I had no idea you and Quinn had to go through that circus."

Davi sat down at her kitchen desk. "We're all fine, John. I had security there to get me through the airport. The twins were great. They didn't notice anything was different from the usual. They're having a nap right now."

"And you?"

Davi sighed heavily. "I'm exhausted. Cat's furious with Quinn, and it doesn't matter what I say. I can't defend him to her. She hates him right now."

"You haven't heard from Quinn?"

"No one has. He's not answering his phone or replying to text messages. He's cut all of us off for now. How about you? Have you heard from him?"

"It sounds like we're all cut off, Davi. He's not talking to me either. I just wish he had said something to me. I thought he could talk to me."

"Me, too, John. He didn't let anyone know about his plans. Everyone is in shock."

"Any idea where he is?"

"Other than Toronto? No, I don't know where he's staying. He's supposed to be back on the set for Monday."

"I should fly up and see him. Find out what's going on."

"John, I don't know if you should. Maybe he needs time to be alone."

"Is he alone, Davi? Have you checked out the internet? He and Rene Adams are trending everywhere. To think that he's left you for that woman. I'm truly embarrassed to call him my son."

Davi heard it in John's voice, the slight hitch as he tried to hold back the tears. It pained her to know that John was suffering through this so soon after losing Margaret.

"John, I'll call you if I hear from Quinn." She heard a call-waiting beep on the line. "I have to go."

"Goodbye, Davi."

"Goodbye, John." Davi ended the call then connected to the waiting call. "Hello?"

"Davina Thomas?"

"Yes. Speaking."

"It's Dr. Nash's office. Dr. Nash has asked that you have an ultrasound to follow your tests taken two weeks ago. There's an opening on Monday. Are you available?"

She didn't need this. Not now.

"I take it they found something?"

"I can't say that, only that a more detailed scan is required. Is 9:00 a.m. good for you?"

"Yes. I can make it."

"Good. We'll send the paperwork to the clinic. Make sure you have your health card with you, and please arrive fifteen minutes before your appointment."

"I will. Thank you."

"Goodbye."

"Bye."

Davi ended the call. She pencilled the appointment time on her calendar, and then she looked around her, feeling lost. For the first time in years, she didn't know what to do.

# XO XO XO

"So this is where you're hiding," Maggie announced from the doorway to Davi's bedroom. "I called out, but I guess you didn't hear me. Where are my god babies?"

"They're with Cat. She's taken them out for ice cream," Davi said, her voice heavy with fatigue. "Come sit with me," Davi said as she patted the space beside her on the bed. "It's getting to the good part."

Maggie walked toward the bed. It pained her to see Davi drinking alone. Davi had her hair in a messy ponytail, and smudged makeup circled her eyes. Maggie recognized the oversized T-shirt Davi wore as belonging to Quinn. She assumed it was his pillow that Davi clutched to her chest as she watched Quinn on the flat-screen television.

"Why are you watching this?" she asked as she sat down on the bed and moved in beside Davi.

Davi held up her hand to stop Maggie from talking. "This is the best part."

Both women watched in silence as Quinn pulled his co-star into his arms and kissed her roughly. He pulled back from her and gazed into her eyes. She reached for his hair and ran her fingers through the long strands. Quinn grabbed her hand and stopped her from continuing.

"Save that for bedtime," Quinn murmured as he picked her up and carried her toward the bedroom.

Davi turned down the volume and proceeded to talk over the movie. "Tigger and I used to watch one of his movies now and then. We'd cuddle on this bed, and she'd cover her face when the sex scenes came up and then I'd tell her how much I'd love to have a man with hair like that. I never dreamed of meeting him, and I sure as hell never thought I'd end up marrying him and having his kids."

"Turn it off, Davi."

Davi ignored Maggie. "There are some things in my life that I couldn't avoid, like sitting beside him on that damned flight to Los Angeles. It was a fantasy come true having Quinn Thomas talk to me. I knew I shouldn't have taken him seriously, but those eyes, Maggie, those eyes just burned right into me and pulled me into him. I should have left it at that. No meeting up with him afterward, no dinner, and definitely no sex. If I'd only acted my age, this wouldn't have happened."

"What do you mean by this? If you hadn't slept with the man, you wouldn't have Jack and Stevie. If you hadn't married him, you wouldn't have been the happiest I've ever seen you since we've known each other."

"I'd still be me. Living my life in my little bubble, content with my life, content with being forty-nine years old and not feeling old. That's what I mean." Davi reached for her glass on the bedside table and took a sip from it. "I meant to call you. It's just that—"

"I know. It's all right, darlin', I'm here now." Maggie took the remote from Davi's hand and turned the television off.

"His mother's death hit him hard. I promised her that I'd look after him and help him deal with losing her, but he shut me out. Quinn made it clear that I can't give him what he needs." Davi saw Maggie's lips form a hard thin line as she fought to keep quiet. "He wants more kids, and I said no. Rene made him an offer."

"What kind of offer?" Maggie's voice was low and angry.

"What do you think? She wants to have his babies."

"He's an idiot to leave you for her. Did he not consider what this would do to your wee ones? Damn the arrogant bastard." Maggie's gaze took in Davi's face. She hadn't seen such pain since Ross had died over five years ago. "When did he tell you it was over?"

"He didn't. He left a note, and all it said was that he was sorry. I tried calling him. He's not answering his phone."

"He promised me he'd never hurt you."

"He made a lot of promises, Maggie." Davi hugged Quinn's pillow tight to her chest as tears started to flow. "I was a fool to believe him. He made me want to believe that he could love me forever. He wouldn't even look at me the night before he left me." Davi wiped away the tears with the back of her hand. "I feel so old, Maggie."

Maggie squeezed Davi's hand. "You're not old, and you're no one's fool. If anyone is a fool, it's that husband of yours for leaving you for that woman."

"What is it about me?" Davi sniffled. "Both husbands cheated on me."

"It's not you. Don't think about either of those fools. Ross is dead, and Quinn—well, he's not worth giving a second thought to, just like he didn't give you and your wee ones a second thought."

"Did you see this coming? You would have told me, wouldn't you?" Davi gazed up at Maggie.

Maggie shook her head. "This took me by surprise as much as it did you. Believe me. I would have told you if I'd known something like this was coming your way."

Maggie had stopped reading her cards where Quinn and Davi were concerned. Once her gift had returned to her, Maggie didn't see Quinn and Davi's future. Her vision now focused on the twins. All she could see was their happiness.

Davi finished her drink and then refilled her glass, emptying the bottle.

"I hope that wasn't full when you started," Maggie said as she took the bottle from Davi and looked at it with concern.

"God, Maggie, I could never drink that much. Do you think I'm that pitiful?"

"No, but I wonder how long your pity party is going to last this time."

"Thanks for your support," Davi drawled. She blew her nose into a tissue then wiped her tears. "Give me today to feel sorry for myself. That's all I have time to enjoy it. Life goes on or something like that. My eldest daughter is getting married, and my youngest still needs me to tie her shoes. I don't have the luxury of feeling sorry for myself and hiding away."

"Would you if you could?"

"Let me see," Davi said before she took a sip from her glass. "The last time I had a pity party, I ended up writing a book. A best-seller, remember?"

"Yes, I do."

"And then I sold the film rights, and I met Quinn, got pregnant and married. Oh, and shot in the head. We can't forget that."

"So you won't be writing another book this time?"

Davi snorted. A smile came to her face as she saw the sparkle in Maggie's eyes.

"I don't think I could handle the excitement. Once was enough, thank you very much. No, I don't plan on doing any writing where my second husband is concerned. My focus will be on my children and myself. Period."

"What about Quinn, though? What are you going to do, darlin'?"

"I'm going to try my best not to think about him and whatever the hell he's doing with that woman. I have enough to think about without wasting my time on him. I'm sure he's not thinking of me right now." Davi saw the look of disbelief on Maggie's face. "You don't think I can do it?"

"I've known you too long to know that I should never bet against you. But—"

"But what?"

"Quinn's a hard man to close your head and your heart to, Davi. Trying your best may not be enough."

# fifteen

**"Ooh, a limo!"** Rene said with mock surprise as she climbed into the backseat of Quinn's stretch limousine. "Planning on having some fun, Quinn?" She gazed at his face. There was no sparkle in his eyes, no hint of lust burning for her. "Or is that only reserved for your beloved Porsche?" she asked, giving him her best pout.

"If you must know, I don't feel like driving tonight. I wanted to concentrate on you, Rene, and not the road."

Quinn took her hand and brought it to his lips. He kissed the back of her hand then squeezed it before releasing it. She hadn't changed. Quinn could still read her. She never stopped acting. The cameras were constantly rolling as far as she was concerned.

"So it's true? You've left your wife?"

"I'm here, aren't I?"

Rene's gaze took in his gorgeous body in one long moment. Yes. He was here, dressed in a black David Paul suit and white linen shirt, and his tie, a perfect blue to match his eyes. His hair hung sinfully messy and sexy to his shoulders the way she liked it. She could smell him, too, fresh and clean, without the scent of another woman, his wife's, to be exact.

"Yes, you are." She noticed his wedding band was absent. A triumphant smile touched her face. "You really are."

Quinn gave her his best Hollywood smile in return. He remembered everything about Rene and what she liked—the smile that turned her on, the wink that promised her more later, and the kiss that made her drop to her knees willingly.

He felt the limousine stop. Looking out the tinted windows, he realized that they had arrived. He hated this restaurant, but he knew it was Rene's favourite. The open concept seating area and the glass windows facing the street offered no chance for privacy by putting diners at the mercy of paparazzi and intrusive fans. It was a perfect location for announcing an affair.

"Nice choice," Rene said as she took Quinn's offered hand as she exited the limo.

"Why keep it a secret?" Quinn whispered in her ear, lingering just long enough to let the paparazzi take their picture.

"I don't know what happened to you, lover, but I like the new you."

"Only for you," Quinn murmured as they followed the maitre d' to their table.

As the maitre d' offered Rene her chair, Quinn had a quick look around him. Perfect. Despite the dim interior lighting, their window-side table would still allow the couple visibility from the street. Quinn sat down beside Rene. She turned to him and kissed him on the cheek. Her hand went to his thigh and squeezed it.

"We're going to have fun tonight, Quinn. I promise you that."

Quinn smiled back at her. "No promises, Rene. I've stopped making promises."

"Don't worry, lover, I won't ask you to make me any. Not tonight. Tonight we're going to have fun just like we used to, remember?"

How could Quinn forget? No matter how much he wanted to, the memories of the endless drinking and the mindless sex still haunted him. Quinn knew no other woman with Rene's stamina or appetite for sex and alcohol. She could put an entire fraternity to shame. Rumour had it that she did just that a very long time ago. Quinn didn't doubt it.

It's not that Quinn couldn't keep up with Rene. He didn't want to. He was a one-woman man, and he didn't like to share. Drunken orgies didn't appeal to him, and soon sex without love lost its appeal, too. Much to the objection of their studio, Quinn walked away from Rene and never looked back. He'd work with her, but their days of being Hollywood's hottest couple were over.  He'd been there, done that, and owned the T-shirt. Then he met Davi.

"Hello, anybody home?"

Quinn smiled as he realized his thoughts had wandered.

"I'm here. I was thinking of the last time we went out to dinner. It was a place very similar to this."

"Yes, it was. Raphael's wasn't it or some Italian name like that?"

"Michelangelo's."

"Right. Didn't we have a drink with Buddy somebody? He stopped by our table. He propositioned me right in front of you."

Quinn chuckled. "He propositioned me. He'd had a bit too much to drink, and so had you. He didn't think you'd mind."

"He did?"

Quinn turned his attention to their waiter and gave him their drink order. "Double scotch, your best single malt, and neat." He glanced at Rene and asked, "Still drinking Cosmos?"

"Not tonight. I'd like to have a Screaming Orgasm."

Quinn's right eyebrow arched with amusement. "Before dinner?"

"I'll take it any time I can get it," Rene said as she winked at him.

"You heard the lady," Quinn said without looking at him.

"Coming right up," the waiter answered before leaving to place their order.

"You haven't changed, Rene. You still like to shock men."

Rene's hand moved up Quinn's thigh to his crotch.

"Admit it, lover, you like it. I bet you've missed it since you married Davina. That's why you came back to work." She squeezed him. "You came back to be with me."

"Is that what you think?"

"Five years is a long time to go without great sex."

Quinn removed Rene's hand from his crotch and brought it up to his lips. He placed a soft kiss on it.

"Any amount of time away from the love of your life is always too long."

# sixteen

**Davi sat apart** from the other patients in the waiting area of the diagnostic imaging clinic. She'd noticed the stares as soon as she entered the room. A glance at the flat-screen television on the wall facing them told her why. There, for everyone to see, on one half of the screen was a picture of Quinn with Rene, his arm wrapped around her waist as he escorted her out of a Toronto nightclub, and a photograph of Davi and Quinn taken in happier times on the other half.

There had been no escape from the press. When Quinn walked through the Boston airport without his family, the paparazzi knew that something big was happening. Within hours of his plane landing in Toronto, Quinn's date with Rene hit the internet. The internet, television, daily newspapers, and the ever-popular celebrity magazines had to have their say on the situation. Fact or fiction, it didn't matter to the press.

She wished she knew the truth. Quinn hadn't contacted Davi, and she couldn't get through to him. He didn't answer his phone, his voice mail no longer accepted messages, and emails remained unanswered. An empty bed, an aching heart, and exhaustion fueled her imagination. As much as she tried, Davi couldn't stop thinking of Quinn and Rene together, only an hour away from her home. She'd be damned if she ran after him to talk to him. Her pride wouldn't let her.

Davi stared at the same page of the book she had brought with her to read while she waited. She was tired, having forgotten how hard it was to get used to sleeping alone. Quinn's pillow and T-shirt were poor substitutes for the man who once held her close every night while she slept.

"Davina Thomas?" a voice called out from the doorway.

Davi stood up immediately and walked toward the technician waiting for her.

"Sorry for the wait," the technician said as Davi followed behind her.

"It's all right."

She didn't mind the technician's chatter as she pored over Davi's chart. Davi appreciated that the woman did not ask if she was the famous Davina Thomas. Today she was only a name on a medical form, a patient scheduled to have an ultrasound.

"So what I need you to do is remove your clothing from the waist up and then lay down on the bed."

Davi did as requested.

"Your chart indicates that you've done this before. However, I have to explain the procedure to you."

As the technician explained the ultrasound and the mass she was looking for, she applied the gel to Davi's breast.

"It's warm," Davi said appreciatively.

"I try to warm it up before I have to apply it. It's the least I can do for you. Now relax, and let's see what we have here."

One hour later, Davi's appointment was over. The ultrasound showed a mass that hadn't been visible in the scans taken a year ago. Only a centimetre in size, it was enough to concern the specialists. She'd be back at the end of the week for a biopsy. As Davi made her way to her truck in the hospital's parking lot, paparazzi surrounded her.

"No comment," was her only reply to the endless questions.

"Keep it together," Davi told herself as she started the ignition and then drove her truck out of the parking lot. She bit the inside of her cheek to stay focused on the road. Davi wouldn't break down. She couldn't. She wouldn't give Quinn the satisfaction of seeing what he was doing to her.

XO XO XO

Quinn sat off to the side of the set, watching Rene run through her scene with Clint. He couldn't let his guard down, knowing that he was being watched and photographed. Watching Rene act was more challenging than working with her. At least when he was working with her, their chemistry brought out the best in Rene's talent. Watching the hungover and ill-tempered actress from the sidelines, Quinn fully appreciated what the crew had to endure every damned day they had to work with her.

This time he was the one to blame for her mood. Every night he had taken Rene out on the town. They dined, danced, and drank. When Rene's hands started to wander and her eyes focused on his crotch, Quinn knew it was time to leave. He'd take her back to her hotel room, make up an excuse as to why he had to go and then he'd kiss her good night. Quinn hadn't partied this hard since the last time he was with Rene over five years ago. What was he thinking? He barely survived back then. What made him think he'd get through it this time? He had to. There was no other choice for him.

Clint called for a five-minute break while he consulted with his crew. Rene sauntered over to Quinn, giving him a forced smile.

"How's it going?" he asked as she fell into his lap and wrapped her arms around his neck.

"Terrible. Clint doesn't know what the hell he's doing. And that idiot who's in the scene with me—"

"His name's Bradley."

"Bradley," Rene repeated with disdain. "He can't act his way out of a paper bag."

"I think his Oscar would say otherwise."

Rene glared at Quinn. "It's a stupid award. It doesn't mean a thing."

Quinn pouted playfully. "Oh, I guess I should throw mine out then if you think they're stupid."

Rene kissed Quinn softly on the cheek. "Not yours, lover. Bradley's. He didn't deserve his."

"Okay."

"You left me last night. I slept alone. Again."

"So did I." Quinn wrapped his arm around Rene's waist. "You had to get here early, and I have to work late tonight. We both needed our beauty sleep."

"Tomorrow then? We can spend the night together. It's time."

Quinn didn't answer her. He felt the vibration of his cell phone in his pants pocket.

"I have to take this," he apologized as he set Rene on her feet. "It's business."

"I'll see you later?"

"I'll call you. You're doing great, babe. Show Bradley how to act."

Quinn pulled his cell phone out of his pocket and answered it. "Luke."

"What the hell's going on? I'm out backpacking in the Rockies for a few days. I finally make it back to civilization, and I find out that you've left Davi for Rene! Are you out of your mind?"

"Luke—"

"I called Jake, and he said you've fired everyone—Sue, Sarah, even him. Is something wrong with your head? Is it a delayed reaction from that asshole Tremblant attacking you? Is it because of your mom?"

"Luke—"

"We'll get you checked out by the best specialists. Don't worry. We'll find out what's wrong with you."

"Are you finished?"

"Yes."

"I need to talk to you, Luke. You're the only one I can trust."

Luke hesitated before he asked, "Are you saying that to your best friend, your business manager, or your lawyer?"

"My lawyer."

"Damn it, Quinn, don't—"

"Divorce, Luke. I need to talk to you about divorce."

# seventeen

**"Davi, I'm so sorry,"** Sue's voice cracked over the phone. "None of us can get through to him. He's lost his mind. That's the only possible reason why he's doing this."

Davi stared at her computer screen, looking at a popular entertainment website that had posted the latest news of Quinn with Rene. Pictures of the two of them working on the set for the movie were now available for everyone to see. There were various shots of Rene sitting on Quinn's lap whispering in his ear and of Rene holding Quinn's hand while they walked to her RV. He was shameless in his affair with her. Davi stared at the pictures, hoping for a sign that this wasn't her Quinn, that it was the Hollywood Quinn putting on a front for everyone but her. Yet, she couldn't see it, not one clue to tell her that he was acting. Davi exited the website.

"What about Luke? Does he know what's going on? I can't remember when he was coming back to civilization." There was a silence that Davi didn't expect. "Sue? Does Luke know?"

"He called yesterday. Jake told him as much as he could, and then Luke said he'd try to get through to Quinn."

"Did he call back? Did he get through to him?"

"Yes, he called back, but I don't know if he got through to Quinn."

"What's that supposed to mean? Sue, just say it. Whatever Quinn told Luke couldn't be any worse than what I'm thinking."

Sue sighed before she answered. "Quinn played the lawyer-client privilege card. Anything Quinn told Luke is off-limits for the rest of us." Now it was Sue's turn to listen to the long silence. "Davi? You know that it doesn't mean anything. Quinn could be asking Luke to look over a contract."

"In secret? Nice try, but I don't think so. He's checking with Luke to see how much it's going to cost him to walk away."

"No—"

"Damn him for doing this now. Did he give Cat any consideration? She's nervous enough about marrying an actor, and now she has Quinn's public infidelity rubbed in her face. Why couldn't he wait? Two weeks, that's all we needed. Two weeks and then Cat would be married, he'd be with his blonde bimbo, and I'd know—"

"You'd know what, Davi?"

"I have to go, Sue. I'll talk to you later."

"Davi, don't hang up on me. Tell me what else is going on."

Davi hung up the phone. She couldn't tell Sue about the biopsy and how she was sure it would be cancer this time. She knew how their small group of friends operated. Everyone knew everyone's business. There were no secrets except for Quinn's secret with Luke and now hers. Cat's wedding and the twins were her only concern right now.

Her cell phone rang. Davi looked at the caller display.

"Foxx," she answered wearily.

"How are you, or should I even ask?"

Davi took a deep breath. "Foxx, I'm sorry. I didn't get back to you on the tour proposal."

"Not to worry. That's not why I called. Look, I'm heading up to my cottage in Haliburton for the weekend. Why don't you and the twins join me? I thought you might want to get away."

"Foxx, Cat's wedding is next week."

"Knowing you, everything has been looked after. You're just putting in time until the big day."

"Not quite. The bachelorette party is this weekend."

"Davi, I won't lie. I've seen the tabloids. I'm offering you an escape for a couple of days. There is no internet or television. Think about it—you, me, the twins, and a big beautiful lake to enjoy. Do you want to spend the weekend with a bunch of young women talking about love and marriage and all that girly stuff?"

"Not really. I'm not a good advertisement for happily ever after right now."

"So say yes and come with me. You'll get to relax and get energized for the big day. I can be at your place in an hour. Swimsuits and shorts, that's all you'll have to pack. I'll look after everything else." He sensed her hesitation. "I'm offering this getaway to you as a friend, Davi. I promise. I won't make a move on you."

"Foxx, the thought never crossed my mind."

"Good. Then I'll be there in an hour. See you soon." Foxx ended the call before Davi could respond.

Foxx left a voice mail for Rene, "Davi will be with me for the weekend. He's all yours. Good luck."

He palmed his keys and picked up his duffle bag filled with a few clothes for the weekend. Foxx locked the door behind him as he exited his bachelor's apartment. He smiled as he made his way to the elevator.

Foxx didn't mind playing Davi. He found her attractive and enjoyed her company. He was intrigued to discover what Quinn saw in his older wife to be so captivated by her. Foxx was sure it was the sex, and he was eager to find out for sure. He looked forward to being able to compare the two women.

**XO XO XO**

Davi didn't take long to pack a few things for her and the twins. While the twins played quietly on the floor of the office, Davi opened her email. There was nothing from Quinn. She typed Quinn's name into the address box then typed a message to him –

> *Congratulations! You look very happy with Rene.*
>
> *I know you, or at least I thought I did. You don't do anything without giving it a lot of thought. You plan. How long have you been pretending that you still loved me? Did your love for me change before or after you started working with Rene again? Bravo, Quinn. Your performance is Oscar-worthy.*
>
> *I wonder if you gave any of us a second thought. Did you think of Jack and how he would call out for you every night? Did you think of Stevie, who can't understand why her daddy isn't home to kiss her goodnight? Did you think of me?*
>
> *I only asked two things of you— to love me and to never cheat on me. There's no going back now. You broke the rules and my heart. —Davi*
>
> *P.S. Ryan called. He thinks you're an asshole. I have to agree. He's number one on my list again.*

Davi clicked on send then closed her email. She looked at Quinn's framed photograph beside her monitor. He was in his early twenties and had just made it onto the Hollywood scene. Davi loved how his eyes bore right into her, eyes that were only for her. She paid twenty-five thousand dollars for that picture at a charity event. He was supposed to be hers and only hers.

"Damn you," she said as she took the framed photograph and jammed it into her wastebasket.

## XO XO XO

Cat entered her mother's office to look for the phone number of the caterer. When she sat down at the desk, she noticed Quinn's framed photograph staring up at her from the wastebasket.

"Oh, Mom," she said, reaching for the photograph and placing it on the desk.

Cat didn't have access to her mother's email account. However, she could check her browser history. With a couple of clicks, Cat found what websites her mother had visited.

She mouthed the words as she read the various websites listed. "What the hell?"

# eighteen

**Rene had the day off** and was making the most of it at the hotel's spa—manicure, pedicure, facial, and a Shiatsu massage. Lord knew that she needed it after the past few days. Quinn was difficult. Sure, he'd left his wife for her, but Rene wasn't getting the complete package. Quinn was holding out on her, and Rene's patience was wearing thin.

Fatigue, stress, or too much alcohol—Rene knew all of the excuses why a man couldn't have sex. However, men rarely used them on her. Men were usually too embarrassed not to perform for her. Not Quinn. He didn't seem to care that she challenged his manhood. He would give her his best smile, kiss her, and then say goodnight. Well, not tonight. If he tried to leave her high and dry, there would be hell to pay.

Foxx's message gave Rene hope. If Foxx bedded Davi tonight, there would be no going back for Quinn. Rene would be his only option, the way it should have been from the beginning.

Rene liked Foxx. She'd known him for a few years. They had met at a mutual friend's party and instantly felt an attraction. Foxx was sexy and very capable between the sheets. They also enjoyed sharing.

One night, after celebrating the end of a challenging workday, Rene and Quinn decided to let loose in her hotel suite. The liquor flowed, and Rene managed to sneak one of her favourite drugs of choice into Quinn's drink. Quinn didn't mind when Foxx turned up unexpectedly at Rene's door. Nor did he care when Rene started to make love to him while Foxx watched. Rene convinced Quinn to let Foxx join them, using words of encouragement and a mouth that gave him unending pleasure. The sex was the hottest she'd ever had. How could it not be with two well-endowed and skillful studs working on her?

Rene couldn't remember when they finally fell asleep in her king-sized bed. She only remembered the curses of disgust and outrage when Quinn woke up and found himself curled up beside a naked Foxx. Quinn scrambled out of bed, furious with Rene for what had happened. He dressed quickly, told Rene it was over, and then told Foxx to go to hell before punching him in the face. Quinn wouldn't talk to Rene again unless they were on the set.

Neither Rene nor Foxx wanted a committed relationship and continued to be bed buddies when their paths crossed. When Foxx became Davi's agent, Rene was ecstatic. She wasn't surprised when Quinn didn't mention Foxx's name to her when they started to work together on this film. She was sure he hadn't said that he knew Foxx to Davi either. Foxx convinced himself that Quinn had forgotten the incident until Rene told him that Quinn had a photographic memory and he didn't forget anything or anyone. Quinn was keeping that night a secret, and Rene was sure she knew why.

XO XO XO

Quinn saw her from across the street. He could always spot her in a crowd, no matter how she dressed. She had her hair tucked into a baseball cap pulled down on her forehead. Oversized sunglasses covered most of her face. Her favourite T-shirt covered her curves, tucked into the waistband of her favourite faded bootcut blue jeans that covered her black cowboy boots. He hardened at the sight of her. God, he had missed her. Quinn couldn't hide the sparkle his eyes gave off whenever he saw Davi.

She knew that he'd seen her, but she didn't let on that she knew. She stayed motionless as she watched him work through three takes of the same scene. When Clint finally called for a break, she waited for Quinn to come to her. She let the crowd walk around her while she kept her eyes focused on him.

He didn't hide his excitement from her. She licked her lips then bit down on the bottom lip. That was something he'd expect to see, something that would make him smile, and he did. He was close to her, almost close enough to touch her. It was time. She took off her sunglasses and then pulled off her cap, smiling all the while.

He stopped. The sparkle in his eyes died instantly.

"Cat!"

"Asshole," she answered as she flipped him the middle finger. Quinn grabbed Cat by the elbow and led her away from the crowd. "Careful, Hollywood, someone might photograph us," Cat said under her breath.

"I don't give a damn," Quinn bit out.

He didn't stop until he reached his RV. Quinn pulled out his key from his pocket, unlocked the door, and then ushered Cat up the stairs.

"What the hell are you playing at?"

"What the hell am I playing at?" she stormed as she fell into the nearest chair. "I saw the look you gave me. You're still hot for my mother. No one gets those eyes except her. I won't even mention what you did below the belt. Admit it, Hollywood. You still love her."

"I never said I didn't," Quinn said as he poured himself a glass of scotch.

"Well, actions speak louder than words, and you've been showing a lot of action with the blonde slut lately. How is your latest fuck buddy?"

"Stop it, Cat!" Quinn said as he took a beer out of the fridge and opened it for her.

"No, you stop it! Stop fooling around and come home before it's too late."

Quinn handed Cat her beer then sat in the chair facing her.

"This doesn't concern you."

"The hell it doesn't! You've left my mother, and you're fooling around in public. I'd say it concerns me."

"What's going on between your mother and me is private."

"When you are publicly flaunting your affair with another woman, it's no longer private, asshole." Cat took a swig from her beer and stared at Quinn. Fury blazed in her eyes. "Why are you hurting Mom? Did she do something that you can't forgive?"

"What did she say?"

"She said not to take it personally. It has to do with the two of you."

"She's right. Stay out of it."

"Fuck off."

Quinn stared at Cat. Any other time he would have laughed at her. She took herself too seriously at times. Except for this time. She was right. This was serious. He drained his glass, then stood and headed to the kitchen to pour himself another.

"Why haven't you called Mom? Have you been too busy with blondie to pick up your phone?"

"I'm giving Davi time to think."

"Think about what? How much of an asshole you are? I think she knows, Hollywood."

"Look, Cat, if you've come here to call me an asshole, I get it. You can leave anytime."

"I logged onto Mom's computer and checked her browser history. Why is she researching pregnancy in older women? Is she pregnant, and you're not the dad? Is that it? Mom got caught fooling around, and you've left her?"

"No! Your mom is not pregnant. She doesn't want more kids. She's waiting for grandkids."

"So it's you." Cat snorted. "You want more kids, and Mom said no, so you left her. You really are an asshole, Hollywood." Cat placed her unfinished beer on the table beside her. "I didn't know you could be so selfish. You were right to leave. Mom doesn't need your shit." Cat stood up and headed toward the door.

"Why is it so wrong to want more kids," he asked as he faced her back. "What's wrong with wanting to have another Davina or Quinn in the world?"

"Mom's already given you five. She's not breeding stock that keeps adding to the herd."

"Two," he corrected her. "She's only given me two kids."

Cat turned to look at Quinn. "She's given birth to five, and two of them are biologically yours. Don't you consider the three of us your family, too?" She saw the answer on his face.

"Cat—"

"I get it. We don't count. We're not related by blood. Well, you know something? I'm glad to hear this now instead of after you walked me down the aisle. That privilege is for family, Hollywood, something you no longer have."

"You don't understand."

"There's nothing to understand. My God, Quinn, my mother was shot because of you. We almost lost her. She gave you Jack and Stevie, and now you want more? When will it be enough for you? She has a right to say no. It's her turn."

Cat turned and opened the door. She walked down the steps with Quinn close behind her.

"Wait," Quinn said as he grabbed her arm.

"Let go of me," she hissed as she turned toward him. "I thought Mom was rushing it by going away with Foxx, but now I'm all for it. By the way, she's also been looking up divorce attorneys. The sooner she's over you, the better."

Cat pulled her arm out of Quinn's grip and walked away, flipping him the bird once again.

Quinn slammed the door to his RV. He cursed as he poured himself a full glass of scotch. His phone vibrated in his pants pocket. Quinn pulled it out, seeing that Davi had sent him an email. He opened it and read it.

"Damn it, Davi!"

"Quinn!" The voice of one of Clint's assistants interrupted his thoughts. "Clint wants you outside now!" he shouted from outside the RV door.

"Hold on!" Quinn yelled back as he jammed his cell phone into his pants pocket.

He should have known better. Instead of trying to win Quinn back, Davi was letting him go. She didn't play games. She had told him that. Why hadn't he listened? Because he was an idiot too caught up in his grief and selfish needs that he couldn't appreciate what he already had.

His phone vibrated in his pocket. He pulled it out and looked at the message on the screen. "Plot Twist."

# nineteen

**"This is nice,"** Davi said as she pulled her sweater around her shoulders and gazed out at the orange-pink sunset over the still lake.

Foxx's cottage was spectacular. The interior was warm and inviting with comfortable furnishings that allowed one to sit down wearing a wet bathing suit or track in the sand on bare feet. Foxx had called it his man cave, where all he had to do was open the door and sweep the sand out to clean the floor. The wrap-around deck offered a full view of the lake and the surrounding forest. It had comfortable outdoor furniture and a rustic stone fireplace that warmed the seating area in front of it.

"I knew you would like it," Foxx said, giving her a warm smile. He offered her a glass of honey-flavoured Jack Daniels. "Try this."

She took a sip then looked up at him. "It's very nice. Thank you."

"You are welcome. We aim to please."

Foxx sat beside her on the outdoor sofa. They gazed out at the lake and listened to the call of the loons.

"I love the loons," Davi said softly. "Their call is so haunting."

"I agree. I used to think the loon mated for life, like the Canada goose, however it doesn't."

"Really?"

"Loons average about seven years together before another mate makes his appearance, fights for the female and then takes over the lake."

"Assuming he wins."

"He'll be younger, more virile, and so more apt to win. Or, he'll be older and wiser and have a few tricks under his wing."

"Seven years. That's not bad. They're close to human marriage."

"Eight years for first-time marriages. Second marriages are supposed to last longer."

Davi smiled at Foxx with amazement. "Where did you read this, or are you speaking from experience?"

"I'm an agent, remember? You'd be surprised at the books I've had to read. As for my own experience, my marriage lasted five years."

"Well, my first marriage lasted twenty-five years. No divorce there. My husband died. My second marriage lasted less than five. I think they skew the average."

"So you're calling your marriage quits then?"

Davi looked back at the lake and focused on the loon swimming near the shore.

"My husband called it quits the moment he decided to sleep with Rene. He knew the rules. No cheating."

"No second chances?"

"My first husband cheated on me, Foxx. He loved me, and yet he still cheated. He couldn't give me a reason why he did it other than it was hard to refuse sex when offered to him." Davi snorted. "What kind of reasoning is that? Because it was offered?" She shook her head, still bristling from his reasoning.

"You didn't divorce him, though."

"No. We tried counselling. We both wanted to get past it, but it wasn't easy. It's hard to love a man when he's broken your trust in him." Davi finished her drink and put the glass down on the table. "Quinn knew that I wouldn't tolerate cheating."

"What about his movies? Could you watch him make love to women in movies?"

Davi nodded. "The on-screen Quinn isn't my Quinn. I can see the difference. His on-screen love scenes are part of his work, and I didn't mind sharing him with his co-stars. Although sharing him with other lovers was forbidden."

"You're a one-man woman. I get that, but he's Hollywood, Davi. The temptation is always there. Surely you knew that."

"He convinced me that he was a one-woman man. We've been together for almost five years, and not once did he ever look at another woman."

"Until Rene Adams."

"Yes, until Rene. I don't know how long he lied to me about her. I can't believe that he fooled me. When he'd come home and tell me about the stunts she was pulling to seduce him, I never thought he was telling me what they were actually doing." Davi shook her head. "Once a fool, always a fool, I guess."

"I'm sorry. I shouldn't have brought it up."

"Don't be. It's not your fault." Davi nodded toward her empty glass. "Mind pouring me another? I think I've found my new favourite drink."

Foxx rose to his feet and picked up Davi's glass.

"Are you going to get drunk on me, Davi?"

"Would that be so bad?" She gave him a mischievous smile.

Foxx smiled back at her. "Keep that smile on your face while I get you a refill."

Davi watched Foxx enter the cottage. He was nice to look at from behind with broad shoulders that tapered down to a narrow waist on long muscular legs. Well-fitted jeans hung low on his waist, allowing her to appreciate his backside. The man was a hunk. He wasn't as big as Quinn, but then, not many men were. Quinn was one of a kind.

Davi closed her eyes and forced the thought of him out of her head. She wouldn't let him spoil this moment.

"Here you go," Foxx said as he returned with her drink. Foxx noticed Davi's closed eyes. "Are you okay?"

"Yes," she answered as she opened her eyes. She took the offered glass and sipped it slowly. "I was just thinking."

"Anything you want to talk about?" he asked as he sat beside her.

Davi shook her head. "No."

She shivered slightly, and Foxx instantly put his arm around her shoulders and pulled her in close. Davi couldn't help but nestle into his shoulder. She felt comfortable with Foxx. Since his confession of wanting to sleep with her, Foxx had been the perfect gentleman and the friend she needed.

"Why did you and your wife divorce? If you don't want to tell me, I'll understand."

"I discovered that I'm not into long-term relationships."

Davi turned her head to look up at Foxx. "You cheated?"

Foxx laughed and then smiled. "No, I left her before either of us did any cheating. We both realized that we married for great sex, and when that faded, we saw that we had absolutely nothing in common. We could barely carry on a conversation."

"I'm sorry."

"Why?"

"It must have been painful to realize that you had lost at love."

"But it wasn't love, Davi. A strong like, maybe. Certainly lust, but there was never love. It's easy to tell someone you love them without really knowing if you do. We say what we need to get us what we want."

"That sounds awful. When I tell a person that I love them, it's because I do."

"And perhaps the next time I tell a woman that I love her, I'll mean it."

"I hope you do. No one likes to be lied to. Trust me on that. So in the meantime, what are your plans? Are you seeing anyone?"

"I do see someone when the opportunity arises. We're a lot alike. No strings and no expectations."

"And no kids?"

"No kids. Your two are the only ones I tolerate. They are perfect."

"You had to say that."

"No, I didn't. Jack and Stevie are perfect. You have raised them well, Davi Stuart. A man would be a fool to pass you by because of those two." He felt her tense under his arm. "What is it?"

"You called me Davi Stuart. I haven't heard that name in a long time."

"Geez, Davi—"

"No. It's okay. I'll probably have to get used to it again."

"You don't have to divorce. It's only been a week. The man may come around and realize his mistake."

"It doesn't matter. Quinn knows the rules."

Foxx kissed the top of Davi's head. "He's a fool. You're a gorgeous and intelligent woman. Any man would consider himself lucky to have a chance with you. Don't give up on the rest of us males."

"Revenge sex," Davi said softly.

Foxx turned to face Davi and leaned in toward her. "Will you forget I ever mentioned that? I know that any relationship with you would be long-term."

Davi reached out with her right hand to touch his hair. She'd always wanted to feel the silky red strands. She held his gaze as she ran her fingers tentatively through his hair.

"Foxx—"

He didn't wait for her to finish. His kiss was soft and warm. Foxx's arms wrapped around Davi's waist and pulled her into his embrace.

She knew her body was betraying her, giving in to another man's kiss. She sighed as she closed her eyes and forgot about everything. Davi tasted bourbon on his breath. She liked the familiar taste. She pulled on the silky strands, and then her hand moved from his hair and touched his ear, tracing the outside edge down to his lobe. She tugged on the lobe and felt the sharp end of his earring stud as it pricked her finger.

"No," Davi said, breaking away from Foxx's kiss. "I can't do this."

"Yes, you can," he said as he took her hand and kissed it. "You can do anything you want to, Davi. There's no one here to judge you. It's just the two of us."

"No, it's not." Davi pulled away from him. "I wear his ring," Davi said as she touched it on her finger. "Quinn's leaving me hasn't made me any less married than I was two weeks ago or two years ago. I can't be with another man. It's wrong."

"It's not wrong. Not anymore. Quinn's made it clear that he's moved on."

"He may have, but until I have a piece of paper that tells me that I'm no longer his wife, I will keep my promise to be faithful to him. I may hate him for what he's doing and want to tear a strip off him, but I won't go against my vows."

"He's playing you for a fool."

"Then let me be a fool. It's my choice."

Her cell phone rang with Quinn's ringtone.

"Don't answer it."

"I have to." Davi reached for her phone. "Davina Stuart," she said as she answered it. "Hello?" she asked again when there was no response.

"You're back to using Stuart, are you?"

"I won't share my name with anyone, Quinn. Once you give Rene your name, I won't be the other Mrs. Quinn Thomas."

"Davi, we're not getting married."

"You're not bringing bastard children into the world, Quinn. You marry her if she's having your children."

"You and I have to talk."

"No. Not until after Cat's wedding."

"Why?"

"I have enough to deal with—Cat's wedding and our children who you so easily abandoned. I don't have the energy to deal with your lies at the same time."

"Davi—"

"Not one phone call or email to ask about your children since you left us, and now you want to talk? I don't think so, Hollywood. Our world does not revolve around you, and you've made it quite clear that you don't want to be a part of ours."

"Please listen to me."

Davi laughed bitterly. "Listen to you? I tried for days to get you to talk to me, but you wouldn't. Instead, you were planning to leave us for your blonde bimbo. You can't dictate the rules, Quinn. I gave you plenty of opportunities to talk to me. Now you have to wait until I say you can."

"Mommy?"

Davi turned to find Jack standing in the doorway.

"Jack, honey, what's wrong?" She lowered her voice so Jack wouldn't hear her. "I have to go. You're not the only one with a lawyer. Luke can contact mine after the wedding and not before. Good night." Davi ended the call then pocketed her cell phone. "Jack?" she asked as she moved toward him.

"Bad dream," he cried out.

"Oh, Jackie, Mommy's here," she cooed as she picked him up and hugged him.

"I want Daddy," he cried.

"I know, honey. Daddy's not here."

"I want my Daddy."

His sobs increased, tearing at Davi's heart.

"Is there anything I can do?" Foxx asked as he got to his feet and walked over to Davi.

"I think I'll say goodnight and take Jack back to bed. I'm sorry for the drama, Foxx. You shouldn't have had to hear that."

"It's okay. I'm glad I wasn't the one getting the earful. You know who deserved it." He leaned down and kissed Davi on her forehead and then patted Jack gently on the head. "Good night, Jack. Mommy will look after you. Sweet dreams."

XO XO XO

Quinn stared at his cell phone. There'd be no more talking to Davi unless a lawyer was involved? How did he let things get so out of control? He thought she'd come after him. Two days. That's how he had planned it. Two days apart, and then she'd show up on the set and tell him that she loved him and would do anything to keep him. They would make love in his RV, and then within the year, they'd make another baby. It was so simple. It was so stupid. Now she was with Foxx, and he was stuck.

His cell phone rang. Quinn looked at the caller display.

"Rene," his excitement forced.

"Where the hell are you? I've been waiting for over an hour." He knew that tone of voice. Rene was drunk and mad.

"Something came up."

"Like hell it did. You know that I've been waiting for you."

"Rene, I'm sorry. Tonight's not going to work."

"Yes, it is, Quinn. I've spent all day at the spa getting ready for tonight."

"Rene—"

"You promised me! You've put me off every night with an excuse for why we can't have sex. Not tonight, buddy, you're making love to me tonight or else!"

She was right. Every night he'd been able to talk his way out of not having sex with her. He was too tired from the day's work, stressed from his separation, too drunk to get it up, or too busy to see her. He was good at playing her. She believed him every time, but not now. It was time to keep his promise.

"Not tonight."

"No. You listen to me, Quinn Thomas. You are not leaving me high and dry. I've been patiently waiting for you to bed me, but not anymore. You get your ass over here now. Do you hear me?"

"Rene, I'm not coming over. I'm going to bed alone. Goodnight."

"Don't you hang up on me. You made me a promise."

"If I can break my promise to my wife, I can break my promise to you. Get used to it. Good night."

Quinn ended the call then threw his cell phone onto the bed.

XO XO XO

Davi cuddled with Jack in her bed. He wasn't settling. His body trembled as he sobbed for his daddy.

"You'll see him soon, Jack. I promise. Go to sleep, sweetheart."

She hated lying to Jack. She'd say anything to get him to relax and fall asleep. She hated Quinn for what he was doing to his family, leaving them so that he could start another with Rene. Did he not care about his children? Did he not realize how much he was hurting them? She thought back to Margaret's funeral when Quinn had talked about responsibility and family. It was clear to her that he didn't believe in what he said. They were just words from a man who knew how to act.

Finally, after long minutes of singing to her little boy, Davi felt him relax in her arms and let sleep take him. She held on to him, needing him just as much as he did her, because now, more than ever, Davi needed comforting.

**XO XO XO**

"Open the door, you bastard!"

Quinn woke to the sound of fists banging on his door and the angry voice of one drunk and pissed-off Rene. Cursing, he dragged himself off his bed and made his way to the door, opening it quickly.

"Rene, what the hell are you doing here?"

"Let me in, or else I'll wake up everyone on this floor."

Quinn stepped aside and allowed her to enter his suite.

"Where is she?" she yelled.

"Who?"

"The slut you brought back to your room. You've still got your clothes on, so she must be here."

"There's no one here. I fell asleep on my bed," Quinn called out to Rene as she inspected his hotel suite, including the bathroom and closets.

"You stood me up, and you had no right. We were supposed to spend the night in bed. Together. We had a deal."

Quinn looked at his watch. Four o'clock in the morning. He must have passed out. That was fine with him. At least he got some sleep. He made his way to the bar and took out a bottle of water from the fridge. Then he palmed a couple of Advil from a nearby bottle and downed them in one swallow.

"You realize we have to be at work in two hours," he grumbled as he fell into the soft comfort of his suite's sofa.

She stopped in front of the sofa and glared at him. "I don't give a damn about work! You said you'd spend the night with me, and you didn't. Do you know how much time I spent getting ready for you? I spent the whole damned day at the spa!" Rene undid the belt to her wrap-around dress and let it fall open, exposing her naked body.

Not again. Rene's desperation embarrassed Quinn. Davi didn't spend a day at the spa unless she needed what she called me time to get her thoughts together for writing. She didn't go to the spa to get ready for sex. She was always ready, always naturally beautiful.

"I apologized."

"Apology not accepted. Make love to me now, Quinn."

"Rene, it's not going to happen."

"Why? Are you too tired or too drunk to get it up, or has your wife made it shrivel up, and you can't have sex anymore?" She snorted. "I bet that's what it is. You really can't get it up anymore, can you? Your precious wife has made you into one of her steers."

He wouldn't take the bait. There was no arguing with Rene when she was drunk. He held her gaze until she fell onto the sofa beside him. Her hand immediately went to his crotch and squeezed.

"You still have it, lover. Even limp, you're quite the size. Come on. Let's do it here on the sofa like old times."

Quinn removed her hand and got to his feet quickly. He winced as the pain from his headache shot through his temple.

Rene laughed as she leaned into the back of the sofa. "You're pathetic. You know that?" She pulled at her dress and refastened the belt.

"I'm pathetic and a lot more. Keep adding to the list if it makes you feel better. God knows you won't be hurting my feelings, and you're probably right."

He walked off to the bathroom and locked the door behind him. Quinn turned on the faucet and splashed cold water on his face. What he needed was a shower, but he couldn't risk it with Rene still in his room. Quinn picked up the hotel's phone and called room service, ordering coffee and lots of it.

"What does she have that I don't?" Rene called out to him from the other side of the door. "I know you still love her, Quinn. There's no other reason for the way you've been treating me. You still love her."

Quinn heard her sobs, and they tore at his soul. She didn't deserve this. He opened the door and found her sitting on the floor, leaning against the wall.

She looked up at him with mascara-smudged eyes. "I thought we were friends. Friends don't treat friends the way you've treated me."

"You're right. I'm sorry."

He sat on the floor beside her and took her hand.

"You were supposed to give me babies. We talked about having babies."

Quinn sat silently beside her. He'd lied to her and himself, thinking he could leave Davi and start a family with Rene. The instant Rene climbed into the back of his limousine, Quinn realized he was a fool. He could barely put up with Rene in front of the camera. What made him think he could do it when they were alone?

He remembered how Davi used to kid him about how hard it was to act. Quinn made it look so easy. It was easy unless what he was doing challenged everything he believed in, such as marriage and fidelity.

Quinn heard the knock at the door and the unmistakable call of, "Room service!"

"Coffee's here," he announced as he got to his feet and went to the door.

Quinn tipped the waiter generously then wheeled the cart into the room. He didn't want the waiter to see Rene.

"Here, drink this," he ordered as he handed her a cup of hot coffee.

Rene sipped it, seemingly lost in thought. Quinn joined her on the floor.

"You're the only man I know who doesn't think with his dick."

Quinn choked on his coffee. "Come again?"

"You don't think with your dick. Getting laid isn't your priority. It has never been."

"Is that good or bad?"

"Bad for me and good for what's her name. If you thought with your dick, we'd be lovers by now. Instead, I'm sitting here, drunk, and you're sitting next to me while you're thinking of her."

"How can you be drunk and think like that?"

"I'm not that drunk. It takes more than one bottle of champagne to make me dumb. You should know that."

Quinn chuckled. "You're right. You handled the tequila like a pro."

Rene drained her coffee cup and then held it out to Quinn. He reached for the carafe and refilled her cup.

Rene sipped her coffee. "You played both of us. Why? If you had no intention of staying with me, why would you pull this stunt?"

"I don't know."

"Cut the bullshit. You know why."

Quinn ran his hand through his hair as he acknowledged the stupidity of his actions. "I was mad at Davi for not wanting to have another child. I thought that if I could make her jealous of you, she'd do anything to get me back."

"Like what?" Rene gazed up at Quinn and then laughed when she realized his plan. "You're a moron."

"I gather that."

"I don't even know her, and I know she wouldn't agree to have another baby for you. What were you thinking?"

"I wasn't."

Rene's eyes lit up. "Oh my God, you were doing that give and take thingy." Rene laughed as Quinn's face reddened from embarrassment. "I read that in a tabloid. I never thought you'd take me seriously! Oh, Quinn!" Rene laughed hysterically.

"I'm glad you think it's funny."

"Oh, shut up! You owe me that much after what you've done to me." Rene shifted and turned to face Quinn. "All the time you were with me, were you thinking of Davina?"

"Yes."

"I thought so."

"You didn't let on that you knew."

"A woman has to have some pride, you know." Rene motioned for Quinn to refill her cup. "That first night, when you arrived in that stretch limo, I thought you wanted to relive what we had before you met her. We had lots of fun on that backseat." Rene sighed heavily. "But you wouldn't touch me, at least not the way you used to. I thought you were tired. You'd been through a lot to leave your wife. I understood."

"I was tired. I hadn't slept in days." Quinn said as he topped up her cup.

"Don't give me that, lover. You can go all night without an hour's worth of sleep."

"I'm older now," Quinn said as he refilled his cup.

"Fuck you. You could do it if you wanted to."

"Do you want to sit on the sofa?"

"I'm fine here."

Quinn shrugged then shifted his position to get comfortable.

"When you didn't pick me up in your Porsche, I knew you weren't going to try anything. I remembered what you said about that car. You drive it to be in your wife. You'd only bring that car if you wanted to erase that memory. It was clear that you didn't."

"God, Rene—"

"I'm not the stupid blonde you think I am."

"I never thought of you as stupid. Honest."

"No, I'm just the blonde bitch from hell."

"You do have that reputation."

"I would change for you."

"I don't want you to."

"You don't want me. Period."

"You're right. I'm sorry."

"I thought that if I could just have you once, I'd get you back."

"You're that good?" Quinn teased.

She stuck her tongue out at him. "Prick. Yes, I am that good. You don't remember. That's all."

"I'm sorry. I shouldn't have said that. You're mistaken, though. I do remember, and you were good."

"And Foxx, do you remember him?"

"Damn it, Rene."

"You do remember that night, don't you?"

"Every fucking minute of it. I wish I could forget, but I can't."

"You did nothing wrong, Quinn. You were quite amazing."

Quinn glared at her. "You put something in my drink. That's the only way I would have consented to that night."

"Oh, get off that high horse of yours. It was just a bit of fun, and no one got hurt. You just broadened your horizon a bit." They sat in silence for a moment, and then Rene asked, "Is that why you broke it off with me? Did I go too far?"

"No. We were heading to the finish line. It's just that I saw it coming before you did."

"You're a gentleman again."

"I try." Quinn winced. "My ass is getting sore. Mind if we move to something more comfortable to sit on?"

"Like your bed?"

"More like the sofa." Quinn stood up and offered his hand to Rene. "Up you come."

She took his hand and let him lead her to the sofa. They sat down together, and Rene nestled into Quinn's chest.

"Foxx is going after Davi. He's supposed to be bedding her this weekend."

"She doesn't know about him, about the three of us."

"I figured as much when I found out he was representing her. Why didn't you tell her?"

"I may disapprove of his bedroom antics, but his reputation as an agent is above reproach. I couldn't let my personal feelings get in the way."

"Just like she lets you work with me."

"Exactly."

"Except that now she thinks you've been unfaithful, and Foxx is going to try his damnedest to make sure that she is, too."

"Tell me. Does Foxx have any feelings for my wife, or is she just another notch in his belt of sexual conquests?"

"I don't know."

"Rene, I've just broken my wife's heart. I need to know if Foxx is going to help fix it or smash it into smaller pieces. Tell me the truth."

"I wish I could tell you, lover. Foxx keeps his cards close—always has. She was just a challenge to him, but now I don't know. You'll just have to wait and see."

"Damn it."

"Hurts to be on the other end, doesn't it?"

Quinn didn't answer her. They sat in silence for a few moments.

"Can we stay here like this until it's time to go to work? I don't want to leave."

"Sure."

"Do you think Davina will forgive you? You are going back to her, aren't you?"

"I'd go back to her in a heartbeat, but I've crossed the line. She won't forgive what I've done to her. At least, she won't make it easy."

"If it's any consolation, I wouldn't take you back either, and my standards aren't as high."

"I thought I was the only one for you."

"You are."

"Ouch."

"Get used to it, Quinnie. I'm sure you'll get worse when you try to get back with your wife."

# twenty

**"Tell me you bedded her,"** Rene said without offering him a good morning.

"You don't sound pleased, Rene," Foxx teased as he sat up in his bed.

"Well, did you?"

"No, I did not."

"How hard is it to get her into bed? Damn it, Foxx, you told me you'd get it done."

"She's not as easy as you'd like, Rene. Davi won't cheat on her husband, even if she thinks he's sleeping with you. The woman has rules."

"You should have convinced her."

"Oh, like you've convinced Quinn to have sex with you? By the tone of your voice, I can tell you still haven't closed the deal."

"He still loves her."

"Then why is he with you?"

"He's playing games with her."

"She doesn't know that. Davi believes Quinn's chosen you."

"If you'd bedded her, I might have had a chance. She may not take him back."

"Rene, don't be his second choice. Don't be anyone's second choice. You're better than that."

"I love him."

Foxx grimaced. "I know, sweetheart, but it's not going to happen if he loves her."

"I'm not giving up. There's still a chance he'll leave her."

"Rene—"

"Trust me. I know what I'm doing. Do what you do best, Foxx. Bed that woman today." Rene ended the call.

"Fuck this," Foxx said in frustration as he tossed his cell phone onto his desk.

There was no reasoning with Rene. She put it all on the line—her career and reputation for that damned actor. Even now, when she knew he was using her, she wouldn't give up. What was it about Quinn Thomas that made women put up with his shit? He was damned if he knew.

Foxx looked out his window and saw the early morning mist hover over the quiet lake. It was the perfect time for a swim while he revised his game plan.

XO XO XO

Davi woke to find Jack stretched out asleep in the bed beside her. He looked so much like his father with his mouth slightly open and his perfectly mussed head of thick brown hair. She kissed him lightly on his forehead and then eased out of bed. After pulling on her sweat pants, T-shirt and hooded jacket, Davi made her way into the early morning quiet of the cottage. She was surprised to find a pot of coffee already made and still hot. Davi poured coffee into two travel mugs then made her way out to the deck.

She watched as Foxx took his morning swim. His strong arms made his breaststroke look effortless as he cut through the flat glass-like water. When he turned and headed toward the dock, Davi took both travel mugs with her and made her way to meet him.

"Good morning," she said, greeting him cheerfully when he arrived at the dockside ladder. "I brought you coffee."

Foxx smiled sheepishly up at her. "Thanks. I wasn't expecting company this early in the morning. You didn't happen to bring a towel with you by any chance?"

"No, why?" She chuckled as the answer came to her. "Skinny dipping, eh?"

"You could come in here with me if you'd like. The water's nice."

"Thanks, but I'm not a lake type of girl. I prefer swimming pools, and showers, and bathtubs."

"Afraid of drowning? I'd hold on to you real close." He eyed the mug of coffee lustfully. "You won't mind if I come out, will you? I'd like to have that coffee."

"I promise I won't stare. I think I've seen it all before. That is if you don't mind."

Foxx answered her by climbing out of the water onto the dock. He raked his fingers through his thick wet hair to stop the water droplets from running down his face and then took the offered coffee.

Turning his attention to the lake, Foxx said, "I love this time of day when the lake is so calm and quiet. It's my very own quiet time."

Davi did her best not to look. However, she couldn't resist a quick once over as he stood beside her. It was true. Every hair on his perfect body was red from the top of his head to the fine hairs on his big toe. She couldn't help staring at the red bush around the base of his penis. She smiled, impressed that the cold water hadn't shrunk his impressive manhood.

"Great view, eh?" Foxx asked as he smiled down at her, catching her ogling him.

Davi's cheeks reddened as she looked up to meet his gaze. "I like your tattoos. May I ask what they are?"

"They're Celtic tribal tattoos. My parents are from Ireland."

"No kidding," Davi teased. "As if your name didn't tell me that."

Foxx reached for Davi and caught her by her wrist. She yelped in surprise as he pulled her toward him.

"The name, Foxx, tells you a lot of things about me. It means sly, cunning, smart, and that's just for starters. So be wary, Davina. Then there's O'Connell, which means strong like a wolf, probably as smart as one, too. As a bonus, I've got the red hair that I know you like. Don't deny it."

"I don't," she answered as she reached with her free hand and ran her fingers through the thick wet strands.

Foxx leaned down, bringing his mouth down to Davi's. His lips lightly brushed against hers.

"You want me to kiss you, don't you, Davi."

"Yes," she whispered against his lips.

They both dropped their coffee mugs, oblivious to the sound of the heavy plastic hitting the wooden dock. Foxx gripped Davi's waist and pulled her in tight against him as his mouth covered hers. Her arms wrapped around his neck as she gave in to his kiss. It was an unfamiliar kiss, yet inviting. Davi closed her eyes as she let Foxx explore her mouth and taste her. Her body moved against him as it desperately tried to fit with his. Her hands instinctively found his hair, her fingers threading through the cold, wet strands then down to his ears. She played with the lobes and once again pricked her finger on the back of his earring. Davi broke away from his kiss.

"Foxx, no."

"Why?"

"I can't." Davi pushed away from him. "You know why I can't. I'm married."

"In name only. The man's left you for another woman, and you have every right to move on with your life. There's nothing to stop you, Davi. There's nothing to stop us from happening."

"There is," she said as she bent down to pick up the dropped coffee mugs. "I don't cheat, and I don't play by other's rules. I play by mine." Davi straightened. "I'm sorry, but that's just the way it is."

"Don't apologize for how you feel. You're honest."

"Perhaps you should take us home today."

"Why? Don't you want to stay? We have two more days here. I promise. I'll make no more moves on you. If you want me, it's your call."

"Foxx—"

"Let's just call this a simple case of mixed signals. You brought a naked guy his morning coffee, and he took it as an invitation to kiss you."

"You asked, and I said yes."

"Not the way I remember it." Foxx held out his hand to her. "Do we have a deal? You and the twins will stay with me for a few more days. We'll be two friends hanging out with two adorable four-year-olds."

Davi smiled at him. "You may get tired of us."

"Never," he said as he nodded toward his offered hand. "Friends?"

Davi took his hand and squeezed it. "Friends."

"Come on. Let's get back to the cottage. It's not fair that only one of us is naked."

Davi walked ahead of Foxx, not wanting to stare at his fine naked ass as they walked back to the cottage. She admired how relaxed he was around her. There was no modesty and no pretense. Whether it was in the office or the cottage, he was the same man with her. Davi liked that, not pretending to put one face on for the public and another on for her. She thought of Quinn, how easily he could shift from Hollywood Quinn to her Quinn. She wondered how long he'd been doing it to her—giving her Hollywood Quinn when all the time she thought he was hers.

"How is Jack? Did you manage to settle him?" Foxx asked her.

"Yes. It took a while, though. Jack's missing Quinn."

"What about Stevie?"

"She's a trooper. She doesn't say much unless something is bothering her."

XO XO XO

"I don't want to go home," Davi said as the foursome strolled along the shoreline.

"Then don't. There's no rush."

"We've already been here longer than I planned. My daughter's getting married in three days. I think she'd hate me if I missed her wedding."

"Hate is a strong word. How about disappointed? She'd be disappointed in your non-appearance."

"Yes, and then she'd hate me."

Stevie and Jack ran back to Davi to show her their discoveries in the sand. She bent down to inspect them.

"What have you got there, Jack, a snail? What do you have, Stevie, a feather? I wonder what kind of feather it is."

Foxx squatted to talk to them at eye level. "That's a Red-tailed hawk's feather. They nest up on the bluff over there," he said as he pointed down the shore.

"You know your birds, don't you, Foxx?"

Foxx chuckled. "Not all of them. There's still one I would like to get to know."

Stevie and Jack left their treasures with Davi then ran off ahead of them, splashing in the water along the way.

"They have enjoyed themselves. Thank you for inviting us."

"What about you? Did you enjoy yourself?"

"Yes, I did."

"I'm glad to hear that." He took her hand and squeezed it. Feeling her tense in his grip, he said softly, "Before you pull your hand away, remember that I'm holding it as a friend, not as someone trying to get you into bed. Not right now, anyway."

# twenty-one

**As she walked with the twins** toward the house, Davi watched Maggie's car make its way along the driveway. Jack and Stevie ran to greet Maggie once the vehicle came to a complete stop.

"Oh, how I missed you," Maggie said as she bent down to kiss the children. "Did you have fun with Mommy?"

"Yes!" they exclaimed with excitement.

"I know that Mommy had fun," Maggie said as she focused on Davi. "Maybe too much fun."

"What's that supposed to mean?" Davi asked as she gave Maggie a quick hug.

"Come on, let's get inside and put the kettle on. I've brought some cookies for you. Here, Stevie, you can carry this, and Jack, you can take this for Auntie Maggie," she said as she handed them two small bags just right for little hands to carry.

"We arrived home about an hour ago. Jack and Stevie had to check to see if there were any newborn calves. They won't settle until they check the barn."

"Just like their mother."

"Yes, just like their mother."

Davi held the kitchen door open for the twins and Maggie.

"Don't forget to put your boots away," Davi said as the twins pulled off their rubber boots.

"Okay," they chorused as they picked up their boots and put them away in the closet.

"Thank you. Now go play until Auntie Maggie and I have the tea ready."

"Okay," they chorused again as they headed into the family room.

Maggie sat at the kitchen table while Davi filled the kettle and prepared to make tea. When Davi came back to the table, Maggie opened her purse and fished out a magazine.

"This came out yesterday," she said as she handed it to Davi.

Davi took the magazine, read the front cover, and then dropped it on the table.

"Nothing happened. Foxx likes to skinny dip in the morning. I met him at the end of the dock with his morning coffee. He hugged me and then kissed me. That's all it was."

"You hugged and kissed a naked man who isn't your husband."

"While my husband is doing who knows what with Rene Adams. I didn't do anything wrong, Maggie. I won't apologize for a picture that invaded my privacy."

"They say you started fooling around on Quinn first. That he left you because you were unfaithful."

"Oh, give me a break," Davi groaned. "You know that's not true."

"I know that. I'm telling you what's in the tabloids."

"Do the girls know?"

Maggie nodded her head.

"Damn it. I need to talk to Cat."

"Cat's fine. You know her. She's not a big fan of the press on their best day."

"What about you? What do you think?"

"Me?" Maggie nodded toward the magazine cover. "I think that man has an adorable arse. Now get off yours. The kettle's boiling."

Davi smiled in agreement. "I think so, too." She got to her feet and walked over to the kitchen counter to prepare the tea. "Foxx is a friend. He was kind enough to invite us to his cottage to get away from the mess Quinn dumped us in."

"Looks like it followed you. Any idea how that happened?"

"No," Davi said as she prepared a tray of goodies for the twins. "Nothing surprises me anymore when it comes to the paparazzi."

Davi took the tray out to the twins and returned to continue their conversation. Maggie had taken the liberty of pouring the tea. Davi sat down at the table.

"So you and Foxx—"

"No comment."

"Davi?"

"There's nothing to say. We kissed. Foxx asked for more. I said no. He didn't push the matter. We had a great time at his cottage."

"What about Quinn?"

"He wasn't there."

"Davi?"

"Maggie, what is it with you and your questions?" Davi took a bite from her cookie. She knew Maggie was watching her and waiting for an answer. "He called. He said he wanted to talk, and I told him I wouldn't talk to him until after the wedding. I said that our lawyers could do the talking."

"Lawyers?"

"He's contacted Luke. The only friend in our group he contacts is the lawyer. It can only mean one thing, Maggie. Quinn wants a divorce."

"You're not going to let him go that easily are you?"

"I won't embarrass myself by begging him to come back to me. Besides—"

"Besides what?"

"I don't know if I want him back. Not now, anyway."

# twenty-two

**"And that's a wrap!** Thank you, everyone," Clint called out as the filming of the last scene came to an end.

The crew let out a loud, "Hallelujah!"

The past couple of days hadn't been easy or enjoyable for any of them. Rene had surpassed her usual bitch queen routine with her constant tantrums and demands. Quinn hadn't been much better as he sulked around the set, barely speaking two words unless it was in front of the camera.

"Wrap up party in an hour! I want to see everyone there," Clint barked. "And that means the two love birds."

Quinn scowled at Clint. "Not funny, old man."

"What's wrong with you, son? You've been moping around for days with your head stuck up your ass."

"Complaining about my work?"

"Nope. You're always one hundred percent in front of the camera. It's what you're doing off-camera that has me concerned."

"It's not your concern."

"Like hell, it's not." Clint stuck close to Quinn as they made their way to Quinn's RV. "I'm the one who got you into this mess by insisting you work with blondie."

"It's not Rene. I did this all by myself."

"Then let me help you. Talk to me, Quinn."

Quinn unlocked the door to his RV, and Clint followed him inside. Quinn headed for the kitchen and opened a cupboard filled with liquor bottles.

"What's your poison? Tequila?" he asked as Clint sat down on one of the kitchen bar stools.

"Hell, no. I can't stand the stuff. Just give me a beer if you have it."

Quinn poured a tumbler of scotch for himself then took a beer out of the fridge.

"That's a pretty big drink you have there, kid," Clint said as he eyed the large glass.

Quinn held out the unopened bottle of beer and the glass of scotch. "You want yours or mine?"

Clint took the beer and twisted off the cap. "It seems like you're the one who wanted something that wasn't yours." He took a swig from the bottle. "Not working out for you as you'd hoped?"

Quinn leaned against the kitchen counter and faced Clint. He took a drink from his glass then placed it on the counter.

"What are you doing with blondie? Everyone knows you can't stand to be around her. What the hell were you thinking?"

"I wasn't thinking," Quinn drawled.

"Did she get you drunk, and you slept with her? Feeling guilty? Is that it?"

"We haven't had sex. Not in over five years."

"I don't know who is more confused, you or me?"

Quinn cleared his throat. "I got mad at Davi. She said no to more kids. I wanted to make her jealous. Jealous enough that she'd agree to have another child with me. I used Rene to try to get her to see things my way."

"Well, I'll be damned." Clint took another swig of his beer. He looked at Quinn with bemusement. "Did blondie know you were using her?"

"She knew I wanted more kids."

"She said she'd give you kids?"

"She wants them as much as I do."

He looked thoughtfully at Quinn. "You're an asshole for playing such a stunt, kid. Davi would never go for it."

Quinn shook his head. "It seems everyone knew that, but me."

"She's your wife. You should have known that, too."

Quinn got on the defensive. "Why? Why am I in the wrong for wanting more kids? Why am I in the wrong for trying to get her to see things my way?"

Clint put down his beer bottle and leaned toward Quinn.

"If she had another baby at her age, and I'm not saying that she's old, hell if all women looked as good as she does, a lot of men would stay with their wives without looking sideways. If she had another baby, it would make her look desperate to keep you. She'd look like a pathetic cougar that would do anything to keep her young husband happy. Rumour has it that's why the two of you got hitched in the first place."

"No! I asked her to marry me before she got pregnant."

"You don't get it, do you? Having a baby would make it look like your marriage was in trouble and that one of you or both of you were grasping at straws to keep your marriage together."

"How do you know that?"

Clint gave him a knowing smile as his eyes showed a hint of sadness. "I've been there. Stuck in a marriage that was floundering, and neither one of us dared to call it quits. We had another baby, and for a brief moment, we were happy, and we pretended that we were in love. It doesn't last, son. Having another baby doesn't bring you closer. It pushes you further apart and faster."

"Our marriage was strong. Davi wouldn't have thought that."

"Really? What about everything that's been in the press for the past few months? It's been nothing but you and blondie reuniting. It didn't matter if it was true or not. The point is your wife had to hear about it every damned day."

"We talked about it. Davi knew what Rene was up to, and she knew nothing was happening."

"Right," Clint drawled. "Until your latest experiment, Einstein. Now, your wife thinks you're a liar and your desire to have another baby was a feeble attempt to keep your marriage together."

Clint eyed the celebrity tabloid on the counter and picked it up. On the front page, there was the photograph of a very naked Foxx O'Connell kissing Davina Thomas. "It looks like she's found your replacement. Nice ass." Clint dropped the tabloid on the counter. "What does it feel like to be on the receiving end?"

"Hurts like hell."

"Serves you right. So, do you think your wife is in love with this man with the bare butt?"

"I have no idea." Quinn took another drink from his glass. "I fucked up."

"No argument here."

"She won't talk to me until after Cat's wedding, and then it has to be through our lawyers."

"When's the wedding?"

"Tomorrow. The rehearsal's tonight."

"What are you doing here then? Shouldn't you be there?"

Quinn shook his head. "I think I'm persona non grata."

"Look, son, you need to get home and talk to your wife. Apologize to her for being an asshole and ask for her forgiveness."

"She thinks I cheated on her. That was Davi's only rule. No cheating."

"Convince her that you didn't. Swear on whatever you hold nearest and dearest to your heart. Make her believe you're telling the truth."

"I don't know—"

"The way I see it, you've only got one chance to make things right. After the wedding, it's going to be two lawyers talking, and you won't like what hers has to say."

XO XO XO

Quinn stopped his Porsche at the farm gates. He gazed up the lane toward the farmhouse. So much had changed since he had married Davi and begun his life as the farmer's husband. They erected a fence around the farm to keep paparazzi and overzealous fans off the property, including security gates with video surveillance. Davi had balked at the added protection, but Quinn and Jake managed to convince her that the twins' safety demanded it after the latest threats made against Hollywood celebrities and their families.

She'd given up so much for him—her carefree lifestyle and her privacy without complaint. Davi accepted it all with only one condition: he didn't bring Hollywood home with him. No interviews or television cameras were allowed on the farm to film her family or her home. No one needed to know anything about the couple's private life, including what their kitchen or bedroom looked like. She would be at his side when he travelled, and she would pose for pictures and take part in interviews, but Hollywood stayed right where it was.

Davi hated Hollywood. She hated what Guy Tremblant had almost cost them. She hated how the studios loved scandal and anything that would put their favourite stars in the news. Quinn hated it, too, and he wasn't alone. Many of his peers loved making movies and not the trappings that came with Hollywood.

Hollywood. He knew the meaning of the nickname when Davi and Cat called him that. Hollywood was a put-down, a name that let him know they weren't happy with him. He preferred the nickname Big, a term of endearment the family gave to him when he sang a Big and Rich karaoke duet with Rich at Davi's and his wedding.

Quinn took a deep breath and let it out slowly. He had no idea if he was welcome. He'd messed up big time. A couple of cars were parked in the driveway, fewer than he expected. Had there been a change in plan? It didn't matter as long as Davi was home, and he could talk to her, explain, and then beg for her forgiveness. There was no sense in putting it off any longer. It was time to face the music. Quinn reached out and swiped his gate pass through the scanner. The gates opened, and he drove up the lane slowly.

Cat was the only one to hear the familiar rumble of Quinn's Porsche as he drove up to the farmhouse. She exited the kitchen and headed toward the car as Quinn parked it.

He saw her coming. Quinn climbed out of the driver's seat, then closed the door and leaned casually against it. Quinn crossed his ankles and dug his hands into his jeans pockets. He was far from relaxed, and yet he couldn't let Cat see that. She was Davi's first line of defence. If he couldn't get Cat on his side, he knew he wouldn't get to Davi.

Cat glowered at him. "You have some nerve showing up tonight. Drive back to your blonde bimbo and get the hell out of our lives."

"Where's the rest of the welcoming committee, or are you the only one who'll talk to me?"

"Jake and Sue are still here. Everyone else has gone back to the hotel. The party's over, Hollywood."

He looked at the diamond ring on her left hand. "Are you still going through with it? You can always back out, you know."

"Yes! We're still getting married, and you are not on the guest list." Cat saw it in his eyes, the quick flash of pain. She stepped closer toward him. "Seriously, Hollywood, what are you doing here?"

"I came to apologize and to wish you and Chas all the best. I mean it, Cat. Congratulations."

"You could have sent a card."

"Would you have read it?"

"No." She smiled up at him.

"I thought so." Quinn looked over her shoulder. "I have to talk with your mom."

"She's putting the twins to bed. Don't talk to her tonight. She's upset enough."

"I thought an apology would help. I want to come home, Cat. I know I screwed up, but I didn't do what you think I did." Quinn shook his head. "We were never a couple. Nothing happened between us. I swear to you that I didn't touch her."

"It didn't look like that to us. You and blondie were very affectionate in front of the cameras, all lovey-dovey. Did you not like how Rene made the bed afterwards? Did she not give you the warm fuzzy feeling inside that family gives you or should give you? Oh, wait, we're not family, so I guess you don't know what that feels like."

"I deserve that. I'm sorry if I hurt you, Cat. That was never my intention. I—"

Cat held up her hand to stop him. "We know what your intention was, Hollywood. Is she pregnant yet? Tell me how that works. Do you go off to a clinic or have a vial or two couriered in, and you do it your-self with a straw? You've seen it done plenty of times to the cows. I'm sure you'd be a pro at breeding blondie."

Cat's quick wit and sharp tongue stung. He couldn't let her see that she was leaving marks.

"I told you. Nothing happened between us, and nothing will."

Cat snorted, incredulous. "So all of those pictures are fakes even though your hands were all over her and she was—"

"Like a bitch in heat," Davi answered from behind her.

"Davi." Quinn straightened at the sound of her voice.

"Mom, you don't have to talk to him."

"It's okay, Cat."

He recognized the dress she was wearing. It was a David Paul design. Davi only wore David Paul. Many designers had asked to have the opportunity to dress Davi for various celebrity gatherings only to be turned down politely. She was loyal to the first man who had offered to design for her, the man who designed her wedding gown. She was like that in her loyalty. Once given, Davi didn't look any further unless that person betrayed her. Quinn hoped she'd make an exception to her rule with him.

Quinn's gaze drank in the design now as she walked toward him. The multi-coloured dress clung to her curves in all the right places, stopping a couple of inches above the knee. David Paul liked to show Davi's assets—her well-rounded breasts, trim figure, and long legs. Quinn loved the look on her. She'd never worn designer clothing until she met him. She willingly accepted all of it—five-inch heels, designer dresses, and expensive jewellery, when all along, she was most comfortable in her jeans, favourite cowboy boots and T-shirt.

"Wow, Davi. You look amazing."

"Thank you." Davi stopped in front of Quinn and looked up at him with serious eyes. "Why are you here?"

"I need to talk to you. I have so much to say, to apologize. I'm sorry for how I've behaved, Davi. Please."

Davi reached out and cupped his face with her hand. "Not tonight. I can't talk to you tonight. It's Cat and Chas's time, not ours."

He leaned into her touch and placed his hand over hers. "You said there wouldn't be time after the wedding. I have to make things right. Now. Please."

"No." She gazed into his tired eyes. "Neither one of us is up to talking to each other right now."

"You don't understand."

"I do understand. The answer is still no. You can't pick and choose when you can come home, Quinn. It's not your call. Cat and Chas are getting married. They are the only two people who matter tonight and tomorrow. Not me and not you."

Quinn wanted to take Davi in his arms and kiss her and never let her go. He wanted to taste her and inhale her scent. He'd missed her more than he knew possible. He needed to feel that tingle again.

"I'm sorry for hurting you. I was an idiot."

"You still are." Davi dropped her hand and looked toward her daughter. "Cat, we have company. Say goodnight to Quinn, then come back to the house. Goodnight, Quinn."

She turned and headed to the house.

"Davi," he called out to her.

Davi didn't stop, unable to let herself do that. Her heart was breaking. The tingle they had always had between them was gone.

"Not the reunion you were expecting?" Cat asked as she watched her mother return to the house.

"Not quite."

"You really are an arrogant asshole. You know that, Hollywood?"

"I made a mistake. I thought your mom would see things my way. I didn't realize what I was doing to her."

Cat snorted. "You didn't realize that you were embarrassing her? Hurting her? Breaking her heart? Didn't you realize that every picture of you and blondie was cruel? You're amazing. You idiot."

"What do you want me to say, Cat? I fucked up? You're right. I fucked up. I hurt the only woman I love because I wasn't mature enough to take no for an answer. I cut off all my family and friends to get my way, and I failed. I hurt everyone. I know I hurt you, and I am sorry for that. I have always considered your family, my family. I only wanted more. I didn't think of anyone else."

"What about blondie?"

"I never wanted her. She knew I was playing her."

"So she's pissed at you, too?"

Quinn grimaced. "Let's just say we won't be working together again. I don't work well with blondes. Brunettes are more my style. They tend to keep me in line and kick my ass when I need kicking. They're also good at accepting apologies, heartfelt apologies especially when I'm the one who introduced them to their husband-to-be."

Cat gazed at Quinn for the longest time. He held her gaze then started to smile as he could see her fighting to give him one in return.

"What do you want from me?"

"I want your forgiveness."

"Fine, but you aren't walking me down the aisle. I asked your dad to do the honour."

Quinn nodded in agreement. "I'm sure he's thrilled. He thinks of you as his granddaughter."

"I don't know if Mom will let you come to the wedding."

"She's right. It's your day. I won't ruin it for you."

"You hurt a lot of people. You've got a lot of ass-kissing to do."

"If I don't get your mom to forgive me, I know no one else will."

XO XO XO

"Davi, what's wrong? You look like you've seen a ghost!"

Davi kept walking. She couldn't speak. She stopped when she found herself at the bar, poured herself a double scotch, and drank all of it.

"Davi," Jake's soft baritone voice resonated through her.

She felt his hand on her elbow as he guided her to the sofa and made her take a seat. Kneeling in front of her, Jake held her gaze, forcing her to answer him.

"He's back. Cat's talking to him now." Davi noticed the brief look of surprise cross Jake's face.

"Do you want me to deal with him?"

"Cat's doing a pretty good job of it herself. You can go if you want to. Talk to him if you want. I can't. Not right now."

Sue, Jake's wife, sat beside Davi and held her hand as Jake exited the house. He didn't have to hurry. He knew the son of a bitch would be waiting for him.

"Go inside, Cat. It's time for Jake and me to talk in private."

Cat turned to see Jake walking toward them, and he didn't look pleased. She started walking toward him.

"Get inside," Jake barked as he neared her.

She called out to his back as he passed her, "Don't wreck his face, Jake, just in case Mom takes him back. I want him looking pretty for my wedding."

Quinn watched as Jake approached him. He knew the look on his face, the stony glare as he focused on Quinn. Jake was pissed, and there would be no way Quinn could talk his way out of what was about to happen. He took his hands out of his pockets, braced himself against the Porsche door, and waited. Within seconds, Jake lashed out with a left hook to Quinn's face.

"I deserved that," Quinn said as he rubbed his smarting jaw. "But that's it. Next time I'm hitting back."

"What the hell, man? What are you doing here?"

"I want my family back. I'm here to apologize."

"You swore to us. There'd be no more screwing up. You promised never to break Davi's heart. Good God, man, Rene Adams! What were you thinking?"

"Whatever it was, I was wrong. I know that." Quinn stepped toward Jake. "I didn't sleep with her. No matter what it looks like, I didn't have sex with Rene. I swear it."

"Then what the hell were you doing with her? You left Davi and the twins without saying goodbye!" he yelled at him angrily. "You fired all of us. You fucking fired all of your friends. Why?"

"I couldn't risk having you around me. I knew you'd see that I was faking it if I let any of you near Rene and me. Sarah would have known right away."

"Faking what?"

"I was using her to get to Davi. I wanted to make Davi jealous of Rene."

Jake shook his head, confused by what he was hearing. "Why on earth would you want to make your wife jealous over someone like Rene?"

"I want more kids, or at least I thought I did."

Jake stared at Quinn as he thought about what he was hearing. "You asked me about kids at your mom's funeral. Something about who got to decide, and I told you it was all up to Sue."

Quinn nodded in agreement. "Davi said no, and I tried to change her mind."

"Whatever made you think it would work?" He held up his hand and stopped Quinn from answering. "The lady's got class, man. Any fool knows she'd never run after you. You chased her, remember?"

"I know."

"This is so messed up. Everyone thinks you screwed around on Davi. We were ready to cut you loose."

"Give me a chance to make it up to her. If she doesn't forgive me, then it doesn't matter what the rest of you do."

# twenty-three

**"Hello?"**

"Here's the deal. You make my mother happy tonight, and you can come to the wedding. Make her very happy, and you can walk me down the aisle and be in the family wedding pictures. Let me down, and I will hunt you down. You won't need to worry about finding another girlfriend, Hollywood. I'll castrate you before you know it. What do you say? Are you in?"

"The wedding's in twelve hours."

"You have a problem with that?"

"I'll have to come over now."

"She's drinking and keeping me awake. I want to be a happy and beautiful bride tomorrow, Hollywood. If I don't get my sleep, I will be neither, and I don't want that to happen. Chas won't want that either. Got it?"

"Are we BFFs again?"

"I'm letting you come to the wedding. Don't push it. The lights are on, and the door is open. I have your ETA in twenty minutes. Don't disappoint me."

The line went dead.

"Cat?" Jake asked, knowing that Best Friend Forever only applied to Cat or Tigger, and Tigger wouldn't talk to Quinn in that tone of voice.

"I'm needed. I have to go," Quinn said as he stood up from the bar. "Are we good, Jake?" He extended his hand to his best friend.

"We're good." Jake shook his hand. "Sue and Sarah won't let you come back unless you've made up with the lovely lady. Make it right."

Quinn left the hotel in a hurry. Davi didn't get drunk. She cried when she got upset and even uttered a curse word or two, but she never turned to the bottle. Getting drunk was his fault, and it tore at his heart to know it.

Quinn walked through the farmhouse without turning off the lights. He didn't know how long he'd be allowed in the house. Davi could kick him out as soon as he stuck his head through the bedroom door. He made his way up the stairs and resisted the urge to look in on the twins. He longed to see their faces once again, but he knew Davi needed him in the room across the hall from them. Quinn opened the door to the master bedroom and poked his head through first. The room was dark except for the glow from the television screen.

"Davi?" he called out quietly as he walked in and closed the door behind him.

"Are you and Cat BFFs again? It didn't take long for her to call you," Davi said dully from the comfort of her king-sized bed.

"I'm on probation. It all depends on how well tonight goes." Quinn leaned against the doorframe. "What are you watching?"

"Epic Cougars. It's a reality show about women like me who go after men like you or much younger. It's a real eye-opener."

"You aren't a cougar, Davi, far from it."

She ignored him as she took a sip from her glass. Quinn saw the half-full bottle of scotch by her bedside.

"Mind if I join you?" he asked as he walked toward the bed.

Davi gestured toward the television with her glass. "That's how everyone sees me, you know. Look at her. She's way too old for that man. He has his whole life in front of him. Why would he want to be tied down to her?"

"Can't he love older women?" Quinn asked as he sat down beside her on the bed and faced the television screen.

"She's old enough to be his grandmother! God, what is she thinking? What was I thinking?"

Quinn read the caption on the screen aloud, "Audrey age seventy-five with her fiancé, Greg, age thirty."

"That's forty-five years difference. Grandmother. I told you."

"You're not old enough to be my grandmother, Davi."

"No, but I'm old enough to be one. That's why you left me. You say it was to have more children, but I know the truth. Greg will smarten up, too. One morning he'll wake up and see Audrey's face on the pillow beside him, and he'll ask himself what the hell he got himself into. He'll think that she looks like his grandmother. He'll see every wrinkle and whisker, and then he'll slip out of bed and run for the hills."

"His loss. He didn't see the woman inside."

Davi took another sip from her glass. "Here's the best part. Audrey's family tries to have an intervention. They don't want her making a fool of herself."

"You've seen this one before?"

"There's always an intervention. Someone tries to talk sense into the woman and the man, but they won't listen. They're in love." Davi snorted. "I needed someone to talk some sense into me."

Quinn reached for the remote and turned off the television.

He turned and faced Davi. "You don't mean that."

"If you'd been a one-night stand, I would still be happy. I wouldn't be the old lady left by her younger husband. I wouldn't see myself as a pathetic fool."

"You aren't an old lady, and you aren't pathetic. If anyone's been the fool, it's been me." Quinn took Davi's left hand in his. "You're still wearing my ring."

Davi pulled her hand away.

"It won't come off. My fingers swell in the summer. I see you didn't have that problem. When did you take yours off? Before or after you left Boston?"

Quinn reached down the neck of his T-shirt and pulled out his wedding band attached to a platinum chain around his neck.

"You know I wear it like this when I'm working. It's always close to my heart. I swear to you, Davi, not having your ring on my finger hasn't made me any less married to you."

Davi laughed bitterly. "Married but still a cheater. I know that one. I even got the T-shirts stashed somewhere. One's white, the other's baby blue."

Quinn winced at the reference to her favourite T-shirt of his.

"I never cheated on you. I swear it."

"Define cheat for me. Maybe we have different definitions."

"I didn't have sex with Rene in any form. No intercourse, no oral sex, no hand jobs, not even a French kiss."

"What about the pictures of the two of you? Every day there was a new picture of you and Rene getting cozy at some restaurant or on the set. You can't deny them. You were cheating on me."

"I was playing her. And I was playing you. Nothing happened."

"Not even one thought about having sex with her? Come on, Quinn, you thought about it, didn't you? I mean, why not go all the way once everyone in the world, including your wife, thinks you're sleeping with her?"

"I know what your rules are, Davi. No cheating. Well, they're my rules, too." Quinn exhaled roughly. "You were supposed to come after me. You were supposed to tell me you loved me enough to try to have another child with me. I was playing the fool's game, and I lost.

"We all lost. Even Jack and Stevie."

"No. It doesn't have to be that way. Forgive me. Let me come home before it's too late. If I could take it all back, you know I would."

"But you can't take it back. It's over. That's it."

"I won't accept that."

"Sometimes, we don't have a choice."

"There's always a choice, Davi. There's always a way to fix things."

Davi pushed back the blankets as she tried to get out of bed. Quinn grabbed her hand to stop her.

"I have to pee. Then I'm coming back to bed to sleep. Sometimes we can't fix things. We fool ourselves into thinking we can make things like they were before, but we can't."

"We can at least try. Maybe we can make things better than they were."

"I didn't think we could get much better than what we had. I guess we saw our marriage differently." She looked down to where his hand held hers. "You can't feel it can you? Our tingle's gone, and you can't bring that back. Admit it. That's why you wanted another baby. Plan B for when plan A stopped working. Now let go of my hand and let me go to the bathroom."

"It's always been Plan A. It was working until I screwed it up," he called out to her as she shut the door behind her. "Damn it, Davi, listen to me!"

Davi washed her hands and stared at her reflection in the bathroom mirror. She was a mess—bloodshot eyes from too much crying and too much scotch. She rubbed at the ache in her chest. Seeing Quinn again and having him so close to her hurt. She'd never hurt like this before, not even when she first found out that Ross had cheated on her. She remembered feeling stunned and betrayed, but her heart never hurt, not like this.

"Get a grip, Davi," she said to her reflection. "You'll get through this. You always do."

She splashed cold water on her face. Then she ran her brush through her hair, wincing as the brush pulled on her scalp. Her head ached. She reached for the bottle of Advil, opened it and palmed two tablets, swallowing them quickly. She needed sleep and not the fitful sleep she'd had for the last few days. She doubted tonight would be any different, especially with Quinn back in their bedroom.

Davi opened the bathroom door and gazed toward the bed. Quinn had straightened the bedding for her and plumped her pillows just the way she liked them. He was gone. She looked at their bedroom door. It was open, letting in the light from the hallway.

She found him in the twins' bedroom, kneeling beside Jack's bed. Davi stood in the doorway and watched as Quinn tucked in his sleeping children.

"I didn't realize how painful it would be not to see them every day," he said, knowing that she was watching him. "I missed them. I missed you."

"Why didn't you come home then?"

"I couldn't," he said as he picked up a stuffed toy dinosaur from the floor and then straightened. "I was in too deep. I was waiting for you."

"One phone call. That's all it would have taken for you to know that I wasn't coming for you. I thought I knew you, Quinn, but the man you've turned into is a stranger to me. The man I knew would never have done what you've done." Davi sighed heavily. "I'm going to bed."

"I can leave if you want me to," he said with reluctance.

"Do what you want. You don't care what I think anyway." Davi turned and headed for their bedroom.

He caught up with her, grabbed her by the elbow, and turned her to face him.

"I've always cared about what you think. No one's opinion matters except for yours."

She looked down where he held her. "Let go of me, please."

"Not until you hear me out. I've never loved anyone but you. Not once while I was with Rene did I stop thinking of you."

She wouldn't look at him. She couldn't. Not if she wanted to stay in control of her emotions. Her heart cried out to her, demanding that she forgive him. Her pride wouldn't let her.

"Ross said the same thing to me when he asked for forgiveness. You two are more alike than I thought."

She couldn't have hit him harder if she'd slapped him. Quinn's hand dropped to his side. "Do you want me to leave? I will. Just tell me what you want me to do."

"I don't know what I want you to do. I'm too tired to fight with you. Stay. It's late, and we both need our sleep. Cat will be happy to know you stayed the night."

Davi walked to her side of the bed and slipped in under the covers. Quinn closed the door behind him and then walked to his side of the bed. He undressed quietly, joining Davi in their bed. She turned her back to him.

"Don't get any ideas, and don't you dare touch me."

They lay quietly for a few moments, and then Quinn heard the soft sounds as Davi sobbed into her pillow.

"Oh, love, don't cry, please don't cry." Quinn wrapped his arm around her waist and pulled her into him. "I'm sorry for what I did. I never meant to hurt you."

"You knew what it would do to me. You knew you were hurting me."

"I was stupid to think I could get you to change your mind. I wasn't thinking clearly. I love you, Davi. That's all that matters. I love you, and I want you to take me back."

He kissed the back of her head. He closed his eyes and inhaled the sweet fragrance of her hair. He'd missed her scent and the warmth of her body as he held her close. His hand cupped her breasts in the familiar way when he held her close from behind.

"Take me back, Davi. Love me again. I promise I'll never leave you. Never."

"I can't," she sobbed.

"You can. I know it will take time, but you'll learn to trust me again. You will. I know you have it in your heart to forgive me. Just go to sleep. We'll talk tomorrow."

"You don't understand."

"Sleep, Davi."

He held her while she cried. Each sob tore at him. He'd never seen her like this, and he knew he was to blame. Quinn cursed himself, ashamed of his cruelty and his stupidity.

Before sleep finally came to her, Davi whispered, "Foxx."

Quinn heard her as clearly as if she had shouted at him.

# twenty-four

**Davi felt Quinn's hard chest** cushioning her cheek. She kept her eyes closed, reluctant to open them and find herself alone again. Quinn's pillow comforted her every night since he'd left her. She changed the bedding except for that one pillowcase. She was afraid that if she washed it, she'd forget his scent and never dream about him again.

For over four years, he had kept her warm in her bed. He'd been her lover, her bed buddy, and her teddy bear. Every morning she awoke with a smile on her face as she remembered their lovemaking from the night before and thought of what was to come— Quinn's breakfast in bed, a morning quickie to start their day.

She liked this dream, the one that felt so real. She imagined Quinn with her in the bed, feeling the warmth of his body. Davi let go of her pillow and reached out beside her. She felt his stomach and the firm muscles of his abdomen. One thing about her man was that he kept himself in shape, whether in real life or fantasy. Her fingers traced the outline of his six-pack then moved slowly down to his belly button. He was ticklish there. He tensed as her nail scraped the inside of the tender spot. She knew he'd do that even in her dreams. Her hand continued its journey down to his crotch.

Her hand stroked his erection. She didn't have to fantasize about his size either. She knew every hard velvety inch of his length—how it felt and how it tasted. He had what she needed. She stroked him as she imagined him lying beside her, whispering words of encouragement.

"Easy there, love," he said softly. "Don't start something unless you want me to finish it for you."

Davi's eyes opened wide and she looked up at Quinn.

"I forgot you were here."

"It didn't seem like it by the way you were touching me. Or were you having a fantasy about someone else?"

"I don't fantasize and tell, Quinn."

"Ryan or Foxx? Let me guess. This time you were dreaming about Foxx."

"Why would you say that?"

"You know damned well why."

Davi pushed away from him when she realized the answer.

"Sucks to get a taste of your own medicine, doesn't it, Hollywood? Seeing your spouse in the arms of another on the cover of every tabloid?"

Davi threw the covers back as she tried to climb out of bed. Quinn grabbed her hand.

"Not so fast there, Davi."

She looked down at his hand then back at him.

"What?"

"Tell me you didn't sleep with Foxx, and I'll believe you. I won't bring the subject up again."

Her eyes opened wide in disbelief. "Do you think I had revenge sex with Foxx?"

"You said his name in your sleep last night."

"So what if I said his name? You talk all the time when you're working on a movie. I've had to listen to entire scenes while you slept."

"That's not what we're talking about, Davi. Did you have sex with Foxx? It's a simple question."

"It's not a simple question! It's an insult. Do you think that I would have revenge sex with him just because you were sleeping with Rene? Do you think I would turn my back on my vows and everything I believe because you had? How could you?" Davi closed her eyes and forced back the tears. "I don't play that game, Quinn. I never have." She looked up at him. "Please let me go." Davi pulled her hand away from his. "I've got to get ready."

"Maybe it wasn't revenge sex. Maybe you've fallen for him."

"What if I have? You only have yourself to blame. Unfucking believable," she muttered as she stormed into the bathroom and slammed the door behind her.

Davi leaned against the door.

"Please give me strength to make it through this day. It's Cat's wedding day. Give me strength for Cat."

Davi turned on the shower and stepped into the ice-cold spray, welcoming the shock to her system. Today would be busy. A limo would take the bridal party and Davi to the salon to have their hair and makeup done. According to Cat's plan, they would have one hour to get dressed and ready before the photographer arrived once they returned home. Quinn's father had volunteered to get Jack dressed while Davi concentrated on Cat. Now with Quinn home, those plans may have to change. No, she'd let things remain as planned. Cat still had the option of asking Quinn to leave, but if he stayed, he'd have to deal with his father.

When Davi opened the bathroom door, she saw that Quinn was gone. Sounds of the twins' laughter and high-pitched squeals filled the upstairs. Davi found Quinn in the nursery armchair, hugging and kissing his children.

"They missed you," Davi said as she stood in the doorway watching them.

"I missed them, too," his voice rasped as his eyes filled with tears. "They asked about you every day."

"What did you tell them?"

"You were at work, or you were late coming home. I hated lying."

"I'm sorry."

"Apologize to them. I lied to your children for you."

Davi turned and walked back into her bedroom. She dressed quickly in jeans, buttoned shirt and then made her way to Cat's bedroom.

Davi sat on Cat's bedside and kissed her on the forehead.

"Wakey, wakey, kitty cat. Someone's getting married today, and she has things to do."

Cat's eyes opened as she stretched. Without hesitating, she asked, "Is he here? Did he spend the night?"

"Yes. Quinn's with the twins right now."

"Are you two—?"

Davi shook her head. "He's pleading his case. I'm deliberating right now." Davi saw the disappointment on Cat's face. "It's okay if you want him to be a part of the wedding, Cat. He came back for you."

"And you."

"Yes, but today's your day, and whatever you wish is your command. If you want him to leave, I'll ask him to leave, and if you want him to be here on the sidelines, fine. If you want him to do his stepfather of the bride thing, that's okay, too."

"But—"

"No buts. Whatever you want is fine with me. It's your wedding day."

"He's staying," Tigger said from behind Davi as she stood in Cat's doorway. "And there will be no discussion."

Cat smiled in agreement. "We talked about Quinn last night, Mom. Tigger and I would like him to stay. I hope you don't mind."

"No, it's okay."

"Besides, he's here to stay, Mom. I can feel it. You're not going to send him away." Tigger rushed to Davi and hugged her from behind. "Please forgive him. We all love him."

The honking of the limo's horn from outside interrupted them.

"Jake's here."

"Shit, we're late!" Cat yelled as she scrambled out of bed.

"I'll look after Jake while you get dressed. Tigger, help your sisters."

Davi took the fastest route to the kitchen—the back stairway. Three sets of eyes focused on her, eager to see a clue about Quinn's return. Sue, Jake and John sat at the kitchen table and watched while Davi eyed the tray of Tim Horton's coffee and the opened box of muffins. She helped herself to a banana walnut muffin and a coffee, taking her time, knowing that her audience was growing impatient.

"He's with the twins. Cat wants him here for the wedding, and we're talking. That's all I can tell you right now."

"So you didn't kill him," Sue said.

"Not yet."

"Where are the girls?" Jake asked. "We're running late."

"We're coming!" the girls' voices chorused down the staircase.

Quinn walked in through the other doorway with the twins on his shoulders. He stopped when he saw the group.

"Whoa. It looks like the posse's here for a hanging."

"Not a hanging, but a castration. You remember our agreement, don't you?" Sue said. "You break Davi's heart, and your balls are ours."

"Yes, but—"

"No excuses, Quinn, your balls are ours."

Davi watched as the two best friends argued. Sue loved Quinn, but what he had done not only affected Davi but all of them. Sue was sure to let him know that.

"When do you want us to do this, Davi?"

"Oh, I get a say in this?" Davi asked with her mouth full of muffin. "I didn't know that," she said after she swallowed. "Wait until after the wedding. If he's going to walk Cat down the aisle, we can't have him holding an ice pack while he's doing it."

"Thanks for your support," Quinn said as he put the twins down on the floor.

"If I had anything to do with it, they'd be bronzed and swinging behind my pickup truck by now, so consider yourself lucky," Davi said before she kissed Jack goodbye. "Look after Daddy while we go out to get our hair done, okay?" Davi looked up at Quinn. "Feed Jack his lunch at eleven, then bathe him. His clothes are in his closet if you have the time to dress him. We'll be home close to noon. Please don't tire Jack out. I need him energized for this afternoon." Davi opened the refrigerator door and pulled out a juice box and yogurt for Stevie. "Mommy's got breakfast for you, sweetie. You can have it in the limo." Davi turned and kissed John goodbye before she exited the kitchen with Stevie holding her hand.

Quinn watched as the ladies of the household left in the limo with Jake.

"She's not going to make it easy on you, is she?" Sue asked as she put her hand on Quinn's shoulder.

"No."

"Are you surprised after the stunt you pulled?"

"I thought she'd understand, just like she always does or at least used to."

"If Jake had done to me what you've done to Davi, I'd never speak to him again. He'd be history."

"But, you're not Davi."

"Lucky for you that—"

"I want pancakes!" Jack sang out as he pulled on Quinn's pant legs.

"Pancakes? Of course, we'll make pancakes," he answered as he smiled down at him.

Quinn got busy gathering the ingredients and the cookware to make breakfast. He noticed that his father hadn't said a word to him while he sat at the table watching them.

"Anything I can do to help?" Sue asked him.

"No. I have it. I've missed this. Dad?"

"What?"

"We'll talk later, okay, so would you mind not glaring at me while I work? Talk to your grandson. I'm sure you have a story or two to tell him about me when I was a kid, something really embarrassing."

"Why?"

"Because anything you tell him won't make me feel as foolish as I do right now."

XO XO XO

"So, what happened?" Jake didn't wait for the limo to pull out of the driveway before asking Davi the question.

"They're back together," Tigger announced with certainty.

"For today," Davi corrected her. "He's back for Cat's wedding."

Davi focused on Stevie, ensuring she was eating her yogurt without getting any of it on her shirt.

"No, it's not just for today. I could see it in Quinn's eyes, Mom. You are still the only one for him."

"Yes, but what does your mother think? That's what's important."

"I'm trying not to think about him right now. We didn't say much. I was too drunk and mad to talk to him. We have little ears listening. Watch what you say, please."

"You said something, Mom. You wouldn't let him back into your bed without a word."

"He slept in the bed with me, but we didn't do anything. Do you think I'm that easy? Give me some credit."

"Way to go, Davi," Jake said from the driver's seat. "Make the bastard suffer."

"Jake! Language!"

"Sorry. Well, Quinn deserves it, and you are the best person to put him in his place."

"She's the only one," Cat agreed.

"Will you please give it a rest? Today is Cat's day, not mine or Quinn's. From here on, we will only be talking about Cat. The first one to break the rules gets kicked out of the limo. Got it?"

"She's going to be in his arms in no time, Cat," Tigger whispered in her sister's ear. "Wait and see. Before the day is over, Mom's going to be in love with him all over again."

Davi sat in stony silence as she looked out the limousine's window. She had never stopped loving him, but the hurt inside was tearing her apart. Although her heart ached to forgive him, her head wouldn't let her.

XO XO XO

"Let's take a walk," John said to Quinn once they'd finished washing the dishes and the kitchen was back in order. "Sue will watch Jack while we're gone."

Quinn folded the dishtowel then nodded to Sue in agreement.

"We won't be gone long," John told her.

"We'll be fine."

They walked in silence for a few minutes. Quinn knew that his dad would be the first to speak. It was always like this. Walk, listen, and then talk. Quinn was good at the listening part. He'd had plenty of practice.

"Did your mother's death have anything to do with your leaving your wife?"

"No."

"I guess that's some sort of relief. It would kill Margaret again to know you'd hurt your family because of her death."

Quinn knew there was more to come. They walked in silence for another moment.

"You were an accident. The condom broke."

"What?" Quinn stopped and faced his father. "Mind saying that again?"

"You weren't planned. When your mother found out she was pregnant, we both went into shock. Neither of us wanted a child. We had made plans to travel the world and work on our doctorates. It took us a while to get used to the idea of becoming parents. However, as your mother's belly grew, so did our desire to see what we had created. The day you were born was the most memorable day of our lives."

"I never knew."

"There was no reason to tell you. The point is after you were born, your mother decided that you would be an only child. She didn't want to share herself with anyone but you and me. Call it selfish, but she knew what she wanted and what she could handle in her life. I tried a few times to convince her that she was a wonderful mother and that we should give you a sibling. However, she was adamant that our family would remain the way it was."

"Dad—"

"I'm telling you this so that you know that you're not the only man whose wife said no to him regarding having another child. Saying no didn't make her wrong, and it didn't make me leave. Your mother knew what she could handle and what she wanted. Davi knows the same about herself. You had no right to try to make her change her mind. What you did was cruel and heartless. It's her body, her life, her choice. She's an amazing woman, Quinn. Consider yourself lucky that she lets you be a part of her life. You had no right to be a selfish prick."

"Don't you think I know that? As soon as I left her, I knew I was wrong. Blame it on the Thomas gene for stubbornness. I couldn't go back to her, not right away anyway."

"More like Thomas pride. You inherited your stubbornness from your mother. You and Rene were quite the news item."

"I take it that everyone knows why I left."

"Not everyone. Davi only told those who had to know. No one in her family knows except for her kids and Maggie."

"I wonder what she told them."

"She told them it was a studio publicity stunt and all that shit. She did her best to protect Cat. She didn't want her daughter's wedding day ruined by you and Rene. Who knows if it worked? You and Rene were pretty damned convincing."

"I didn't sleep with Rene. There was no sex of any kind."

"So you let everyone in the world think you cheated on your wife? You've made a real mess of things, son."

"I know."

"Make it right with Davi no matter what you have to do."

"Cat wants me to walk her down the aisle. I know she's asked you."

"If walking Cat down the aisle makes it right for you and Davi, then do it."

"I don't know what will make it right for Davi. All I know is that I have to try. I can't lose her, Dad. I just can't."

Quinn's cell phone vibrated in his pocket. He pulled it out and read the text from Rene. *Say hi to the wife for me.* Quinn deleted the message and then found a previous text message he'd saved on his phone.

"Great timing. Thanks." Quinn showed his father the text message.

John read the message and then laughed. "When did you get that?"

"A few days ago. It's Mom's number. You're the only one who could have sent it."

"Sorry, son, I didn't do it. I cancelled your Mom's number shortly after she died."

"Then who?" Quinn ran his hands through his hair as he thought about the possibilities.

"Consider it a gift from your mother. It doesn't need explaining as long as it worked."

# twenty-five

**"This is how we do it, Jack,"** Quinn said as he sat with his son in the living room while they waited for the rest of the family to arrive. "A man always faces the doorway as he waits for his lady love to make her entrance. He is the one who she sees first. It's the expression on his face that will let her know that she's the most beautiful woman in the world."

"Bootiful," Jack repeated.

"Yes, beautiful. Mommy's the most beautiful woman in the world. However, today is Cat's day, and it's her day to be the most beautiful woman in the world."

"Cat's getting married."

"That's right. Cat's getting married to Chas. So today is going to be a big party for Chas and Cat."

"Will there be cake and presents?"

"Yes, Jack, there will be cake and presents and lots of dancing. Daddy likes to dance with Mommy. Daddy hopes Mommy will let him dance with her today."

Quinn handed Jack a glass of chocolate milk.

"Drink up, little man. Finish your drink before we have to go." Quinn touched his glass of chocolate milk to Jack's. "Cheers."

"Cheers," Jack said happily.

He'd done everything right. He and Jack were fed, bathed, and dressed before Davi and the girls returned home. He'd even had snacks ready for them if they had time to eat before they had to dress. Quinn received an appreciative thank you from Davi but no kiss. Now he and Jack waited.

The wedding planner flitted about, talking on her cell phone while checking her watch. Everything was running on schedule.

"Here they come," she announced as the bride and her entourage made their way down the staircase.

Quinn took Jack's empty glass and put it on the coffee table. Then he and Jack stood and watched the ladies enter the living room. Cat was the first to make her entrance, wearing a gown designed by David Paul. There was no mistaking the designer's handiwork, a long gown made of cream lace with a gold satin sash around the waist. Cat didn't want a poofy dress, adamant that she didn't want to look like a princess bride. She made it clear, also, that she wanted a dress she could walk in and dance in without looking like a mermaid out of water. David Paul gave her exactly what she wanted, showing off every curve and asset Davi's eldest daughter possessed in the most subtle and feminine way.

"Cat, you are simply breathtaking. Chas is a lucky man."

"Bootiful."

Cat smiled at both of them. "Thank you."

Tigger entered the room with Stevie by her side. The tallest of the three Stuart women, Tigger shared the same slim and curvy build as Davi and Cat. She wore a soft pink dress that fell just above the knee, and Stevie wore a cream dress with pink bows. A floral headband kept her dark curls in place.

"Look at you two."

"Bootiful," Jack offered.

"Exactly, Jack. You took the word right out of my mouth."

"Thank you, little man," Tigger gushed as she bent down to kiss her little brother. "You look very handsome. Daddy doesn't look so bad either."

Quinn was about to speak when Davi entered the room. He couldn't take his gaze off her. She was simply stunning. All eyes would be on the mother of the bride today, and Quinn knew that not all would be admiring Davi's beauty. Only Cat, Maggie, Quinn and his gang knew that Ross, Davi's first husband cheated on her. She didn't want it to tarnish her family's memory of him. It was Quinn's latest stunt that would have her friends and family talking about her. She didn't deserve that kind of attention. Davi was right. Today was Cat's day, and all eyes should be on Cat.

Davi's dress was the perfect shade of blue to match her eyes. The hemline was just above the knee, showing off the bare sexy legs that made Quinn hard the first time he laid eyes on them. She wore the shoes he helped her pick out–silver with four-inch heels and open toes to show her pink nails, not the red she had always worn for him.

His gaze made its way up to her chest. The neckline was not too deep, but enough so that her sapphire pendant was framed perfectly by the curve of her breasts. He remembered when she first wore the sapphires. It was the premiere of *Lovestruck*. He couldn't wait to share the evening with his beautiful bride. Then all hell let loose when Davi watched in horror as Quinn made love to Jocelyn Love on the silver screen. He had promised Davi that she would never see him touch another woman the way he touched her. Their private life would remain just that—private. It was one of the worst nights of Quinn's life. He thought he'd lost Davi all because of a little lie. A lie was never too little as far as Davi was concerned. She hadn't worn the sapphires again until today.

Her make-up was perfect, and she had her hair styled in the sexy up-do that always turned him on. This time it was different. She was showing off the silver hair that grew from where the bullet had entered her skull. She called it the dragon's bite. Davi had the hair braided into a single plait and woven into her up-do.

Quinn knew what she was doing, receiving the message loud and clear. From the tips of her toes to the top of her head, Davi let him know that she was moving on, and yet she still wore his rings.

"Davi, you look incredible."

"Bootiful, Mommy," Jack said.

"Thank you. You look pretty good yourself."

Quinn's tuxedo fit him like a second skin. His thick dark hair hung perfectly to his shoulders, framing his famous chiselled face with brilliant blue eyes. Quinn noticed Davi give him the look of approval—the one with the soft smile telling him that she still thought he was gorgeous and that he belonged to her. Belonging to Davi and wearing her ring was all that mattered to Quinn. Why he tried to make her believe anything else would haunt him for the rest of his life.

He stood still as Davi approached him. She reached out to make the last adjustment to his perfectly tied bow tie. It was a habit of hers that Davi couldn't resist. When Quinn lowered his head for the thank-you kiss, she only smiled at him.

Davi turned her attention to Jack, saying, "Jackie, you look very handsome today. Mommy is so proud of you."

"It's time for pictures," the wedding planner announced from the doorway.

"One minute," Quinn said. He faced Cat and pulled out a jeweller's box from inside his tuxedo jacket. "I want you to have this, Cat. It's an apology from me to you for what's happened the past two weeks. I know that I hurt your feelings, and I know I probably added more stress than you needed so close to today." Cat accepted the velvet box and opened it. "It belonged to my mother. My dad gave it to her on their wedding day."

Cat looked at the gold locket and read the inscription aloud, "Forever Yours." She looked up at Quinn. "I can't accept this. You should give it to Stevie. She's your daughter."

"And so are you, Cat, in every way that matters. You're my Best Friend Forever, too, and I know Mom would agree with me in giving you this. Please accept it."

"Thank you. Will you put it on me? I'd love to have Margaret close to me today. She was an extraordinary woman."

"Yes, she was," Davi said. "Thank you, Quinn, for your thought-fulness."

The gardens by the pool made the perfect backdrop for photo-graphing Cat and her sisters. Her bridal party was small, with Tigger as her Maid of Honour, Beth as her bridesmaid, and Stevie as her flower girl. Jack, of course, was the ring bearer, and Rich and Taylor Manning were Chas's groomsmen.

"Mom, let's get you in here with your girls."

Quinn stood back and smiled as he watched the young ladies smile for the photographer. They were all relaxed in front of the camera. Davi was the only one needing coaxing to smile.

"I'm out of practice," she joked with the photographer.

Quinn knew it was more than that.

"Quinn, it's time to join your family."

"I want a picture with Quinn first," Cat told the photographer as she took hold of Quinn's hand. "I have to have one with my BFF."

Quinn's eyes sparkled. "Are you sure you want me? It's going to be a hard decision for you later—which picture you like best, the one with you and Chas, or the one with you and me. Chas isn't going to have a chance, Cat."

"Let me be the judge of that," Cat said, smiling.

Rich stood by his mother off to the side. "Thank you."

"For what?"

"For letting Quinn be a part of today. I know you're only letting him stay because of Cat."

"It's not just because of Cat."

"So, you've forgiven him?"

"Not quite. It's complicated, Rich."

"Is anything ever not complicated when it comes to the two of you? Both of you should come with a handbook and let the rest of us in on the rules."

"What are you talking about?"

"Mom, it's been in your eyes since you met the guy. It's in his, too, whenever he's around you—that thing you have for each other. No one else has it. Cat's pretty close when she's with Chas, but you and Quinn own it."

"We used to, but not anymore."

"That's where you're wrong, Mom. Look at Quinn when he's near you. Really look at him, and you'll see. He's still got it for you big time."

# twenty-six

**All eyes were on Davi** when Rich escorted her to her seat in the front pew of the church. Davi learned from the best how to tune everyone out and concentrate on what was important. Today was Cat's day, and nothing would ruin it for her. The song for the mother of the bride ended, and then the bridal march began. The congregation stood, and all eyes focused on the twins making their way down the aisle.

Stevie beamed with pride as she scattered rose petals onto the aisle. She linked her arm through Jack's as he walked beside her. It wasn't the plan, but the twins insisted they were a team and did everything together.

Tigger followed once the twins had made it halfway down the aisle. She was smiling broadly, happy for her sister and pleased that Quinn had returned for this day. True love was alive and well again in the Stuart-Thomas household.

Once Tigger and the twins arrived at the altar, all eyes turned and focused on the church entranceway. There was no disguising the sounds of surprise escaping from the guests as Cat stood in the doorway with Quinn at her side.

"It's never too late," Quinn whispered in her ear. "Chas will understand. It may take him a lifetime, but he'll get over you."

"Same to you, Big. Give Mom some time. She'll come around. Now get me down that aisle before Chas comes to get me."

Quinn chuckled then escorted Cat down the aisle to her waiting groom.

The minister asked, "Who supports this marriage to this man?"

Davi stood up and joined Quinn.

"We both do," they replied as Quinn put Cat's hand in Chas's.

Quinn escorted Davi back to their pew, taking her hand in his. He kept hold of her hand once they took their seats. Davi kept her attention focused on the ceremony.

When Chas started to recite his vows to Cat, Quinn remembered his vows to Davi. *I offer you my solemn vow to be your faithful partner.*

He leaned over and whispered in Davi's ear, "I'm sorry I broke my vows to you. Forgive me."

Davi turned to Quinn with tears in her eyes. She placed her finger against his lips.

"Please. Not now. Not here."

She turned her attention back to Cat and Chas.

XO XO XO

"What's he doing here?" Quinn asked Davi when he noticed Foxx join the other guests for the receiving line.

Davi smiled when she saw him. She knew the guests would be talking about this handsome red-haired stranger. She wondered if anyone would recognize him as the naked man she hugged in the photograph that spread across the internet only a few days ago. Foxx wasn't as big as Quinn, although he matched him in height. His build was leaner, and Davi had witnessed for herself that under his designer suit was a defined six-pack and a lovely ass.

"He was invited. You invited your lawyer, and I invited my agent. It's only fair."

"Luke's one of my best friends. And yours, too."

"You're the only one with lawyer-client privileges. Well, Foxx is one of my best friends with some privileges, too."

Quinn winced. Davi could put him in his place faster than anyone he knew. He should have realized that when he played the privilege card, his friends would make assumptions about pre-nuptials, divorce, and child custody. They'd be correct, but they'd be wrong, too. There was no pre-nuptial. Quinn would give it all to Davi if she wanted it. That is, if she wanted a divorce. Quinn didn't contact Luke to start divorce proceedings. He told Luke there'd be no fighting her if Davi refused to let him back into her life.

"It's not what you think."

"It's a bit crass talking about lawyers at a wedding, don't you think?" She looked up at him with the slightest hint of tears forming in her eyes. "This is Cat's day. Don't ruin it for her, please."

"Quinn, Davi, congratulations," Foxx said when meeting them.

"Foxx, you look better with clothes on," Quinn said dryly.

"That's a matter of opinion, and yours doesn't count." Foxx turned to Davi, leaned down, and kissed her lightly on the lips. "You're too young and beautiful to be the mother of the bride. Congratulations."

"Foxx, thank you for coming."

"I wouldn't have missed this. It's going to be a day to remember. Save a dance for me?"

"Of course."

Foxx winked at Davi and then moved on to congratulate the bride and groom.

Davi and Quinn did their best to welcome their guests as the happy parents of the bride. Staying true to her promise, Davi wouldn't let anyone or anything interfere with Cat's day. She was all smiles and hugs as she greeted family and friends alike. Quinn did the same, putting his Hollywood charm on full throttle.

"Quinn, you're a terrible man, making us all believe that you'd left our Davi. That movie better be worth it. When do you think it will be in theatres? I'd love to know what all the fuss was about."

"You know how it goes. It could be a year or two before it makes it to the theatres."

"So, are you going to tell us what it was like working with Clint? I bet you've got some stories."

"Well, you know what they say—what happens on the set stays on the set."

"Unless you've got someone videotaping you! Save me a dance. You can tell me all about it then. I can keep a secret."

"So you came home."

"Maggie. It's good to see you."

"I bet it is. Save the charm for someone else."

Davi held out her arms to Maggie and hugged her. "Not now, Maggie. Leave Quinn alone. I promise you can tear a strip off of him when there's no audience."

"Davi, you look lovely, darlin'. It was a wonderful service. Where are my godchildren?"

"They're with Rich and Beth having a snack."

"I'll catch up with you later. You, too, Quinn. Don't be disappearing on me."

"I'll be in clear view all night, Maggie. You have my word."

"Like that means something."

"Well, I guess I'm not one of her favourites," Quinn muttered as he watched Maggie give her congratulations to Cat and Chas.

"She's just getting started. You know Maggie. What did you expect?"

**XO XO XO**

"We're up," Quinn murmured in Davi's ear as the families of the bride and groom joined the newlyweds on the dance floor. Quinn pushed his chair back from the table, stood up, and offered Davi his hand. "Mrs. Thomas, may I please have this dance?"

Davi looked around her—all eyes were on them. She gave Quinn her hand and let him lead her onto the dance floor. His hand found her waist, and he pulled her in close to him. Davi felt the heat emanating from his hard body. She closed her eyes and willed her feet to move.

"Relax, love. I've got you."

Quinn moved expertly around the dance floor. His lips brushed the top of her head. He'd missed this—the feel of her in his arms, the soft feminine curves that moulded perfectly to his body. He inhaled deeply, breathing in the perfumed scent of her hair.

She'd missed his arms wrapped around her, holding her close and making her feel as though they were the only two people in the world. No matter how hard she tried not to think about it, their talk from last night had stayed with her.

"Tell me something?"

"Anything."

"Were you unhappy? Did I not see the signs that our marriage was in trouble?"

"I was never unhappy, and our marriage wasn't in trouble."

"Then why did you run away?"

"I thought you knew. It was your turn."

"My turn?"

"I chased after you when we first met. So, I thought that it was your turn to chase after me."

"Like a game of tag?"

"Something like that. I know it sounds silly, but—"

"So when I caught up to you, I was supposed to tell you that you'd won and that I'd do anything to keep you?"

"Yes, and that you would have another baby with me because you loved me."

"You are such an ass. I didn't chase after you because I loved you enough to let you go. I wasn't going to beg you to stay with me if you wanted Rene."

"Davi—"

"You can't change the rules when it suits you. Why on earth would you ever play games with our marriage when you said that there was nothing wrong with it? You should have stayed, and we could have worked this out."

The music ended, and Davi let go of Quinn's hand immediately. She gazed up at him with sad eyes. "You promised to love me forever. Why would you ever want to make me think that you'd stopped?"

"May I?" Foxx's voice was a welcome interruption.

"We're talking. Get lost, ginger man."

"Of course, Foxx, your timing is perfect." Davi took his offered hand and danced away with him.

"Not going as planned?" Jake asked as he offered a drink to Quinn.

"Every chance I get to explain myself, Davi shoots me down and makes me see how stupid I've been. I don't know, guys, if she'll ever forgive me."

"You'd better act fast before it's too late. It looks like your wife has someone already waiting on the sidelines," Luke said as he gestured to Davi and Foxx with his drink. "Haven't I seen that ass somewhere before?"

XO XO XO

"So? I see the wayward husband has returned," Foxx said as he led Davi out onto the dance floor. "How's that going?"

"I don't want to talk about it if you don't mind."

"That good, huh? Okay, let's talk about something else. You and that dress, Davi. Wow."

"Foxx."

"Sorry. I couldn't resist. Tell you what, let's just dance. I won't say another word unless you talk first."

"That book tour you were proposing. Can we move it up? I'd like to start as soon as possible."

"Sure, Davi, whatever you'd like. I'll get started on it Monday."

## XO XO XO

Quinn noticed the group of women watching him and most likely talking about him. They were Davi's sisters and other extended family members, all of whom were probably wondering if he had cheated on Davi. It was time to put on his best Hollywood face again and play the perfect host. It was Cat's wedding day, and he'd be damned if he let them spend their time gossiping about him and Davi instead of celebrating Cat's marriage.

"Showtime," Quinn muttered as he walked toward the women. "Okay, who's first on my dance card? Don't be shy, ladies. I'm sure you've worked out the pecking order, just like you did at my wedding. Babs, let's go, sexy, time to dance with your favourite brother-in-law."

Quinn knew how to do it right. It didn't matter if the music was fast or slow. He held Babs close enough to make her forget everything else around them. His expertise made her look light on her feet. He didn't flinch when she stepped on his foot more than once, nor did he let it show when she zigged when she should have zagged. Quinn made her laugh when he gave her the little tidbits of gossip about

Rene and Clint that he knew she craved. In one dance, Babs had dismissed any doubt she had about her sister's husband. He couldn't possibly do what the tabloids had claimed.

Quinn maneuvered Babs across the dance floor in perfect time to arrive at the group of waiting women. He kissed Babs on the cheek, thanked her for the dance, and then offered his hand to the next woman. He made a quick calculation that it would take forty-five minutes before he would get the chance to dance with his wife again.

He watched Davi when she danced by him. She smiled and talked with her dance partners. No one to get jealous of—all family members or close family friends. Except for Foxx. Quinn noticed Foxx had more dances with Davi than any man, including Quinn. He was always holding her, smiling at her, touching her. And she was smiling back and laughing. Quinn wanted that for himself. He'd give anything to have her smile at him and tell him she loved him.

Having finished his obligatory dances, Quinn headed to where the twins were dancing with Cat and Chas. He scooped up Stevie, and Cat picked up Jack and danced with them. She danced close so that she could talk to Quinn.

"Why aren't you dancing with Mom? Show everyone your romance is still hot. Show them the love."

"They're more interested in you and Chas tonight, Cat. You're the newlyweds. You're the ones who have to show the love."

"You know what I mean, smart ass. Show everyone that you and Mom are together for real. Make them forget about you and the bimbo. Dance with Mom."

"Haven't you noticed that I've been busy with your aunts? Your mom told me to keep everyone happy, and that's what I've been doing. PR is a lot of hard work, you know."

"I know, and thank you for dancing with them. My aunts will be talking about you for days."

"I want them to talk about you and Chas and your epic wedding."

"Oh, they will, but you'll be the icing on the cake, as always."

"I don't want to be the icing on the cake. I want to be with your mother. She's all I care about."

"Give her time, Quinn. She'll forgive you. Look, maybe this isn't the best time to make it right with Mom. Try to enjoy yourself. Party with the gang. You can fix things with Mom tomorrow."

"I can't do that. Not right now. Something tells me that I'll lose Davi if I don't set things right with her tonight. I have to keep trying."

Quinn gave Cat a wink then danced off with Stevie.

"Come on, sweetheart, let's see if Mommy will dance with us." Quinn worked his way toward Davi. "Care to dance with us, Mommy?" Quinn swayed with Stevie in his arms, making Stevie giggle.

Davi smiled at her youngest daughter having so much fun with her father. It seemed like too much time had passed since Quinn had last played with his children and made them laugh.

Quinn shifted Stevie to one arm then took Davi into the other. He held his two ladies close as they danced. Stevie leaned her head against Quinn's shoulder as if she knew to do it for a slow dance. She patted Quinn's other shoulder to show her mother what to do.

"Did you tell her to do that?" Davi asked in amazement.

"No. I can't help it if Stevie knows the proper way to slow dance. Come on, Mommy, put your head here, and I'll dance my girls around the floor."

Davi did as requested.

"We can stop if your arm is getting tired."

"We'll dance as long as Mommy lets us, won't we, Stevie? Relax, Mommy, we're just dancing, Daddy and his girls." They danced in silence until Quinn whispered in her ear, "This is all I've ever wanted —you and the twins, our perfect family. Forgive me. Please."

Davi felt the words cut through her heart. Dancing with Quinn was a bad idea. She felt trapped with him, and there was nowhere to run, nowhere to hide. Davi squeezed her eyes shut, trying to force the tears away.

"Davi? What's wrong? What did I say?"

"You wanted more kids. That's what you told me the night before you left us. Now you're here holding your daughter and telling me that Stevie and Jack are all you've ever wanted. You can't use children as an excuse to leave and then use them as a reason to come home. One way or another, you're lying to me, and you don't seem to realize it." She pulled away from Quinn. "I have to go. Thank you, Stevie, for the dance, but Mommy needs to go to the little girls' room." Davi kissed Stevie then left as quickly as she could.

XO XO XO

Davi stared into the mirror, dabbing carefully at her makeup with a tissue.

"Here, you'll need this," Maggie said as she offered Davi her compact.

Davi smiled her thanks and fixed her makeup while Maggie watched. Davi waited for the lecture to come once they were alone.

"You haven't told him, have you? Is that why you're in here crying?"

"No, I haven't told him, and that's not why I'm in here. I've got something in my eye."

Maggie ignored her lie. "He deserves to be told what's been going on with you. He needs to know that he left you when he needed to be at home with you, supporting you."

"No. Don't you see? I didn't tell him because I didn't want him to come back to me because of guilt. My self-esteem is bruised enough, and I don't need to make it worse. I won't be the pathetic wife who keeps her husband by playing the cancer card."

"Maybe he needs to be told if only to knock some sense into him. Resuming his film career was a big mistake. He should have stayed at home with you and his children."

"I convinced him to go back to work, Maggie. I wanted him to work with Clint. If anyone is to blame, it's me."

"You didn't force him to sleep with Rene." Maggie put her hand on Davi's shoulder. "Tell him."

"There's nothing to tell him. I've only just had the biopsy done."

"When will you tell him, Davi?"

"I don't know. Promise me you won't say anything to Quinn, Maggie. Promise me."

XO XO XO

Maggie tapped Quinn on the shoulder. "You owe me a dance, Mr. Thomas."

"I've been looking for you, my Irish beauty. Where have you been hiding?"

"I've been in the ladies' room with your wife. She seems to be having trouble with her makeup."

"How is she? She won't talk to me, and the more I try to talk to her, the more upset she gets." Quinn took Maggie in his arms and started to dance with her across the dance floor. "Before you tear a strip off me, let me tell you that I know what I've done. I've messed up with my wife, put my marriage and my family in jeopardy, all because I'm an idiot who doesn't know when he's got everything he will ever want or need in his life. I've hurt Davi. I can see it in her eyes. I don't know if she'll ever forgive me, but I'll do my damnedest to win back her love and her trust."

"That's a tall order to fill, even for a man like you, Quinn Thomas."

"Do I have a chance?"

"Are you asking me as her friend, or are you asking the cards?"

"Both."

"I don't read your cards anymore. I stopped reading you once my god babies were born. It's their future I see now."

"Okay, so what do you see for them? Two parents in a loving home?"

"My god babies will be fine no matter what happens." Maggie saw the disappointment in Quinn's eyes. "I'm sorry, but I don't know what Davi's going to do. I don't think she knows herself."

Quinn saw them out of the corner of his eye. There was no mistaking the woman's bare back in the blue dress or the hand of the ginger-haired man resting on her backside. He guided Maggie expertly toward the couple and then stopped, blocking them.

"Get your hand off my wife's ass, ginger man."

"Jealous, actor man? Your wife doesn't seem to mind."

"Quinn—"

"Stay out of this, Davi. Foxx, you're crossing the line. I'm asking you to stop before—"

"Before you do what? Cause a scene? You've caused enough scenes in the last few days, Thomas. Would one more matter?"

"This one would. Show Cat and her mother some respect. Dance with Davi if you want to, but keep your hands to yourself. Be a gentleman. Stop groping my wife in front of everyone here."

"You mean, stop making a public display of affection for a beautiful woman? You've got some nerve considering what you've been up to with Rene. A bit of a double standard, wouldn't you agree, Davi?"

"Enough, you two, this is not the time or the place. Lower your testosterone a bit and simmer down." Davi looked at Quinn. "I was dealing with the errant hand. I didn't need your protection."

"Davi—"

"Gentlemen, I think this dance is over," Maggie said as she hooked her arm through Davi's. "Come with me, Davi. Let's go check on my god babies."

Quinn and Foxx stood staring at each other while Davi walked away with Maggie.

"Keep your hands off my wife. I won't tell you again."

"You can't have them both, Thomas. Davi or Rene? Make up your mind."

"If I'd chosen Rene, would I be here? It's always been Davi."

"Not according to Davi. She was sure you'd left her. She even talked about divorce."

"I'm sure you loved that."

"You walked away from her, not me. It's not my fault if she let me comfort her." Foxx smiled suggestively at Quinn.

"Why you—"

"May I suggest you break this up before you bring more attention to yourselves?" Jake's quiet but strong baritone interrupted them.

"I don't think Thomas minds the attention." Foxx chuckled as he faced Jake and met his threatening glare. "Fine. I could use a drink."

Quinn and Jake watched as Foxx left the dance floor and headed toward the bar.

"What the hell are you thinking?"

"He's making a move on my wife in plain sight. His hand was on her ass."

"Just like yours was on Rene's. I think that picture was on Tuesday's news."

"Go to hell."

"Doesn't feel good, does it, seeing someone else grope your spouse in public?"

"I should be dancing with her. My hand should be on her ass, not his."

"Then go get her. Apologize to her. Do whatever it takes to get her to forgive you."

# twenty-seven

**Cat and Chas were dancing** their last dance before they left their wedding reception. Everyone held hands to make a circle around the dancing couple. Quinn held hands with Davi and Tigger, and Maggie held Davi's other hand. They swayed in time to the love song as the newlyweds made their way around the circle.

"Mind if I cut in?" Foxx asked as he took Davi's hand and cut in between her and Maggie.

Quinn tensed at the sound of Foxx's voice. His grip tightened on Davi's hand.

"I'm going to miss her," Davi said softly, holding back the tears.

"She won't be far away, love. We can visit her anytime you want."

"It's not the same."

"I know."

"Mom," Cat gushed as she stopped and hugged Davi. "Thank you. Today's been perfect."

"Anything for you, sweetheart."

"Forgive him, Mom. Let Quinn back into your heart. You know you want to."

"Cat—"

"That's all that's missing. You and Quinn have to get back together. Please."

"Cat, it's time to go," Chas said as he tapped her on the shoulder. "Thanks, Davi," he said as he took his turn to hug her.

"Love her and be good to her."

"I will. I promise." Chas kissed Davi on the cheek. "Quinn?" he said as he held out his hand to him. "Good luck, buddy."

"Look after her, Chas. She deserves the best."

"I will, and you look after my favourite mother-in-law."

Quinn hugged Davi from behind as she watched the couple make their way out the door. He kissed the top of her head. "She'll be fine, you know. He'll look after her."

"They'll look after each other. The way it's supposed to be." She stepped out of Quinn's embrace. "I'm going to check on the twins."

"Do you want me to come with you?"

"No. Some of our guests may start to leave. Say goodbye to them if they do. I'll only be a couple of minutes."

Quinn watched Davi as she walked to the private lounge where the twins slept safely.

"I'm going to head home now. It's getting late for your old man."

Quinn turned to face his father. "I saw you dancing with the ladies. You were quite the mover and shaker on the dance floor tonight. Care to have a nightcap with me?"

"If I'm still up when you get back to the farmhouse, I'll have one with you then. I've got a limo heading home right now." He looked at Quinn with concern. "How are you and Davi? I didn't see the two of you together much tonight."

"I'm still working on it, Dad. She's not making it easy."

"Fight for her, son. Don't give up."

John Thomas hugged his son then headed home.

For a moment, Quinn stood alone. He watched the guests on the dance floor. No one liked to leave their parties. They were always fun, and the music was perfect for dancing. Epic— that's what Cat called them.

"So? Where is she?"

"Davi's checking on the twins. She should be back any time."

"How about Foxx? I haven't seen him in a while. Did you run him off?" Jake teased.

"He was here when we said goodbye to Cat and Chas." Quinn looked around the room. His gaze stopped at the closed door to the lounge. "Damn it."

**XO XO XO**

The twins slept soundly on the sofa. Each had a new stuffed toy, a gift from Chas and Cat, tucked under their arm. Davi pulled the blanket over them and then sat on the sofa facing theirs.

She sighed heavily, feeling the happy sadness that comes when a child leaves home and embarks on a new and wonderful stage of life. She was delighted for Cat and Chas and yet sad that Cat wouldn't live at home anymore. She'd miss Cat and her witty and sometimes heated banter. Never one to hold back, Cat was the only one of her children who always kept Quinn on his toes. Cat kept the conversation lively, whether it was a comment on the latest Hollywood gossip or Quinn's favourite sports teams.

Davi leaned back and rested her head against the soft cushion of the sofa. She was mentally exhausted, tired of answering questions about Quinn. She was tired of explaining who Foxx was and why he was at the wedding. Most of all, Davi was tired of being told to forgive Quinn.

*"Forgive him, Mom. Let him back into your heart."* Cat's words repeatedly played through Davi's thoughts. Of all those who pleaded Quinn's case, Cat's opinion was the one that mattered most. She was the only one of Davi's children who knew that their father had cheated on Davi, and although she couldn't forgive her father for cheating, Cat could forgive Quinn.

It wasn't easy for Cat to forgive. She didn't forgive her father, nor did she forgive the so-called friends who teased Cat about Quinn and Davi's marriage, especially those who suggested Cat should make a play for Quinn. Cat didn't forgive lightly, and neither did Davi. If Cat thought Davi should forgive Quinn, then maybe—

"So this is where you're hiding?"

Davi looked up to find Foxx standing in the doorway. His bow tie hung loosely, and his hair had that sexy, messy look as though someone had run their fingers through it many times.

"I'm not hiding. I'm thinking. It looks like you've been having fun."

Foxx closed the door behind him and walked casually toward Davi.

"One of your sisters thought I was some bald actor from an HBO series. I let her run her fingers through my hair to prove that my hair was real." Foxx sat down beside Davi. "Believe me. I'd rather have had your fingers running through my hair, preferably as you were kissing me."

"Foxx—"

"The wedding is over. Your daughter is married and is now enjoying the beginning of a romantic honeymoon. Your wedding obligations are now a memory. Now you can think about what you are going to do with your life, especially what you are going to do with me."

"What about remaining my friend and my agent? I thought we'd agreed that—"

"Change in plans. I want an answer tonight."

"No."

"Is that your answer?"

"I'm too tired to think about anything tonight. I'm going to say goodnight to the guests, and then I'm going to take my children home and go to bed."

"What about your husband? Are you going to take him home, too?"

"It's none of your concern what I do with Quinn."

Foxx leaned in toward Davi, his lips skimming her ear. "I'm very much concerned about what you do with Quinn. Because, if you're doing it with him, you won't be doing it with me unless, of course, you've changed your mind in that regard."

"Foxx, please don't." Davi shifted uneasily. "This isn't the time or the place."

"Why?"

"Because I said so."

"Not good enough. You danced with me more times than your husband."

"He was a good host, and I was trying to be a good hostess."

"You were. Did you dance with all of your male guests?" Foxx put his hand on her chin and turned her face toward him. "Did they all get to hold you close and inhale your delectable perfume, or was I the only one?" He leaned in to kiss her.

"Foxx, no!"

XO XO XO

Jake cursed under his breath as he followed Quinn to the lounge. For a brief moment, he thought of Guy Tremblant, the first man who tried to take Davi away from Quinn. Jake should have disposed of him that night. He knew better now. There'd be no stopping him if Foxx—

"Stay here. This one's mine."

Jake looked at his friend. Quinn had never had a fighting chance to protect Davi from Tremblant. This time the odds were on his side.

"Wipe that smile off his face, man."

Quinn opened the door. His gaze went immediately to the twins, who were fast asleep on the sofa.

"Foxx, no!"

It only took Quinn three strides to reach Foxx's back. "I warned you to keep your hands off my wife!" Quinn grabbed the back of Foxx's jacket and pulled him off Davi. "Are you okay?" He gazed at her, taking in every inch of her. "Did he hurt you?"

"I'm fine."

Quinn turned to face Foxx. "Whatever plans you have for my wife, they aren't going to happen. Your involvement ends now."

"I think they're just about to begin. Davi's barely talked to you all night, and when she does, she leaves in tears. She said she wouldn't decide until after the wedding. Well, the wedding is over, and the bride has left the building. So, Davi can make her decision now."

"I think her telling you to get off of her showed you that she'd made her decision."

Foxx shook his head and laughed. "That's not the impression she gave me on the dance floor."

"It seems to me that she told you to keep your hands off her."

"Enough already!"

"No. This ends here tonight, Davi. I don't want this man anywhere near you."

"Quinn—"

"He and Rene have been playing you, love. He was supposed to bed you while I was with Rene. They knew that if one of us crossed the line, there was no coming back."

Davi looked at Foxx. "You know Rene?"

"And I've known your husband, too. We all knew each other a long time ago."

"What? Why didn't you tell me?" Davi held his gaze.

"If he hadn't told you, I wasn't going to. I won't go into details."

"Quinn?"

"It's something I'd rather forget. It was the last time I was with Rene."

Davi fell back into the sofa's cushions. "Is there no honesty anymore?"

Quinn sat beside Davi. "You want honesty? Here's honesty for you. I didn't tell you about Foxx because I trusted you to work with him the way you trusted in me to work with Rene. I broke that trust, but not until these two hatched a plan to drive us apart. I would never have considered going back to Rene if she hadn't offered to have my children. My mother had just died, and I wasn't thinking straight. I take full responsibility for being a fool. Rene brought Foxx into this mess and persuaded him to seduce you so that she would have a better chance of keeping me. They both knew that we couldn't go back to each other if we'd cheated. When I wouldn't sleep with Rene, she got Foxx to go after you."

"Is that true, Foxx? Did you use me? For Rene?"

"Davi, it started that way but then—"

Davi held up her hand. "No more. Both of you were playing me. How could you?" Davi got to her feet unsteadily. "The two of you make me sick. I'm going to take my children home. And both of you can go to hell for all I care."

Davi walked to the door and opened it. She knew that Jake would be waiting on the other side.

"Lovely lady?"

"Please help me with the twins, Jake. I want to go home now."

"I guess that's my cue to leave," Foxx muttered.

"Not so fast, ginger man. You and I have some unfinished business." Quinn stood up and glared at Foxx. "Don't even think about leaving."

Jake gathered up the sleeping twins in his strong arms. He glanced at Quinn before following Davi out the door.

Quinn closed the door and then turned to face Foxx.

Foxx stood watching him with his arms crossed casually across his chest. "She's probably going to fire me. That's a shame because I had great plans for her book."

"I think her book is the last thing on her mind right now."

"Really? Tonight she asked me to move the book signings up. It seems that she wants to get away from you as soon as she can."

"If that's what she wants, then I won't stop her."

The two men stared at each other. Foxx shifted uneasily under Quinn's gaze.

"So, what's the plan, Thomas? I'd like to go home now if you don't mind, or are you going to stare at me all night."

"I'm going to beat the crap out of you, Foxx, and then you can go home."

"May I ask why? You've lied to both women, used them, and hurt them. What have I done other than having a little fun with Davi? You can't blame me for wanting to know why you prefer her over Rene. It must be what your wife does in the bedroom that keeps you interested. Does she like it the way the three of us did it? Maybe that's the problem, she does, and you don't. You can always call me if you need a third person. I can show you how to do it right."

Quinn didn't let Foxx say another word before throwing himself at him and knocking him to the floor. His years of stunt training kicked in as he held Foxx down while he gave him three quick punches to his face.

Foxx underestimated Quinn's fighting ability, thinking that he'd have time to react before Quinn made his move. He struggled against Quinn's weight, his left arm flailing as he tried to make contact against Quinn's head.

"Get off me," he choked out as blood from his split lip filled his mouth.

Quinn took another jab at Foxx, breaking his nose.

"Fuck!"

"I may have played my wife, but you had no right. She trusted both of us, and we let her down."

"Make it fair, asshole. Let me get in a few punches."

"No, Davi gets to do that."

Quinn released Foxx and got to his feet. He headed toward the closed door.

"She told us both to go to hell, remember? What if she won't hit back?" Foxx asked as he wiped his bloodied mouth with the back of his hand.

"Don't worry. She'll hit back." Quinn turned and faced Foxx. "Look after Rene. I don't expect her to forgive me. I could never give her what she wanted. Maybe she can get that from you. You two suit each other."

Jake stood outside the door, waiting for Quinn.

"I thought you took Davi and the twins home?"

"She asked me to stay here just in case Foxx kicked your ass."

"Thanks for the vote of confidence."

"Oh, I knew you'd win. I trained you. But on the off chance that you lost, Davi asked me to step in. Something to do with telling him he's fired while I rammed my fist down his throat. Your wife was very descriptive in her instructions. Man, I wonder what she's going to do to you when you get home."

# twenty-eight

**Quinn found Davi** in the master bathroom, standing at the vanity while she removed her makeup. She wore the black silk dressing gown he had bought for her not too long ago. He'd seen it and its matching nightgown in one of the storefront windows on one of the location shoots in the Toronto Annex. He was immediately smitten with it, wanting to see it on Davi. He remembered how excited she was when he gave it to her, her smile and the hot kiss she gave him in thanks.

"You're staring at me."

"I'm enjoying the view. I was thinking of the night I gave that to you."

"You gave it to me at four in the morning. You'd been up all night filming, and you couldn't wait to see me in this. You woke me up to have me try it on."

"You were beautiful in it. You still are."

"You were drunk when you gave it to me. Are you drunk now?"

"Sober."

"Did you see your dad? He thought you might have a nightcap."

"I took a rain check."

Davi glanced his way. "You've got blood on your collar."

"It's not mine. Ginger man didn't get a punch in."

"Did you two have sex? Is that why you've never liked him? Never mind. I don't want to know."

"I'll tell you if you want."

"No, that chapter is finished. No more Rene, no more Foxx, and no more—"

"Us?" Quinn offered reluctantly.

Davi turned to look at Quinn. "Games."

He saw it in her eyes. She still loved him.

"Here. Let me help you with these," Quinn offered, stepping behind her and helping her with her hairpins.

"I swear there are a hundred of these damned things stuck in my hair."

"Do you want me to count them to make sure?"

"No. Just get them out, please."

"I got your message."

"What message?"

"You rarely show this," he said as he removed the pin from her plait of silver hair. With loving care, his large hands undid the braid. "You're a survivor. I'm sorry for all of the crap I've put you through."

"Sorry doesn't always cut it, stud."

"I know. I really fucked up this time."

"You made me feel old and unwanted."

"I'm sorry."

"I bet Audrey never felt as old as I did. Greg probably didn't want kids, so that was never an issue with them. They'll probably fight over the number of cats she has in the house."

"I'm allergic to cats, but we can have cats if you want them. Just say the word, and we'll go to the animal shelter in the morning."

"I don't want a cat. Are we almost finished? My arms are killing me."

"Let me finish for you."

Davi dropped her arms and stood still while Quinn worked on the remaining pins.

"How bad did you hurt him?"

"Broken nose, split lip."

"Ouch." Davi reached for Quinn's right hand and examined it. "No broken skin. Ooh, you're good, actor man."

Quinn stopped and locked his gaze with Davi's reflection. "You wanted me to fight Foxx, didn't you?"

"Yes."

"Why?"

"It was your turn."

She held his gaze, her blue eyes pulling him in and showing him the love she had buried underneath the pain he had caused her. And then he saw it, the twinkle in her eyes that let him know that she got it—all of it.

"I love you."

"Yes, I know."

Quinn took out the last of the pins and then took Davi's brush and brushed her hair. When he finished, he leaned down, kissed the nape of her neck and then kissed a trail up to her ear. He touched the dangling sapphire earring.

"I think you should give your sapphires away. Maybe one of your sisters would like them."

"Why?"

"Because I don't plan on ever hurting you again."

"I'd like to keep them, if you don't mind, as a reminder."

"To punish me?"

"No, not to punish you. To remind us of forgiveness."

"Oh, Davi," Quinn murmured as he turned her around. His mouth found hers, and he kissed her hard. He was hungry for her taste, hungry for the love he'd denied himself for two long and lonely weeks.

Davi reached up instinctively and found his hair. Her fingers laced through the long dark strands she'd fallen in love with the first time she'd seen him on the silver screen. She tugged on his hair, enjoying the moans she elicited. Then her fingers found his earlobes. She rolled them between her thumb and forefinger.

Another moan escaped from Quinn, vibrating through her mouth, exciting her. His arms wrapped around her, pulling her in tight against him, crushing her breasts.

Davi tensed.

Quinn released her. "What is it?"

There was no point in hiding it from him, no more secrets. Davi untied her dressing gown and exposed the low-cut neckline of her nightgown. Quinn saw the bandage and the bruising on her breast. He looked up at her with questioning eyes.

"I had a mammogram and ultrasound before we left for Boston. When I came home, my doctor said that they'd found something. The biopsy was yesterday."

"Why didn't you tell me?"

"Tell you what? Play the cancer card to make you come back to me? I didn't want you back because you felt sorry for me."

"I'd have come home because I love you. We wouldn't have had to go through all of this mess."

"I didn't know that. I believed you'd left me for good. Besides, you got the chance to kick Foxx's ass."

"Don't make light of this, Davi."

"Quinn, I have to make light of this until I get the results. I don't want to think of the possibilities."

"What can I do?"

"Hold me. I've missed my teddy bear."

He held her in his arms and kissed her tenderly. Slowly and carefully, Quinn kissed around the bruise on her breast, tracing the edge of the bandage with soft kisses. His breath was hot against her skin as he made a line of kisses from one breast to the other.

Davi's fingers laced through his hair. She didn't want to let him go. She couldn't. Not now when she'd been without him for so long. She tugged on his hair as he moved his head down her body.

"No. Not yet. Please." Quinn looked up at her. "Hold me. I need to have your arms around me. Now. Please, Quinn."

Quinn took her in his arms. He kissed the top of her head.

"Anything you want, love. Just tell me what you want."

"Kiss me."

He knew what she meant. She wanted her kiss—the one that sent tingles down her spine to her toes and made her gasp and sigh with the softest orgasm. The tingles she lost because of him. Quinn hesitated for a brief moment, wondering if he could bring it back. He gazed into her eyes, seeing the love she had for him. He saw her tears and knew that she was wondering the same thing.

Quinn kissed her. His tongue played with hers, teasing it. Quinn loved the taste of Davi, so sweet and inviting. Quinn pulled Davi tight against his body. He felt Davi relax against him as her fingers skimmed down his back and then made their way to his hair.

His hair. His ears. Davi played with them with the familiar lover's touch. Her fingers ran through his long strands, pulling gently on them and causing Quinn to moan softly. She loved the soft feathery feel of his hair between her fingers and the slight tickle it gave her. She could play with his hair for hours and never tire of it. Davi loved how it fell across his forehead when he leaned over her to kiss her. She loved how it hung perfectly messy to his shoulders when he wore his designer tuxedo or T-shirt and jeans. She loved how he kept it just for her.

Quinn shifted his embrace, pressing his hand against her lower spine. Davi countered by finding his earlobes and rubbing them gently between her fingers. She knew how he loved to have his ears touched by her and that he hardened when she felt the sensitive lobes. She dug her thumbnails into them.

"Damn it, love," he said against her lips as he broke their connection. "You're going to make me come."

She nipped his bottom lip in response. Davi was doing it to him again, playing with him and daring him to come when it took all of his control not to. She'd done it to him before, more than once. Whether they were on an airplane, in his Porsche, or their king-sized bed, Davi knew how to get to Quinn with the most intimate of kisses.

"Not this time," Quinn warned her as he picked her up and carried her to their bed. "I want to be inside you, loving you. I've missed the feel of you so damned much."

Her eyes sparkled as she gazed into his eyes. Davi opened her legs, eager to feel Quinn inside her. It had been too long to be without his touch. She held his gaze as he lay on top of her, his strong arms framing her as he supported his weight. Davi wrapped her legs around his waist, holding him close to her. Her nails dug into his shoulders as if to keep him from leaving her.

Quinn entered her slowly, fighting the urge to climax. No woman had ever affected him the way that she did. No woman had ever responded to him sexually the way that Davi did. He was a fool to think that he could leave her and be satisfied with anyone but her. Quinn closed his eyes, forcing out the thoughts of what he'd done and what he could have lost.

"Look at me, Quinn. I need to know you're here."

He opened his eyes. "I'm here, and I'm not leaving ever again."

Davi guided his face to hers. She kissed his lips lightly and caressed his lower lip with her tongue. Small nips followed before her mouth covered his, and she kissed him hard. She ached to feel the tingle, to know that they had it back.

Quinn kissed her with the same intensity. His thrusts matched the urgency of their kiss. Davi's legs tightened around him, and her nails dug in deeper. Her orgasm was close, and he wanted to be with her when she went over the edge. She broke away from their kiss, and her back arched as Davi let out a low moan. Quinn followed her with one last thrust. He cursed as his orgasm racked his body, reminding him that this moment had been too long in coming.

Their foreheads touched as they caught their breath and then they kissed each other lightly on the lips. Quinn's gaze searched her face, looking for the final sign that they were all right.

"I love you," he said softly. "Only you."

"I think I got the message."

"We'll get it back, Davi. Let's just not try so hard to find it."

Tears filled her eyes. "I miss it."

"I'm sorry. It will come back. We just have to give it time."

XO XO XO

Davi awoke, hugging Quinn's pillow. For a brief moment, she thought she'd dreamed last night. Her mind was playing games with her again, making her question what was real until she heard the soft voices behind the bedroom door.

"Okay, Daddy's going to open the door, and we're going to be very quiet so that we don't wake Mommy, okay?"

Davi repositioned herself in the bed and then closed her eyes and waited. She heard the click as Quinn turned the doorknob and opened the door. It was hard for her not to smile as she heard Quinn whisper directions to the twins.

"Stevie, don't pick at Mommy's toast. Jack, this side of the bed. No, don't jump up on Mommy. Wait. Jack, don't hit Mommy with the flowers."

She opened her eyes when she felt the soft thump of the carnations against her face. She smiled at the twins, who were almost eye level with the raised king-sized bed.

She sat upright. "Good morning," she crooned. "You two are up early."

Davi gazed up at Quinn and felt a slight tug at her heart, reminding her of what she almost lost. No man looked as gorgeous as Quinn did in the morning with his blue eyes, sparkling with mischief, set on his perfectly chiselled face with the hint of a morning beard. And then that hair, with the just had sex messiness that made Davi want to run her hands through it and have him make love to her all over again. Her gaze moved down to the tight T-shirt and baggy sweatpants that hung low on his hips.

"Good morning, Daddy."

"Good morning, Mommy. We made you breakfast," Quinn crooned as he placed a breakfast tray over her lap.

"Peanut butter and jam on toast, my favourite." She gave Quinn a suspicious glance when she noticed the bites taken out of the two slices.

"Food tasters, Mommy. We had to make sure the lady of the castle wouldn't get poisoned."

"Thank you. Coffee and toast are my favourites."

There were two small glasses of chocolate milk on the tray for Stevie and Jack. Quinn helped them onto the bed, and then they made themselves comfortable in the pillows beside their mother. Davi then handed them their glasses.

Quinn placed the carnations in the vase on the tray.

"Are these from the wedding?"

"It would be a shame to let them go to waste."

"Smart and sexy."

"Thank you." Quinn leaned over and kissed her. "We've had a family meeting."

"What kind of family meeting?"

"A let's take Mommy away on a holiday kind of meeting."

"Oh."

"Yes, really."

"And what did you decide?"

"Punta Cana. Tomorrow. You, me, the twins, and one very long sandy beach for romantic walks and reconnecting."

"Romantic walks with these two?"

"Of course."

"Tomorrow?"

"It's not like you have to go out and buy anything, Davi. It's August."

"It's also hurricane season there."

"I checked the long-range weather forecast. The storms have passed. There might be a bit of rain, but other than that, it will be fine."

"Tomorrow?"

"Yes," Quinn smiled at her. "Is there a problem?"

"Why tomorrow? Why get away?"

"We need a change of scenery. Somewhere that is new for both of us. No phones, no internet, no paparazzi trailing us."

"There are always paparazzi, Quinn," Davi drawled. "Remember our honeymoon?"

"Yes, and you didn't know they were there."

"I'll know this time."

"Come on, Mommy, what do you say? Stevie and Jack are up for a plane ride, and it's been ages since we've been on holiday. I spoke with Rich. He doesn't need you here. Harvesting corn silage won't be for another week or two."

"What about your father? We can't leave him."

"Tigger will be here. She has tickets for the film festival tomorrow night. He'll be her date. Besides, Dad heads home on Monday. He's okay with us leaving tomorrow."

"I wonder how she got tickets on such short notice. You've been busy this morning, haven't you?"

"Please say yes."

Davi bit into her toast. She chewed her food slowly as she pretended to mull over her decision. She swallowed then smiled at Quinn. "Bring me another piece of toast, and I'll say yes."

# twenty-nine

**From the moment the twins were born,** Quinn and Davi didn't shelter them from the outside world. The twins, accustomed to the stares of strangers and the flash of cameras, ignored the chaos surrounding them at the airport. They knew that Mommy and Daddy were special. They thought it was because of Mommy's cows and Daddy's bedtime stories.

Quinn found the perfect getaway for them in Punta Cana, Dominican Republic. Not far from the airport, right on the beach, and large enough that hardly anyone noticed the Thomas family.

Stevie and Jack assisted Quinn in the construction of a sandcastle. Davi supervised their trips back and forth to the water's edge as they collected water in their pails. She knew they were somewhere watching her. She didn't care. Let the paparazzi take pictures and sell them to the highest bidder. There was no story here except for the Thomas family enjoying their holiday.

"What do you think, kiddies? Is our castle finished?"

"Need a dragon," Jack answered.

"Need a cow," Stevie added.

"Hold on," Davi said as she searched her beach bag. "Will these do?"

She handed the twins the plastic dinosaurs that had kept them amused during their flight.

"Dinosaurs?" Quinn asked. "What do you think, Jack? Stevie? We'll have a dinosaur story?"

"Yes!" they shouted with delight.

Quinn started his story, "Once upon a time on a desert island far, far, away, there lived a queen who lived in her castle."

"With dinosaurs," Jack added.

"They lived with her?"

"Yes, they kept her safe," Stevie said happily.

"And she fed them peanut butter and apples."

"And she scratched their backs."

The twins continued with their story. Quinn looked up at Davi with amazement.

"Later," she mouthed.

XO XO XO

When it was naptime, the twins slept in their poolside cabana while Davi and Quinn soaked in the cool water of the poolside spa enjoying their champagne.

"It's later," Quinn reminded her.

Davi shifted in her seat so that she could face Quinn.

"You and Rene were in the news constantly. The phone wouldn't stop ringing, and paparazzi surrounded the farm. It was hell. Foxx was kind enough to invite the twins and me up to his cottage to get away from it all."

"It wasn't kindness."

She ignored him and continued, "Stevie and Jack liked being at the cottage, but it didn't stop them from missing you. Nighttime without having you tell them their story was hard on them." Davi looked over toward the sleeping twins. "I wrote that story, and they told me that I couldn't tell it the right way. They cried for you, especially Jack." She looked back at Quinn. "Foxx stepped in and started telling them a story. It was a silly story about dinosaurs and peanut butter. The twins loved it, and for the rest of the night, they forgot about you. His story was a godsend, Quinn. I don't know how I would have managed without Foxx."

"He used my children to get to you."

"No, he didn't. He was genuine with them. He couldn't fake that, and they would have picked up on it. I needed a shoulder to cry on, and he offered his. If he used me, I used him, too." She searched his face for a sign that he understood. "My self–esteem was in the toilet. You had left me for Rene. Pictures of the two of you together were everywhere. He wanted to sleep with me, but I couldn't. I hate that he was playing me, but in a way, I played him, too."

"Care to explain, love?"

"It felt good to be wanted by another man. He made me feel desirable. He made me believe that I could find love after you."

"You are desirable. More than you know."

Davi gave him a mischievous smile. "We kissed. He is a good kisser."

"I should have knocked out some of his teeth."

"He's not as good as you, though." Davi moved in close to Quinn. "Something was missing."

He met her lips and returned her kiss. They'd been doing that a lot lately. Kissing. Although neither one of them talked about it, the absence of their tingle was a constant reminder that something had changed between them, and they were desperate to get it back.

"I've been thinking," Davi said, breathless from their kiss.

"You're always thinking. Storylines and dialogue, it never ends."

"No, I'm not thinking about that, but you are on the right track. We need to make plans for ourselves. It's our last year of freedom before the twins start school."

"Freedom to do what exactly?"

"You can continue acting."

He rolled his eyes in response.

"Don't give me that look. I've seen the emails. You're in demand, Quinn Thomas. Hollywood wants you back, and you want to go back."

"Davi—"

"It's perfect timing. I'm not needed on the farm anymore. Rich is making all of the decisions now, and he's only running things by me because he thinks he has to. You've enjoyed being on the farm but admit it. It's not your passion. That's okay. You're an actor, Quinn. You should be acting."

"What about what you want?"

"I want this for you. And if you're working halfway around the world, we'll go with you. I've always wanted to travel, and this will be the perfect time to do it."

"What about your writing and your book launch?"

"I'll still write. As far as my writing goes, I'll need a new agent. I think my working relationship with Foxx has come to an end."

"Do me a favour?"

"What?"

"Hire someone who doesn't have red hair."

# thirty

**"I hope your next book** has dinosaurs and peanut butter in it."

Davi looked up at the man who had handed her one of her books to sign.

"Foxx."

"How are you, Davi? You're looking as beautiful as ever."

"Thank you. What brings you here?"

"I work out of New York now. I joined a new agency."

"Glad to hear it. You're great at what you do."

"It's just my bedside manner with my clients that's not so great."

"Foxx—"

"No. It's true. I apologize for what happened between us. I shouldn't have crossed the line."

"I think it was more than that." Davi glanced at the people standing in line. "This isn't the time or place to discuss this, Foxx."

Foxx leaned in toward Davi and lowered his voice, "Just giving you a heads up. The game's not over. Rene's still playing." Foxx straightened and smiled at Davi. "Thanks for the autograph. Say hi to Stevie and Jack for me."

He left without letting her respond. Was he playing with her? Davi had no idea what Foxx meant. Six months had passed since Quinn's stunt with Rene. It took some time for the gossip to die down.

The status of Quinn and Davi's marriage was no longer in the celebrity headlines. Rene had disappeared, leaving many guessing that she was licking her wounds after being rejected by Quinn once again. Others believed she had gone into rehab, given her erratic behaviour the last few days on the set.

Davi didn't care where Rene was or what she was doing. She hadn't given her much thought, especially since Quinn made it his mission to make her forget the two weeks of hell he'd put her through.

It was Valentine's Day. Davi touched the pink diamond ring on her right hand, a present from Quinn, when her test results finally gave her the all-clear after her lumpectomy. It had been a stressful time for him, although Davi refused to think the worst when the specialist recommended surgery to remove the cancerous mass in her breast. Still feeling the loss of his mother from cancer, Quinn couldn't bear to think of losing Davi.

Quinn would be there soon with the twins to accompany her back to their hotel suite. It was the same suite Quinn had when Davi first met him. They had a special attachment to that hotel, despite Davi's kidnapping from its lobby. The plan was for Quinn and Davi to have an early supper with Stevie and Jack and then get ready for the Valentine's fundraising event for an international charity for children. The couple tried their best to fit in appearances at charity events when their schedules allowed. They knew how much it meant in increased publicity and donations when celebrities attended.

Davi heard a woman clear her throat. She looked up at the waiting customer and smiled. "Sorry about that. Happy Valentine's Day."

**XO XO XO**

"Wow," Quinn said lustily when Davi made her entrance into the suite's living room wearing a long dress designed by David Paul.

"Wow," Jack and Stevie chorused.

"You don't think it's too much red?"

"It's Valentine's Day, love. How can it be too much red? You are beautiful, simply beautiful."

He waited for her to come to him.

"Nice tie, Daddy," she said as she eyed his red bow tie that matched her dress.

"I couldn't let you be the only one wearing red."

Quinn gazed down at her with sparkling eyes as Davi adjusted his tie for him. He kissed her softly on the lips to thank her.

"Love the hair. We match."

"I couldn't let you be the only one with a ponytail," Davi teased as she tucked a wayward strand behind his ear.

Quinn's latest role required him to have long hair and light stubble on his face. He refused to wear a wig, and so he let his hair grow longer than usual. Both of them wore a red ribbon to tie back their hair.

"Okay, you two, enough with the lovey-dovey. Jake's waiting for you, and I've got a date to watch a movie with Jack and Stevie. Kiss them and get out of here."

"Sarah, don't keep them up too late. We have a busy day planned for tomorrow."

"Don't worry. My sweeties will be in bed on time. Now go."

Davi leaned down and kissed her children goodbye. "Mommy loves you. Be good for Sarah, okay?"

"Bye, Mommy."

Quinn picked Stevie and Jack up and gave them a whisker rub. They squealed with delight as their father tickled them.

"Love you."

"Love you, Daddy."

XO XO XO

"Aren't you two quite the pair of Valentines? Nice hair, man," Jake teased as he held open the door of the limousine for them.

"You're just jealous you can't grow a full head of hair, buddy."

"Hah, I'm glad I can't if wearing it like that were my alternative."

"Jake, be nice. I think he looks very sexy. He has that Casanova look going for him. Wouldn't you agree?"

"Casanova fooled around with the ladies, didn't he, Davi? Are you sure you want him to have that look?"

"Hey, my wife knows there will be no fooling around with any lady other than herself. If she wants to think of me as the world's greatest lover, who am I to stop her?"

"Oh please," Davi drawled. "World's greatest lover?"

"You're the one who called me Casanova."

"I said you had the look of Casanova, not the reputation."

"Bam! The man's been told." Jake laughed heartily from the front seat.

"I guess you don't want your Valentine's present then," Quinn said as he feigned hurt feelings.

"Quinn! We agreed. No presents."

"No. You told me no more. I disagreed. I only listened. Listening isn't agreeing."

Davi frowned playfully at him. "I don't need anything."

Quinn reached into his inside jacket pocket and brought out a jeweller's ring box. He offered it to her and waited for her to take it from his hand. She stared at it for the longest time. Davi couldn't imagine what he'd be giving her now. Wasn't her pink diamond ring enough?

"It won't open by itself," he teased. "Allow me."

Quinn opened the box.

"Oh my," she gasped as she saw the eternity ring nesting in the box's blue velvet.

"I couldn't wait for our anniversary to promise you forever again. No more mess-ups, Mrs. Thomas. You are my forever Valentine." Quinn took the ring out of the box and put it on the ring finger of her left hand. "It's a perfect fit with your wedding band and engagement ring."

"It is perfect." Davi kissed him. "Thank you."

"Way to go, Casanova," Jake said as he watched them from his rearview mirror. "Make it hard for the rest of us mortals on Valentine's Day."

"You weren't stupid and put your marriage on the line, Jake."

"No more apologizing, Quinn. It's over. It's in our past. I'm not holding it against you."

"And that is one of the reasons why I love you so much."

Quinn wrapped his arm around her waist and pulled her in close to him. He gave her a long and tender kiss. Davi longed to run her fingers through his hair and then remembered his ponytail. She pulled away from him.

"Sarah told me not to mess with your hair. I can only do that if we don't kiss."

"I can kiss my wife whenever I want to. Damn Sarah's rules."

"Not now, folks. We're here."

Quinn groaned.

"Later, stud. I've got something for you when we get home."

"I thought you said no presents?"

"Who said it was a present?"

Quinn's hand rested on Davi's hip as he escorted her into the building. A red carpet waited inside, allowing the guests to pose for photographers without freezing in the cold New York night air.

"I haven't missed this one bit," Davi said softly for Quinn's ears only.

"Smile, love, all cameras are on you tonight."

"I'd rather they weren't. Isn't there someone famous here? I thought Ryan would be attending."

Quinn laughed. Davi never missed the opportunity to mention her favourite movie actor's name. When Ryan stepped in to replace Quinn in *Second Harvest*, Davi's crush on the actor was cemented firmly in her heart. The two Canadians hit it off instantly and became good friends. Quinn kept his jealousy in check, knowing that Ryan was happily married.

"No, you'll have to be satisfied with me. I hope you're not too disappointed."

"How could I be? You're the love of my life."

Quinn looked down at Davi and met her gaze. He couldn't love her more if he tried. She did this to him constantly, teased him, and then said the most heartfelt words to him.

"Mrs. Thomas, once again, you've gobsmacked me."

The couple worked their way along the red carpet, having photographs taken and questions asked. Thankfully, none of the inquiries related to Quinn and Rene.

Davi's attention focused on the couple entering the building. Cameras flashed, and shouts rang out as the press tried to get closer to them. There was no mistaking the man's head of flaming red hair. Davi's gaze went to the woman beside him. Rene. Instantly, Davi felt the knot in the pit of her stomach as Foxx's words hit her, *"The game's not over. Rene's still playing."*

"Damn it," Quinn said as he saw the couple. "We'll leave as soon as we can. I'm sorry, love."

"No. Don't be. We'll get through this, Quinn. Keep your hands off Foxx, and we'll be fine."

"What about Rene?"

"Keep your hands off her, too."

"Not funny."

"Be polite. We'll say hello and then stay as far away from those two as possible."

The organizers had the brilliant idea that they'd have a group picture taken of their celebrity guests. Quinn wanted to throttle the person who came up with that idea. He fumed as he and Davi waited at the end of the red carpet while Rene and Foxx progressed slowly toward them.

Davi noticed it first—the baby bump under Rene's silver body-hugging mini dress. Davi shifted her focus to Foxx. She looked for the sparkle in his eyes or the proud smile that told the world the baby was his. It wasn't there. Foxx looked more the part of the embarrassed escort than the proud father-to-be. Davi squeezed Quinn's hand.

"I see it. Rene and ginger man deserve each other."

"I don't think Foxx is the father."

When Rene and Foxx got close to Quinn and Davi, the questions started to fly.

"Pregnancy looks great on you. Congratulations! Is this your baby's father?"

Foxx shifted uneasily on his feet. He leaned down and whispered in Rene's ear. She looked up at him and turned her gaze to Quinn. Quinn met her gaze and held it until she looked away.

"Is that polite, asking me who the father of my baby is?" Rene asked as she posed for the press.

Her smile was too broad, her demeanour too relaxed for a woman who was protective of her privacy. Davi squeezed Quinn's hand harder.

"I think it's fairly obvious who the father of my child is." Rene turned her gaze once more to Quinn.

All cameras were on them. There was nowhere to turn without a camera lens or microphone in their face.

"Don't make a scene," Davi whispered in his ear. "Don't take the bait."

Quinn stiffened and immediately went into Hollywood mode. He extended his hand out to Rene.

"Congratulations, Rene," he said as he squeezed her hand. "You look stunning."

"Is Quinn the father?" one of the reporters called out from the crowd.

"Who else would it be?" Rene replied.

"We're leaving," Quinn said as he turned away from Rene. He caught the attention of one of the event's representatives. "Get us out of here," he ordered her. "Take us somewhere private."

Quinn's hand pressed against Davi's lower back, guiding her while they followed the woman through the crowd. She took them to a private room off the main foyer. Quinn locked the door behind him then called Jake on his cell phone.

"Jake, we have a problem. We're leaving. Call me when the limo is ready for us." Quinn ended the call. "Damn it all to hell! What does she think she's doing?"

"Quinn," Davi said, gently touching his shoulder.

"There's no way that baby is mine. Why would she lie about it?"

"Quinn. We can't leave."

"Why not?"

"If we leave now, it will look like you are the father. We have to stay and talk to her."

"This is not the time or the place. Let's get out of here, and I'll have Luke deal with her."

"No. We're not involving Luke. Not yet. Quinn, you started this. Now we have to end it. Get yourself together, and let's go find Rene."

"Why?"

"From now on, we face our problems head-on together. No running."

They found Rene and Foxx sitting at their table. Rene was basking in all of the attention while Foxx looked painfully uncomfortable. Foxx pushed himself up from the table. He held out his hand to Quinn.

"I'm not shaking your hand, ginger man," Quinn grumbled.

"Everyone's watching us," Foxx said as he gave Quinn a thin smile. "You don't want to come across as the jealous lover, do you?"

"I am far from feeling jealous." Quinn shook Foxx's hand with reluctance.

"How about a kiss for me?"

"Don't push it, Rene. This isn't a reunion," Quinn answered as he offered Davi her chair.

Quinn and Foxx both took their seats. Quinn stopped a waiter and ordered drinks for their table. He offered the waiter a hundred dollar tip if he brought their order in less than two minutes. They sat in silence while they waited. Once the waiter returned, and Quinn took a long drink from his glass, he talked.

"Out with it, Rene. What game are you playing?"

"I'm not playing anymore, Quinn. You started the game, and I finished it."

"How? By telling everyone that I'm the father of your baby when we all know that I'm not?"

Davi saw it in her eyes. Quinn would have seen it, too, if he weren't so angry with Rene. She was confident and sure of herself as though she were holding the winning hand and daring others to bet against her.

"You're going to pass ginger man's baby off as mine? I don't think so."

"Hey, leave me out of this. I only found out about this yesterday, and no way am I the father."

"It's not Foxx's baby. It's yours, Quinn."

The seriousness of Davi's words hit Quinn as hard as a slap to his face. He looked at her with anger.

"How could you possibly say that it's mine?"

"You probably told her about your soldiers being in cold storage. I bet it didn't take much effort to get possession of a vial or two. Right, Rene?"

All eyes focused on Rene. She returned their stares with a sweet smile.

"You little minx," Foxx said with admiration.

"You little thief," Quinn retorted.

"You promised me children, Quinn. You made me think you left your wife for me so that we could start a family. I told you that I wanted children, and you used that against me for what, to make your wife jealous, to make her want to have more children when it's obvious she's too old to have more?"

"Why you—"

"You hurt me. I thought I had a chance with you when all the time you were only thinking about her. Well, if you know anything about me, Quinn, you know that once I get over being mad, I get even. I took what you owed me."

"I don't believe you."

"It doesn't matter to me if you do or don't. I'm sure when you contact the fertility clinic, you'll find out that a vial is missing, that is, if they'll admit to it."

"Those were mine. You had no right."

"I had every right. You promised me a child, and I took what you promised."

"What do you want from Quinn?" Davi asked.

"I want Quinn."

"That's not happening."

"Then you don't get to be a part of your child's life."

"I should have you arrested."

"For stealing your sperm? Then what happens? Won't the press have fun with that!"

Foxx cleared his throat to get their attention. "You're not going to agree on this. Not tonight. May I suggest that everyone take a deep breath, settle down, and try to get through this evening without giving the press anything more to write about?"

"What's your role in this, ginger man?"

"Quinn—"

"No, it's all right, Davi. Rene and I haven't seen each other since you two got back together. I only found out about the pregnancy yesterday when Rene called me and asked me to be her date."

"Foxx is right, Quinn. We're here for the charity, not to air our dirty laundry in public," Davi reminded him.

"Rene should have thought about that before she decided to announce that I was the baby's father."

"Well, you are," Rene smiled triumphantly.

"Sperm donor and it wasn't given willingly."

"Quinn. Enough."

**XO XO XO**

"This is fucking ridiculous," Quinn grumbled as he cut into his filet mignon. "Why are we sitting with these two when she's just told the world she's pregnant with my child? It's sick, Davi. It makes it look like you're all for it."

"I'm not all for it. If we run, it will make matters worse. Think of what happened the last time either one of us ran. It didn't work out well, did it?"

"This is different."

"What are you two whispering about?"

"Davi's keeping me from strangling you in public, Rene."

"Quinn!"

"Why don't we go out for a smoke?" Foxx asked Quinn as he rose from the table.

"I don't smoke."

"You do now, Quinn. Go. Give Rene and me a chance to talk."

Quinn scowled. "Five minutes. That's it." He got to his feet and followed Foxx out the door.

"If you're about to give me a lecture on pregnancy and drinking, I'm allowed to have one drink."

"I'm not going to give you a lecture about drinking. I'm going to give you a lecture on being a mother."

"Oh please," Rene drawled with disdain. "What makes you an expert?"

"You have no right to make Quinn's child a news item."

"So you believe me."

"Yes, I do."

"You're taking this well."

"You don't know what's boiling underneath. The wife inside me wants to throttle you. The mother inside me wants to protect your baby. So don't push me, Rene."

"I didn't think you'd take him back."

"I almost didn't."

"Why did you?"

"I love him more than I ever thought possible."

"I love him, too."

"You're allowed to love him, Rene. You just can't have him. What he did to us was terrible. He was wrong to pull a stunt like that."

"And yet we still love him."

"Yes." Davi took a sip from her wine and looked at Rene thoughtfully. "Our children deserve better, Rene. It's our job to protect them and to keep them safe. What you did tonight was reckless and hurtful."

"I wanted to let Quinn know that I won."

"Not at the price of labelling his child a bastard. That's no way for a baby to start in life. You could have kept this private and kept your child out of the spotlight. Now you're going to have the paparazzi on you and my family. That's not fair to any of us."

"I thought you'd be used to it by now."

"Being used to it doesn't mean I have to like it. I put up with it because it comes with Quinn. My older children deal with it. They can smile at the photographers or tell them to go to hell. My twins think it's normal to take their pictures every time they go out with their daddy. What they don't understand is why a security guard carried them through an airport when their daddy wasn't with them and why their mommy cried once they made it through the crowd."

"What do you want me to do?"

"Be smart. Protect your child. Think about your baby and my children before you do something thoughtlessly. It's too late to take back that Quinn's the father. There's no fixing that, but you can be a better mother, Rene. Put your child first, not your need to hurt Quinn."

"I'm back," Quinn said as he sat down at their table. "It's fucking cold outside."

"Where's Foxx?"

"Men's room. What did I miss?"

"Your lovely wife and I are now friends."

"Really? I find that hard to believe."

"Let's say that we have come to an understanding," Davi offered.

"About what?"

"No more silly stunts, Quinn. Davi's convinced me that discretion is the best policy from now on."

"Too bad we didn't have this conversation earlier," he bit out.

"Careful, Quinn, since you were the one who started all of this."

"Quinn." Davi touched his arm. "Please, let's try to get through this together. We can't change the fact that Rene is pregnant with your child. Everyone will know about this by tomorrow morning. The best we can do is come up with a plan to deal with it."

"What are you suggesting?"

"Yes, Davi, what are you suggesting?" Rene asked with keen interest.

"If we deny that Quinn's the father, the press will investigate it and find out the truth. It won't take much effort, I'm sure of it. If Quinn admits paternity, he'll be the philanderer, and I'll be the old betrayed wife. We've already been through that scenario before. It won't be hard to pretend."

"You forget one thing. I didn't cheat on you. Everyone will think that I did and that I fathered a love child. I won't be part of a lie."

"So you'd rather let people know that Rene stole your sperm from a fertility clinic and that your child is a product of a crime? No, Quinn, you don't get to have that luxury."

Quinn stared at Davi with disbelief. "I can't believe you would do this. Why?"

"I'm doing it for the children. They aren't pawns to be used in getting what you want. Both of you should be ashamed of yourselves."

# thirty-one

"You're quiet," Quinn said on their way up to their hotel suite.

"I'm tired."

"You're upset, too."

"Well, I wasn't expecting to find out that you're going to be a father and that I'm not the mother."

"What Rene did was wrong, Davi. There's no excuse for it."

"Yes, it was wrong. It doesn't hide the fact that Rene is carrying your child."

"I don't want anything to do with her, and I want you to stay out of it, too."

"What do you mean by that? Stay out of it?"

"I'll call Luke and have him look into the legalities. I'll find out what my responsibilities are if any, and how to best deal with the situation."

"Situation? Quinn, she's having your child. This isn't something you hand off to your lawyer."

"Let me make myself clear. I don't want to have anything to do with Rene Adams or her child. What she did was wrong. She took something of mine when she had no right. What she's done to our family is unforgivable."

"How can you be such a hypocrite? You let both of us believe that you left me for Rene. What you did was cruel. Don't you dare play the holier than thou card because you won't win."

The elevator stopped at their floor. When the doors opened, Davi stepped out without waiting for him.

"Davi?"

"I'm tired, Quinn. It's been a long day, and I want to go to bed."

Sarah met them at the door.

"Tell me she's lying."

"It's true. Rene stole Quinn's sperm, and now she's expecting the child he promised her six months ago. I think that sums it up. How are the twins?"

"They are fast asleep. We watched one movie, had animal crackers and chocolate milk for snacks and then they went to bed. I want details."

"I'm going to bed. Thank you for looking after Jack and Stevie, Sarah. Quinn's all yours."

Davi closed the bedroom door behind her. She wanted to hit something, tear something apart, rip it into pieces as she screamed profanities at it. Instead, Davi headed for the shower. She kicked off her shoes then left a trail of clothing to the shower door.

Cold water cascaded over her as she pressed her palms and forehead against the cool tiles. Damn him. Damn Quinn for his idiotic game. Damn him for putting his family and marriage in jeopardy because of a stupid, selfish need. Damn him for having a vasectomy. Damn him for sitting next to her on that flight to Los Angeles.

She cried out in frustration at being powerless to change what had happened. She hated being the pawn in other people's games. She hated how Ross had played her for a fool and cheated on her for too many months. She was still raw from Quinn's stunt from only six months ago. And now this—having to pretend to be the wronged spouse to protect an unborn child. Davi's frustration turned to anger, and her rage hurt her very soul because the man who made her angry was also the man who was the love of her life.

Strong arms wrapped around her waist and pulled her against his body. Hot lips caressed her ear as he whispered words of love. She let the sound of his voice flow over her pain and soothe her.

"Don't let this come between us, Davi. Please don't."

"What you are doing is wrong."

"What she did was wrong."

"Two wrongs don't make a right, Quinn. Don't turn your back on your child. Please."

"I'm right."

"No, you aren't."

Quinn exhaled heavily. "Please. Can we call it a draw for tonight?"

"This is breaking my heart."

"I don't want to lose you over this. Tell me that I won't."

Quinn turned Davi around to face him. He cupped her face in his hands and kissed her softly. His kiss was warm against her cold lips. He nibbled on her bottom lip, hungry for her to return his kiss.

"Kiss me, love. Let me know that you still love me." He gazed deeply into her eyes, begging her to kiss him.

"I'll always love you."

She let his tongue push past her lips and enter her mouth. Her tongue played with his, tasting him as his warmth flowed through her.

"This water's too cold," he said against her mouth as his arm reached out to the lever and turned the water to warm. "You and your damned cold showers."

"I was here first," she countered as she pushed away from him. "You can always leave."

"I'm not going anywhere. Damn it, Davi." He grabbed her and pulled her against his chest. "Say you won't leave me over this. Say it."

"I won't leave you. I promise."

"Let me love you, please. I need you."

"No. I can't. Not tonight."

He released her, his shoulders slumping in familiar defeat. "I'm sorry."

Davi ignored his remark. She was tired and didn't want to have this conversation, especially now.

"Davi?"

"I know you're sorry. Don't you know that I'm sorry, too?"

"I want us back. I want you to want me like you used to. What am I doing wrong?"

"Please, Quinn, not tonight."

She opened the shower door, reached for a towel and then stepped out onto the cool tiles of the bathroom floor. Quinn followed her, dripping water on the floor as he watched her dry herself.

She handed him a towel. "You're making a mess."

"What's one more? I seem to make a lot of messes."

"I'm going to bed. Good night, Quinn."

Davi crawled into her side of the bed and turned her back to the centre. She couldn't face him, not tonight. She closed her eyes and tried to fall asleep before he joined her.

Once again, his strong arms wrapped around her and pulled her into him.

"No more running away. That's what you said."

"Going to bed is not running away."

He nuzzled her ear. "We used to make love like rabbits."

"Rabbits get old and tired."

"Not you." He nipped playfully at her ear lobe. "You were insatiable."

"You were the insatiable one. I'm the one you wore out."

"You never let it show." He kissed a trail from her ear down her neck.

"You wore rose-coloured glasses so that you couldn't see the real me. You still don't."

Quinn growled with exasperation and pulled Davi around to face him. "I see every inch of you, Davi. I always have. I'm not giving up on our sex life just because we've lost that tingle. I know it was my fault. Blame me all you want, but stop torturing yourself over it. Not having it doesn't mean the end of that part of us. I won't let that happen."

"I miss it," she cried.

"We'll get it back," Quinn said softly. "It's going to take time, but we'll get it back. We're still connected even without that, and it doesn't mean that we give up on each other. We still have our love, Davi. We still have this—you and me."

His mouth came down on hers, kissing her fiercely. His strong arms pulled her in tight against his chest, crushing Davi's breasts. She winced, and yet her arms wrapped around his neck and kept him tight against her.

"Davi," he moaned as his hand slipped between her legs.

"Quinn—" she breathed against his lips. "I—"

"No more talking. Let me love you. Please."

He rolled her onto her back, pressing her into the mattress. Her body submitted to him as he kissed her again. His fingers played with her sex, causing her to writhe as the pleasure rippled through her. Davi's hands worked on the ribbon still tied in his hair until his long hair fell freely past his shoulders. Her fingers wove through the thick strands and tugged hard on them.

Quinn moaned as the sharp pulls caused his cock to harden further. "You don't know how much I need to be inside you," he murmured as he entered her slowly.

She arched her back against his invasion. Her hands moved down to his ears. She pulled on them gently then dug her nails into the sensitive lobes.

"Yes, baby, just like that," he murmured as his right hand cupped her ass and held her while he thrust into her. "Yes."

Davi pulled his face to hers. She kissed him, hungry for the taste of scotch that still lingered on his breath. She wrapped her legs around his waist, pulling him into her, then tightened around him as her fingers squeezed his lobes.

Quinn groaned.

"Harder," Davi cried out. "Harder."

He thrust into her, giving her what she wanted.

"Ah, Davi!" Quinn moaned as she pulled him over the edge with her. His release came hard and fast.

Davi hugged Quinn and held him close.

"Please, don't give up on us," he said, catching his breath. "We'll get through anything as long as I know I have your love."

## XO XO XO

Davi woke up alone. She wasn't surprised. Quinn usually worked out in the hotel's gym before the twins awoke. He'd return in time to have breakfast with his family before he showered and headed off to work. For a brief moment, she forgot about last night and then she heard Quinn's angry voice.

Davi scrambled out of bed, hastily putting on her robe while she headed out the bedroom into the living area. Quinn paced the floor, his cell phone against his ear while he swore at the person on the other end of the call. Stevie and Jack stood in their bedroom doorway clutching their stuffed animals as they stared wide-eyed at their father. Davi walked hurriedly to them, giving them her best smile.

"Good morning, sweethearts. Let's go back to your room and get you dressed while Daddy's on the phone."

"Daddy's mad," Stevie remarked.

"He said the bad word, Mommy."

"Did he? I don't think he meant to."

She took her time as she helped her children with getting washed and dressed. Davi kept the conversation light as she tried to distract the twins from thinking about their father's behaviour.

"What movie did you watch with Sarah last night?"

"It had dragons in it. A boy learned how to ride a dragon, and then he taught the other kids to ride their dragons."

"Did you like it?"

They nodded their heads in approval.

"What's a bastard?"

She knew they wouldn't be distracted from their father's telephone conversation. "It's an old word, Jack. It's what people call someone whose mommy and daddy aren't married."

"We're not bastards."

"No, Stevie, you're not bastards. Mommy and Daddy are married. Come on, let's have breakfast. What would you like today?"

"Pancakes!"

"Again?"

"Yes!"

Davi hoped Quinn had finished his phone call or at least moved into the master bedroom to be out of the twins' hearing range. They found Quinn standing by the floor-to-ceiling window. His hand braced against the glass as he stared out into the cold, dull New York morning.

"I don't know why she turned off her phone. Ask her. No. She's fine. Would I lie to you?"

"Quinn?"

He turned to face them. "Your mom's right here. Ask her yourself." Quinn held out his cell phone to Davi. "It's your eldest daughter. She's taken back my BFF status. Again."

Davi took the offered phone. "They want pancakes," she said to him as he started toward the twins. "Cat?"

"Mom, what the hell is going on? Are you okay?"

"I'm fine, sweetheart. We're okay."

"What's going on with the blonde bimbo? There's no way she can be pregnant with Quinn's child."

"Cat, we're looking into it. She said she managed to get access to his sperm at the fertility clinic."

"She stole his sperm?"

"She feels that he owed it to her."

"That crazy bitch. What are you going to do? Press charges? Mom, you can't let her get away with this."

"We have things to work out, Cat. We're still a bit shell-shocked."

"Do you want me to come over?"

"No. Not today. I'll call you. Quinn's making breakfast. I need to go, hon."

"Give Stevie and Jack a kiss for me, okay?"

"Will do. Bye, Cat."

Davi ended the call and made her way to the kitchen. She handed the cell phone to Quinn.

Quinn pocketed his phone.

"Your cell phone is off. I've been answering calls all morning."

"It's your turn."

"For what?"

"When you left me in Boston, you turned off your phone, and I had to deal with endless calls asking what you were doing. I think it's called Karma."

"Well, Karma shouldn't start at five in the morning."

"You didn't have to answer your phone."

"I did when the first call was from my father."

"Like I said. Karma."

## XO XO XO

Davi helped with the dishes while the twins played in the living room. She and Quinn worked in silence as they both thought of Rene and her unborn child.

"A penny for your thoughts."

"They're not worth a penny. Sorry to disappoint you, love."

"Okay then. Tell me what's on your mind."

"I'm going to fight Rene. I won't let her get away with this."

Davi gasped, incredulous at Quinn's stubbornness. "You don't mean that."

"I'm not letting her put you or our children through this. We're not going to pretend that Rene's carrying my love child. I can't do that to you."

"No, Quinn."

"I've made up my mind. I've got Luke working on it now. We'll demand a paternity test, and then we'll go after the fertility clinic and then Rene."

"No, you won't." She took his hand and held it firmly between hers. "You wanted another child, Quinn Thomas. You made me feel like a fool while you paraded around with Rene to try to make me change my mind. The world already thinks the two of you had an affair and that I'm the desperate wife who took back her cheating husband. Nothing you do now will change what people think of us."

"I can try."

"And you'll fail. No more lies. No more games and wishing for something you don't have or can't get back. You wanted a child. You made Rene think you wanted one with her, and now she's giving you one. Accept it."

"I only wanted a child with you."

"Yes, well, we don't always get what we want, do we?"

"I'm sorry."

"So am I." She reached for Quinn, hugging his waist. "We'll stay here with you and ride it out together. If I take the twins home, it will look as though I've left you."

"So stay here and play the happy family?"

"There won't be any playing. We are a happy family. Nothing will ever change that. Got it?"

He gazed into her eyes and saw the love she had for him. It pained him to know that he'd done it to her again, caused her unnecessary heartache.

"I love you. If it takes me a lifetime to make it up to you, I will."

He kissed her again. His arms pulled her in tight to his body. Davi's soft moans vibrated through him, exciting him as she returned his kiss. He wanted her now. They both felt the vibration of Quinn's cell phone.

Quinn groaned as he released Davi from his kiss. He pulled out his cell phone from his pocket.

"Jake."

"Hey, Casanova, ready to go?"

"Give me five minutes." Quinn ended the call. "Jake's waiting for me."

"Have fun. We'll see you when you get back."

XO XO XO

"So? She's keeping you?" Jake teased when he met Quinn at the limo.

Quinn shook his head. "I don't deserve her."

"That was a given from the day we met her. The lady has more class in her baby finger than someone who I shall not name has in her entire body."

"You don't have to remind me."

Quinn slid into the back seat, and Jake closed the door. As Jake got into the driver's seat, Quinn pressed Luke's number on his cell phone and put it on speakerphone.

Luke answered on the third ring, "There is a time difference, you know. You couldn't have waited another hour or two?"

"For what I pay you? Not a chance. I've got you on speakerphone with Jake."

"Hey, Jake, how's the family?"

"All good, Luke."

"Great! So, what's up? Has Davi kicked you to the curb?"

Quinn grimaced, and Jake laughed.

"No, she hasn't."

"One of these days, you may not be so lucky."

"Which is the reason why I am calling you, Luke. Get onto Rene. I want a paternity test run ASAP. If I am the father of that baby, find out how she got her hands on my stuff and go after the fertility clinic."

"You think it's a stunt?"

"I wouldn't put it past her."

"Rene is smart. She's got too much to lose to lie to you and her fans."

"I think she was hoping for Davi to leave me."

"One last kick at the can," Jake mused.

"Exactly. I'm not going to lose my wife over this, Luke. Let's get it fixed."

"I'll get right on it. What does Davi say about this?"

"We've agreed to disagree."

"You think that's wise? Davi's got a pretty good head on her shoulders, man. I don't think it's a good—"

"She's looking out for me. Well, this time I'm looking out for her. It's my call, Luke. Look after this for me."

"Okay. I'll call you when I have news for you."

"Thanks, man."

"I hope you know what you're doing," Jake grumbled when the call ended. "Something tells me your wife wants more than lip service from you."

# thirty-two

**Davi sat with the twins** on the living room floor as they worked on puzzles of barnyard animals. She enjoyed this playtime with them, teaching them about shapes and animals. She enjoyed the quiet atmosphere, too. She turned off her cell phone and had all calls to her room go directly to voicemail. There was only one person she wanted to talk to today.

The hotel telephone rang. Davi got to her feet and walked over to the table to answer it.

"Hello?"

"Ma'am, it's Sunny at the front desk. We have a Mr. Foxx here to see you."

"I've been expecting him. Please let him come up. Thank you." Davi hung up the phone.

She was happy to hear that he'd received her message. Davi was eager to see Foxx and talk about the events from last night. She had questions for him, ones that only he could answer.

The twins ran to the door when they heard the light rap at the door. Davi followed behind them.

"Foxx," they cried out with excitement when they saw him.

"Hey there, Jack and Stevie, how are my favourite dinosaur lovers?" Foxx squatted and gazed at them at their eye level. "I brought you something." He reached into the bag he was holding and pulled out two stuffed dinosaurs.

"Thank you!" the twins chorused as they clutched the toys to their chests.

"Thank you, Foxx. That was very sweet of you."

"I saw these, and I thought of them and our story. Do the twins remember it?"

"Yes. It's a new favourite." Davi couldn't tell him that it bothered Quinn that Foxx had made an impact on his children.

"No more castles and dragons?" He gave her a knowing smile. "It must piss off actor man."

"He's getting used to it."

Foxx laughed. "Serves him right."

"Would you like some coffee? I've made a fresh pot."

"Yes, thanks." Foxx followed Davi to the kitchen. He sat on one of the bar stools at the counter. "How are you, Davi?"

"How am I in general, or how am I after last night?" She poured his coffee and then refreshed her cup. "I'm fine. Really. It's Quinn I'm more concerned about." Davi took a sip from her cup.

"Quinn? Why?"

"How would you feel if an ex-lover publicly announced that she was carrying your child right in front of you and your wife?"

"It felt pretty shitty for me standing beside her when she announced it, too."

"What did you say to her? I saw you whisper something to Rene before her big announcement."

Foxx put his cup down on the counter and rolled it slowly between his palms. He stared down into the steaming coffee.

"I asked her not to do it. I told her she was making a big mistake." Foxx looked up at Davi. "I didn't want you or the twins to get hurt again, and I knew that it would backfire on her." He rubbed absent-mindedly at his once broken nose. "Rene and I hadn't spoken since Cat's wedding when she found out that I hadn't won you over. She was pissed. I've seen her mad before, but this was different. She wanted Quinn."

"What he did was terrible."

"To both of you."

"Yes, to both of us."

Foxx gazed at her with admiration. "You forgave him. He's one lucky man."

"I love him, Foxx. I can't see that changing."

"Why did you ask me to come over?"

"Is the baby Quinn's?"

"I thought you believed her."

"I do. Quinn doesn't. Did Rene tell you anything?"

"Not how she did it, only that she did. She said it wasn't hard to do, and then she gave me that Rene Adams smile that told me it was true. She won't fight a paternity test, Davi. She isn't lying."

"Does she expect him to leave me for her?"

"She did at one time or that you'd leave him, but not now. She's carrying his child, and she's happy with that. She finally came around to seeing the light. She doesn't want to be someone's second choice. Neither would I."

"Foxx—"

"It's okay. I knew you didn't want me. That night when Jack needed you to comfort him, I heard you crying. I heard you say Quinn's name in your sleep and that you loved him."

"I'm sorry."

"Don't be. Actor man was a fool for what he was doing to you. I decided that I wouldn't do the same thing to you."

"What about Cat's wedding? Weren't you serious?" Davi saw the sparkle in his eyes and the slight twitch of his lips. "You were playing me?"

"Not you. Quinn. He's not the only one who can act. He needed a taste of his own medicine, don't you think?"

"He broke your nose."

"It was worth it."

"Thank you." Davi kissed him on his cheek.

"You're welcome."

"So you're back in Rene's good books?"

"For now. Why do you ask?"

"Will you watch over her for me?"

"In what way?"

"Make sure that she's looking after herself and the baby. And, if she's agreeable, I'd like to be able to contact her myself."

He saw it in her eyes, and he felt it in her touch when she took his hand and squeezed it. She truly wanted the best for Rene.

"You amaze me. You shouldn't be concerned about Rene."

"She's carrying my husband's child. She's giving him something that I wouldn't. I won't harbour any ill will toward his child or Rene."

"What about Quinn?"

"He's not so forgiving. He can't see past his anger."

"This is all on him, you know."

"I know, and so does he. The thing is, I forgave him, and yet he can't seem to forgive himself."

# thirty-three

**Three weeks had passed,** and now the waiting was over. Quinn received the paternity test results. He was the father. There was no doubt about it. Rene hadn't lied, and no matter how hard Quinn had wished the results to be different, he couldn't change that fact. He pulled his fingers through his hair as he heard the news, and then he cursed and threw his cell phone against the nearest wall. Then Quinn focused his anger on a chair as he kicked it and sent it crashing into a nearby table.

Jake stood on the sidelines, watching his best friend and client slowly come undone. Quinn could act. Two Academy Awards along with countless Golden Globes and People's Choice Awards were proof he was one of the best actors alive. He was a pro at hiding himself away and giving everyone Hollywood Quinn, but not today. Two hours into his workday, and Quinn was losing it—losing his focus, losing his temper and losing his wife.

"You should call Davi," Jake suggested as he pocketed the broken cell phone.

"She knows. Who do you think called me?"

"What did she say?"

Quinn glared at Jake. "She said, give him your name. It's the right thing to do."

Jake knew that Quinn and Davi had been arguing lately. They didn't fight or yell at each other like other couples. Maybe if they did, Quinn wouldn't be reacting this way. They talked constantly. Whether it was behind closed doors or in the limo's back seat, Davi and Quinn talked about Quinn's situation with Rene.

Quinn asked Davi to stop all contact with Rene. No more emails, no more phone calls. She understood his concern. However, she told him in no uncertain terms that he was wrong. She didn't tell him who he could have for friends, so he had no right to choose hers. He said to her that it wasn't his child and that Rene's theft of his semen negated any parental responsibility Davi thought he had. Davi responded that Quinn started this mess and didn't have the right to deny his and Rene's child. Quinn told Davi that he'd never change his mind. Davi told him that she would never speak to him again if Quinn didn't claim his child. He didn't believe her. She dared him.

She dared him again two hours ago when he told her that the child's paternity and sex didn't change a thing. Quinn wouldn't claim him. His surname would not go on the child's birth certificate, not if he had any say in the matter, and his lawyers were working to make sure that happened.

"Quinn, you're breaking my heart," she cried over the phone.

"Why can't you see it my way? I am embarrassed by this entire situation. To acknowledge this child puts a face to my embarrassment. I put our marriage in jeopardy because I wanted another child. Rene's child throws what I did back in your face and mine."

"If you don't acknowledge him, then everything you put us through was for nothing."

"I don't see it that way."

For the first time, Davi hung up on her husband. She refused to answer his calls or texts. After two hours, he stopped trying.

## XO XO XO

Davi soaked in their suite's Jacuzzi, appreciating the soothing heat and the jet streams massaging her back. Other than the sound of the water, quiet surrounded her. No telephones ringing, no four-year-olds asking for a snack, and no husband making impossible demands. Davi took a sip from her glass of white wine and closed her eyes. She wouldn't think about Quinn. She was tired of thinking about him and their situation. She wanted to smack him every time he said that damned word. It wasn't a situation. It was an innocent child.

"You're thinking about him," she said aloud, chastising herself for breaking her rules. "No thinking. Stop it."

Davi took another sip of wine and then settled into the warmth of her bath. It was hard not to think of Quinn. She'd never known anyone to be so stubborn and pig-headed. She could deal with determination. Her daughter Cat was the definition of determination, who, from the moment she could talk, would say, "I can do it" to any challenge. But, this was different. Quinn was wrong, and she knew that deep down inside, he knew it, too. If only she could make him admit it.

Davi sighed. She couldn't make Quinn do anything he didn't want to. He had ways to resist her that made it hard for her to fight him. And he was good, the way he could manipulate her with his baby blue bedroom eyes, the mischievous wink and the "I want you now look" that made her weak at the knees. That's all it took, and she quickly forgot what point she was trying to make with him. She should be used to him and his ways after five years together, but no. One look from Quinn or a soft word in her ear and she was putty in his hands, and oh how she loved his hands.

He was doing it to her again, and he wasn't even with her. She thought back to earlier this morning when she awoke to his hot breath against her ear as he whispered something her sleep-muddled brain couldn't decipher. Her body reacted instinctively as it always did to him. Her buttocks pushed back against him, and her left leg raised and rested on top of his. She moaned when his fingers found her and played with her. She moved against his hand, eager for her morning pleasure. Quinn whispered in her ear again, and she raised her hand and found his hair. Her fingers wove through the long strands and pulled gently on them. She remembered hearing him curse softly, and then his fingers entered her. She gasped and her back arched against him. She opened her legs wider, wanting more of him inside her. And then she felt him as he thrust into her. He cursed against her ear again, something about being wet and tight. She remembered countering with, "Got a problem, stud?" and then it was countless orgasms until he had to leave.

Her hand found the spot that Quinn had touched just hours ago. She was still tender. The memory flowed through her as she arched her back. Davi squeezed her legs together and softly moaned her climax.

Suddenly, the door to the bathroom flew open, banging against the wall behind it. Davi startled and sat upright in the tub.

"You're here." The terrified look on Quinn's face told her that he wasn't in any mood for teasing. "Where are my children?"

She took a moment to answer, still feeling the effects of her orgasm. "It's a play date with Sue and her kids. We talked about it this morning."

She watched him as he stood in the doorway, filling it with his large frame. She'd never seen him so upset before or look so sexy. His long hair was a wild mess. She could tell he'd been running his hands through it more than usual, a habit he had when he was upset. His messy hair framed his perfect face. His blue eyes were wider than usual, brilliant from excitement, or was it terror? His lips pressed closed as though he were willing himself not to speak as he tried to calm down. Sweat beaded on Quinn's forehead, and the tight T-shirt stretched across his chest was soaked from sweat. She didn't recognize the clothes he wore. He must have come from work without changing.

"What's going on?"

"You hung up on me."

"You were an ass."

"Why didn't you pick up the phone? I tried calling you for two fucking hours."

"Were you going to apologize and tell me that you'd changed your mind?"

"No."

"Then there was no point in answering your calls." Davi reached for her glass and took a long sip. "Shouldn't you be at work?"

"My mind wasn't on it."

Davi tried not to choke as she swallowed hard. Quinn was the master of focus. He could tune everyone and everything out and focus on what he had to do. There was only one person who could distract him.

"You walked out on everyone?"

"I'm allowed."

He never played the star card, never asked for concessions or stupid must-haves because of who he was. Quinn was a team player, an actor who never left the set until the day's work finished.

"Did you run all the way here? Why are you so sweaty?"

"The elevators were running slow, so I took the stairs."

"You took the stairs? Why?"

"I had to find you."

Davi gazed up at him as the realization hit her. "Quinn, I would never run out on you. Believe me. The day I leave you, you'll know because I'll say it to your face."

"Then you are planning to leave me."

"That's not what I said."

"You said you'd never speak to me again if I didn't give the baby my name."

"When he's born, your name should be on the birth certificate. You owe him that much."

"I owe him nothing."

Davi threw her washcloth at him, hitting Quinn square in the chest. "You owe him everything! Why are you so stubborn?"

"Why do you care so much?"

"What kind of mother would I be if I didn't care about the well-being of a child, especially if that child belongs to you?" Davi's shoulders slumped in defeat. She was tired of trying to make him do what was right and tired of being the nagging wife. "You win. You won't hear another word from me about Rene or the baby." Quinn shifted uneasily on his feet. He didn't expect her to give in so easily. She saw the questioning look on his face. "One day, Quinn Thomas, you will see how wrong you have been, and you will hate yourself for what you've done. And the sad part is that it will probably be too late to make it right."

"Davi—"

"Now, if you don't mind, I'd like to finish my bath before the water gets too cold even for me."

There was no invitation to join her. She didn't want him, and for the first time in a very long time, Davi asked Quinn to leave her alone. He stepped back and closed the bathroom door.

"I take it you found her?"

"She's taking a bath." Quinn turned to face Jake. "She's not going to fight me on this anymore, Jake."

"You don't look pleased about it."

"I could see it in her eyes, the disappointment, and the pain."

"Then why don't you do something about it?" Jake said, exasperated. "Why can't you do what Davi wants for a change?"

"I can't. I just can't."

# thirty-four

**Davi walked with the twins** to the calving barn. One of the cows was about to give birth, and the twins liked to watch the arrival of a newborn calf whenever they could. Davi welcomed the distraction. Foxx had called her an hour ago to let her know that Rene had gone into labour.

She'd kept her promise to Quinn. She hadn't mentioned Rene or her unborn son for four months, and there had been no discussion about Quinn giving the baby his name. However, it didn't stop Davi from contacting Rene and talking about Rene and the baby with everyone but Quinn. She didn't tell Quinn she knew her due date and the hospital she'd use for the delivery. She didn't tell Quinn that Rene had shown her pictures of the nursery. The only thing Davi didn't know was what the baby's name would be. Rene told her she wasn't ready for that announcement.

Jack and Stevie took their place at the calving pen. They stood by the gate, peered through the rails, and watched with awe as the cow lay quietly in the straw. It was always the same with them. They stood and watched with wonder as they saw the appearance of the front feet, the calf's nose, and then the entire body with the cow's final push. Jack nodded as though approving Rich's work with the calf as he cleared the calf's nostrils to make sure it was breathing and then pulled the calf to its mother so that she could start licking it clean.

"What did we get?" Davi asked Rich.

"Heifer calf. Care to name this one, Mom?"

"How about Rene? She's having her baby right now. Maybe this will bring her luck."

Rich shook his head. "You're my mother, and I love you, but there are times that I don't know how you think the way you do."

She knew what he meant. "He's a baby. It's not his fault he got thrown into this mess."

"It's not your mess to clean up, Mom."

"Someone has to, Rich, and I don't see any other volunteers."

XO XO XO

Davi received the news during bath time. She took the call out in the hallway while Quinn supervised the twins in the tub.

"How is she?" Davi asked Foxx.

"She's good. She's resting right now. The baby is fine, too, all seven pounds and twenty inches of him."

"Will you send me a picture?"

"Rene asked that I wait until she looks more presentable."

"I heard that," Rene said in the background. "Hand me the phone, Foxx. Davi?"

"Congratulations, Rene. You're a mom!"

Rene started to cry. "He's so tiny. What do I do now?"

"Love him. I know you'll be a wonderful mother."

"He's perfect, Davi. He has ten fingers and ten toes."

Davi smiled. "Of course, he's perfect. What colour is his hair?"

"He has Quinn's hair."

Davi started to cry.

"Please don't hate me, Davi."

"I don't hate you, Rene."

"Would you like to know his name?"

Davi leaned against the wall and closed her eyes. "Of course I would."

"His name is David Foxx Thomas. I named him after my two best friends."

Davi slid down to the floor. "David?"

"Did you know your name means beloved or friend? This little guy is my beloved, and you've been my friend. You didn't have to be, but you were there for me when no one else was, except for Foxx. That's why David has his name, too. I couldn't have done this without you, Davi. I owe you so much."

"You don't owe me anything, Rene. Promise me you'll be the best mother you can be to David. That's all I ask."

"Is Quinn there?"

"He's giving the twins their bath."

"Tell him I'm not sorry. I won't apologize for what I've done. I love my baby too much."

"I will."

"I have to go now. Bye, Davi."

"Goodbye, Rene. Kiss David for me."

Davi ended the call and stayed seated on the floor. She held her head in her hands and cried.

"Mommy!"

Four small arms wrapped around her neck and hugged her tight. Davi inhaled their scent of soap and all things wonderful that came with freshly bathed children. She wiped away her tears.

"All done? Pick a story for bedtime. Mommy will be right in."

Quinn held out his hand to her. "Davi?"

She took his hand and got to her feet. She wrapped her arms around his waist.

Quinn kissed the top of her head. "He's here?"

"Yes. And he has all ten toes and ten fingers and hair like his father."

Quinn held her tighter.

"His name is David Foxx Thomas, and he weighs seven pounds." Davi cried into his shirt, her tears soaking it. "Don't fight her on his surname, Quinn. Please."

"I won't. No more fighting, Davi. I promise."

# thirty-five

**It didn't take long** for the news to break that Rene Adams had given birth to her love child with Quinn Thomas. Paparazzi and reporters constantly tried to get to the maternity ward of the hospital. Jake and his security team made sure that no one got past them. News trucks and paparazzi parked along the road outside of Davi's farm. Quinn unplugged their landline phone, and still, unwanted calls got through on his and Davi's unlisted cell phones. And through it all, the twins played, oblivious to the chaos around them.

After a couple of weeks, the media frenzy died down, and life resumed to some semblance of normal. Quinn, on a break between movies, stayed at home with his family. The twins enjoyed having their father as their full-time playmate, and Davi used the time by hiding out in her office.

She thought she could do it—play the part of the wronged wife who suffered the public humiliation of having her husband father a child with another woman. The problem was, Davi wasn't an actor. She didn't know how to pretend, and she didn't know how to lie. Countless emails requested her appearance on various talk shows. The requests focused on Davi's books. However, she knew the real reason behind the requests—Quinn's love child.

She gazed at the black and white photograph of Quinn that Cat had rescued from the garbage months ago. She didn't have to wonder how different her life would have been if she'd never met him. She knew that she'd be living alone in her big farmhouse, waiting for her kids to make her a grandmother. Now, she was the mother of two five-year-olds and the wife of one of Hollywood's most talented and gorgeous movie stars. Her husband, the man who had once called her his universe, had in one thoughtless and stupid move sent their world spiralling into a black hole.

"A penny for your thoughts," Quinn said as he sat down in his old tan leather chair situated across from her desk. "You look as though you're a million miles away."

Davi smiled. "You could say that."

"So? What is it?" Quinn propped his feet up on the edge of her desk in the familiar way he'd done so many times before.

Davi gazed at him. He was the living and breathing definition of hot sex, and he was hers. Quinn wore his hair the way she liked it, not too long, just long enough for her to have something to hold onto when she wanted. He was clean-shaven. Davi preferred the feel of soft skin against her body instead of scratchy stubble. Her gaze moved down to the tight T-shirt that clung to him like a second skin. He knew how much she liked to see him in T-shirts.

"You have to stop what you're doing."

"What is it that I'm doing exactly?"

"You're pretending."

"I'm not. You're getting the real deal here, Davi. Nothing more and nothing less, unless you think it's less." He gazed at her with his bright blue eyes. "What's up? You've been hiding out in here for too long. I know you aren't writing, so what is it?"

"I can't do this anymore."

"Can't do what?"

"This."

"This?"

"Pretend."

"Davi, you'll have to speak in sentences if you don't want this conversation to last all day. I've already told you that I'm not pretending, although I don't know what you're referring to."

"I can't pretend that there isn't a little boy growing up without his father."

"Oh."

"I know that it's what you want, and Rene seems to be fine with it, but I can't stop thinking that it's not right."

"I'm not pretending that he doesn't exist, Davi. I know he's out there."

"Then why won't you talk about him?"

"Because I don't want to."

"Doesn't it bother you knowing that he's growing up without knowing who his father is?"

"Davi, he's only a baby. He'll be okay. Isn't Foxx still with Rene?"

"Yes, but—"

"Foxx will be good with him. You said he was good with our two, so why would he be any different with the baby?"

"You hate Foxx. Why would you be happy that Foxx is helping Rene raise him?"

"Because it's better than the alternative. The boy won't know the difference."

"His name is David."

"I know."

"You still can't say his name."

"No."

"He's your son."

"I'm sorry, Davi, but I can't accept him. Not yet."

"Someday, you'll have to."

"Maybe, but right now, I don't."

# thirty-six

**"So, how are my god babies enjoying school?** Has Jack threatened to walk home again?" Maggie asked Davi as they sat at the kitchen table having their second cup of coffee.

"No. Jack knows that he has to stay at school. We asked his teacher to give him something extra to do when he gets bored, and he takes one of his readers with him, too, just in case."

"How can a five-year-old get bored at school?"

"It's easy when there aren't cows at school or a tractor to ride in."

"Do you miss them?"

"More than I did the first three. I didn't think it could be possible, but it is. Jack and Stevie are growing up too fast, Maggie. I hoped I could slow things down a bit the second time around, but it doesn't work that way. The clock keeps ticking no matter what we do."

"What's Hollywood up to? Any movies coming up?"

"He's in New York for the day. He's meeting with the director and producers of his next project. I think they had some final changes to agree on before they start filming in February."

"What's he signed on for this time? Another romance?"

"It's a science fiction film—something a bit different for Quinn."

Davi picked at her muffin while Maggie eyed her carefully.

"Any news from Rene?"

"She sent me a picture of David and her with Santa." Davi reached for her cell phone and found the picture. "Isn't it a beautiful picture of the two of them?"

"He looks like Quinn. There's no mistaking who his father is."

"I know. Isn't David adorable?"

"And she's—"

"It's okay. You can say it. Rene is more beautiful than ever. Motherhood agrees with her."

"Quinn still hasn't come around?"

"No. He's insisting on no contact. He knows now that I email Rene, he can't stop me from that, but he's asked that I don't go visit her, and I respect his request."

"But you'd like to. I can see it in your eyes."

"I'd love to hold him just once."

"You amaze me."

"Don't say that. You'd do the same thing."

"No, I wouldn't. If Charlie had done to me what your husband had done to you, he'd be my first ex-husband."

"Your first?"

"Having more than one ex-husband is all the rage right now. Haven't you been keeping up with your Hollywood peers?"

"I don't think I have any Hollywood peers. I've dropped off the map where Hollywood is concerned, and I have no plans on ever going back there."

"Give it time. You'll change your mind."

Davi shook her head. "I have no desire to walk any red carpet ever again. As far as I'm concerned, bad things happen when Quinn and I walk the red carpet together. From now on, he can make the walk all by himself."

"What about the Academy Awards? Certainly, you and Quinn are going. He's been nominated for an award!"

"He can go, Maggie. I don't need to go with him."

"You have to go with him. Isn't it required?"

"I don't think there's a rule that spouses have to attend. If you recall, I didn't attend when he won his last Oscar."

"You were in the hospital recovering from a gunshot wound that put you in a coma. I think that was a valid reason not to attend."

"Okay, so let's put it this way. I need a pretty good reason to attend this time. Quinn's nomination doesn't count. It has to be bigger and better than that."

"Careful what you wish for, Davi."

"I do not wish for anything, Maggie. I'm only saying that I can't imagine what would ever make me go to the Oscars."

Davi's cell phone buzzed. She picked it up and looked at the caller display.

She answered the call. "Foxx?"

"Davi, is Quinn there?"

"No, he's in New York for the day. What is it?"

"There's been an accident."

"What?"

Maggie reached out and put her hand on Davi's. Davi held her gaze.

"A drunk driver hit us. David's okay."

"What about you and Rene?"

"I've got a broken arm. It's Rene—"

"Foxx? What about Rene?"

"She wants to see Quinn. Can you get him to go to the hospital?"

"How bad is she?"

"Just get him to come here, New York Methodist. I'm sure he knows how to get here."

"I'll do my best."

"Tell him to hurry, please. Thank you." Foxx ended the call.

Davi looked up at Maggie. "Rene's been in an accident. She's asking for Quinn."

"Oh my, do you think he'll go?"

"He doesn't have a choice. He has to go." Davi dialled Quinn's number. "Quinn?"

"Hey, I'm just heading to the airport. My meeting finished earlier than expected."

"You have to turn around. Rene's been in an accident, and she's asking for you."

"What kind of accident?"

"A drunk driver hit them. David's okay, but it's Rene." She sensed his hesitation. "You don't have a choice. You have to see her. She's at New York Methodist. You may not have another chance to set things right with her. Do this for me, please."

"Okay." Davi heard him tell Jake of the change in plan. "I'll call you when I know anything."

"Thank you. Give Rene my love, please."

"I'll call you."

Quinn ended the call and then spoke to Jake, "Rene's been in an accident. She's asking for me."

"I'll get security there right away. We don't need this becoming a media circus."

"That hospital's got the best doctors for trauma. She's in good hands."

"Did Davi say what her injury was?"

"It doesn't matter. Rene will be fine. She has to be."

Quinn looked out his window without taking in the scenery. He recalled Davi's words that one day he'd realize that he was wrong and that it might be too late to make things right. What was the saying,

"Hindsight is twenty-twenty vision?" Of course, it was. If he could undo everything he did that was wrong, how far back would he go?

What would he change if he could? Rene? If he'd never met her, none of this would be happening. No. Too easy an answer and a definite cop-out. As much as he complained about her, Rene and Quinn worked well together. He enjoyed her spark and her lust for life. Quinn realized it was a mistake only when they tried to turn sex into love, especially with Foxx added to the equation. Foxx? Just the thought of the ginger man made Quinn's skin crawl. He would definitely undo his involvement with Foxx.

What else would he undo? He reddened with embarrassment as he thought of his stupid desire to have more kids. What was he thinking? Davi and the twins were everything to him. What made him use them as pawns in a game that no one could win? His mother—was it possible that her death was the catalyst that drove him to try his stupid stunt with Davi? Was it an obsession with his mortality that caused him to want more children? Was it Rene's support and willingness to give him children that blinded him to the insanity of his actions? Quinn ran his hand through his hair. He didn't know what the answer was, only that what he did was madness and hurtful and unforgivable.

Yet Davi forgave him, and that was the hardest part of all. She forgave him, and although she welcomed him into her heart and her bed, he could tell that their relationship changed irrevocably. They had lost their tingle, and Quinn knew deep down in his soul that he was the reason for it. He sensed it when they kissed or when they made love. Quinn knew that she was desperate to feel it again, and then Quinn would see the disappointment in her eyes when it didn't happen. And that was why he couldn't forgive himself. For as much as Davi said she forgave him, her eyes always told him differently.

Quinn exhaled roughly.

"You okay, Quinn? We're almost there."

"Yes. Just thinking."

"Security's in place at the hospital. No one's getting in there unless they're supposed to be there."

"Any word on Rene?"

"Drunk driver T-boned them at an intersection. The baby was unharmed, Foxx received minor bruises and a broken left arm, Rene has multiple lacerations, some broken bones. That's all they'd tell me." Jake watched Quinn from the rearview mirror. "You haven't spoken to Rene since last year, have you?"

"Not one word."

"Any idea what she wants to talk to you about?"

"That's what I'm about to find out."

# thirty-seven

**"Thanks for coming,"** Foxx said as he greeted the two men at the elevator.

"How is she?" Quinn asked him.

"She's scheduled for surgery and won't take any drugs so that she can nurse the baby," Foxx said as he led them to Rene's room. "She's been waiting for you."

"And you?" Quinn asked as he eyed Foxx's cast and bruised face.

"I'm okay."

Quinn hesitated when he reached the doorway. Beeping machines and the flashing lights of the monitors reminded him of when Davi was in the hospital.

Jake's hand rested on his shoulder.

"Are you okay?"

"Yes. I'm fine."

Quinn made his way to Rene's bedside. His gaze went immediately to the dark-haired cherub latched onto Rene's breast.

"This is the best pain medication I could ever want," she said as she smiled up at Quinn. "Thank you for coming."

Quinn took the chair beside the bed and leaned in toward Rene. He took her free hand and squeezed it.

"How could I say no to you?" He kept his eyes focused on Rene and the baby. Quinn couldn't bear to look at the tubes and wires that were attached to Rene's body. "You're looking as beautiful as ever, Rene."

She gave him a weak smile. "Cut the crap, Quinn. You've never been one with the pleasantries with me. Don't start now."

"Rene—"

"It took an accident for you to talk to me finally."

"You were always good at drama." Quinn saw her wince. "I'm sorry. That was insensitive of me."

"No. My little angel has a tooth coming in. He just bit me." Rene sighed and leaned back against her pillow. "I'm sorry for trying to come between you and Davi."

"It's okay."

"No. What I did was wrong. I should have respected your marriage. I should have shown Davi some respect. She's better than either of us."

"I know."

"You don't deserve her."

Quinn smiled in agreement.

"I know now why you love her and why you couldn't love me."

"Rene—"

"Will you please keep quiet and let me talk? It's her heart. She loves everybody even when they've treated her like crap. I'm talking about you and me, lover."

"I know, and you're right."

"She loves David, too, and she's never met him. Did you know she checked up on me all through my pregnancy? She reminded me of my mother, only better. Don't tell her about the mother part. I don't want her to feel old."

"That's a change for you, thinking of someone else's feelings."

"She has this way of getting to you, of making you want to be the best person you can be."

Rene closed her eyes and stiffened.

"Let me call the nurse for you."

"No. She'll only want to give me a needle, and I won't take anything while this little one is feeding."

"I think he's asleep."

"Will you do me a favour? Say his name for me? I want to know how it sounds when you say it."

Quinn swallowed hard.

"Please say his name for me."

Quinn looked down on the sleeping boy and said softly, "David Foxx Thomas."

Rene smiled her appreciation. "It sounds so perfect when you say it."

"Except for Foxx," Quinn grumbled.

"You owe him more than you know. He's a good man, Quinn."

"That's a matter of opinion."

"They're going to operate on me. I want to talk to you before that happens."

"Rene, it can wait. I'll stay here. I promise."

"No. Now. I'm not sorry for what I did to get David. I love him. He's the best thing that ever happened to me." She ignored the whispers of the nurses behind Quinn's back. She squeezed his hand. "That's why I forgive you for what you did. You were awful to both Davi and me, but if you hadn't done what you did, I wouldn't have found out about your sperm bank, and I wouldn't have made this little guy."

"I'm sorry for playing you. What I did to you was cruel. I wish I could say I was insane, but I can't."

"You were insane, or at least not in your right frame of mind. The Quinn I know would never have done what you did. You're too much the gentleman."

"Thank you."

"There's one more thing I want you to do."

"Anything."

"Hold him while I'm in surgery. I don't want David to be left alone. Please."

"Rene—"

"He's your son. Let me see you hold him before they take me away." She watched as Quinn lifted David carefully and cradled him in his arms. "Just as I imagined," she said, pleased. "I'll dream of the two of you while I'm asleep."

Quinn leaned down and kissed Rene on her forehead. "We'll see you when you wake up. Davi sends her love. She told me to make sure you know that you are in her thoughts."

Rene smiled. "Thank her for me. Thank her for everything."

Quinn stood back as the nurses prepared to take Rene to surgery. Foxx followed her.

Quinn sat in his chair and gazed down at his son, who was now awake. He saw himself in the infant. The boy had his hair and his smile. He had Rene's green eyes opened wide as they took in the man gazing down at him. David held Quinn's gaze and gurgled. He reached out, touched Quinn's nose, and smiled.

"Hello, little man. I'm your father. I guess it's time that we got to know each other."

# thirty-eight

**Davi waited in the arrival area** of the Toronto Pearson International Airport terminal 1. She sat on the edge of her seat, sipping her coffee. Quinn's late-night flight was on time, and she was eager to see him. The sliding doors continually opened as travellers made their exit from customs. Her gaze never wandered from the doors.

She knew they were there, circling the waiting area, looking for the best vantage point to get the money shot of Quinn at the airport. Davi was used to the paparazzi. She barely gave them a second look, even when she knew cameras focused on her. She wished they weren't here to spoil the moment—not tonight, of all nights.

The doors opened, and Quinn paused for a brief moment as he searched for her. He stood straight, his shoulders pushed back and chest out as though daring the paparazzi to charge at him. The look on his face made it clear. Quinn Thomas was to be left alone. Davi prayed no one would cross the line with him.

A tired smile crossed his face when he found her. Her heart called out to him. He'd been gone too long. Quinn walked toward her, his gaze never leaving hers as he made it through the crowd. He reached out to her with his free arm and pulled her in close. He was so close to her that she felt the sweet warmth of his breath. She smiled at him and kissed him softly on the mouth. His arm wrapped around her waist and pulled her in tight against his body. His hand pressed on her lower spine in the familiar way that only a lover's hand knows.

Davi moaned softly into his mouth. She pressed against him, wanting more from the kiss than was possible in such a public spot. Her hands found his ears and caressed them, and then her fingers found his lobes and gently pulled on them. His moan vibrated through her and excited her. And then it happened. The slightest tingle ran up her spine and along her arms. She felt it in her lips, and she knew that he felt it, too, because he cursed appreciatively against them.

Quinn released Davi from his kiss and smiled lovingly at her.

"I've got someone I want you to meet. I've told this little boy all about you, and he told me that he couldn't wait to meet you." Quinn reached down into the stroller and unbuckled the safety strap. "Davi, I'd like to introduce you to David. David, I'd like to introduce you to your new mommy."

David gave her his best smile and reached out to touch her face. "He's beautiful."

"Take him. I know you've been dying to hold him."

Davi took the little boy in her arms and hugged him. She breathed in his scent and held it in her lungs as long as she could. She wanted to remember this moment forever.

"Come on, Davi, let's go home."

Davi drove home. Quinn held her hand as she made her way through the late-night traffic.

"Jack and Stevie will be excited to see you in the morning. They've missed their pancakes for breakfast."

"What did you tell them about David?"

"I told them that Daddy was bringing home a baby and his name was David and that he was their new brother."

"How did that go over?"

"Something akin to getting a puppy for Christmas, I think. They talked about where he would sleep and who would get to take him out to the barn to see the cows."

"True farmers," Quinn said, chuckling.

"How's Foxx?"

"Better. None of us ever thought Rene would die. Her injuries weren't life-threatening. She went under to get her damned leg reset. Who'd have thought she'd never wake up?"

"She did."

Quinn looked at Davi and nodded his agreement. "We talked about you. She thought the world of you. She apologized for trying to undermine our marriage." Davi kept her eyes on the road. She was sure he was wiping away tears. "She forgave me for treating her like shit. Not her words, but that's what I did. She said I wasn't myself. The Quinn she knew would never have played a stunt like that."

"She was right."

"I knew what I was doing. I played both of you against each other, and what did it do? Almost ruined our marriage and turned her into a thief."

"I prefer to think of her as an angel who answered your prayer."

# epilogue

**Davi didn't fight him** over attending the Academy Awards ceremony. Quinn's movie had received four nominations—Best Actor, Best Actress, Best Director, and Best Film. There was no acceptable excuse not to attend, and surprisingly, Davi didn't try to offer one. They had to go. It was the right thing to do.

Rene won Best Actress, and Quinn accepted her award on her behalf. He told the audience that Rene was the most difficult actress he had ever worked with, yet they had that on-screen chemistry that brought their characters to life. She challenged him every day to be the best he could be, and he made a promise that when their son was older, he would tell him all about his mother, the movie star.

Davi was the first to stand and give him a standing ovation. Quinn's speech was his first public admission that David was his son, and with it, the heavy burden of denial lifted from his shoulders.

Clint won the award for Best Director, and he also accepted the award for Best Movie. The film clip played for both awards was the bar scene fuelled by tequila.

Quinn didn't win Best Actor. Davi's crush, Ryan, took that honour. Quinn and Davi were the first to congratulate him as he made his way to the stage. While Ryan gave his acceptance speech, Quinn was sure he saw him wink at Davi.

"He's dead," Quinn muttered under his breath.

"Don't worry, stud. I'm a one-man kind of woman. You're it for me."

When the ceremony ended, Quinn and Davi disappeared. They slipped out of the theatre and headed back to their hotel suite, where three children waited to hear the story about the knight and his lady and their adventures with the dragons, dinosaurs, and cows.

# author's note

**In 2014,** when I wrote *Love's Games*, I didn't think that one of the scenes would become real. Since this note is at the back of the book, it's not a spoiler for you, the reader.

Little did I know that in 2020, my mother would choose a similar ending to her life. Mom, at the age of 93 years, developed a cancerous tumour on her windpipe. Even with the assistance of oxygen, she was slowly suffocating. Mom applied for MAID—medical aid in dying. Our family thought it would take weeks to get approval. In Mom's case, it took a few days.

Our family made the preparations, organizing final visits and goodbye hugs. Then on the appointed day, my sisters and I, along with our spouses, had our last visit with Mom in her apartment. We talked and listened to Mom's favourite recording of my nephew when he featured as a guest pianist with the city's orchestra, and then Mom said she was ready.

By that time, the doctor and her assistant had arrived and had made the necessary preparations. Mom went to bed. We hugged her and told her we loved her, and then we left the room. The process was over faster than we had imagined. When the doctor called us into the room, Mom was gone. Just like that.

For those who had made peace with her dying, knowing that it was the right choice for her, it was a blessing. Others in the family wished they had more time, hoping that Mom's health would improve. However, Mom was ready to leave this world and go to sleep. I am thankful that she was able to do as she wished.

# Book Club Questions

1. How did the book make you feel?

    • Were you amused, bored, intrigued by Quinn and Davina's story?

    • Are you glad you read it?

2. What did you think about the main characters?

    • Were they believable?

    • Which character did you relate to the most/least?

    • Was Quinn's desire for more children justification for his actions?

    • Was Davina's reaction to Quinn's relationship with Rene believable?

    • Was Davina's acceptance of Rene's pregnancy believable?

    • If you were to be one of the characters, who would you be? Why?

3, Which parts of the book stood out to you?

    • Are there quotes, passages, or scenes that you found particularly compelling?

    • Were there scenes that you thought were unique, out of place, thought-provoking or disturbing?

4. What themes did you detect in the story?

    • What were the main points you think the author was trying to make?

    • Was there symbolism that you noticed?

- Have you ever been in a situation where it was essential to do the "right thing"?
- Have you ever had to "overlook" something so that you could forgive another?

5. What did you think about the ending?
    - Were you satisfied or disappointed with how it ended?
    - How do you picture the characters' lives after the end of the story?

6. What changes/decisions would you hope for if the story were made into a movie?
    - Is there anything that you would cut from the book?
    - Who would you cast to play the main characters?

7. How does this book compare to other romance novels you've read?
    - If you have read any of the other books in the Davina and Quinn series, did you like it more or less that *Forever Love*? *Love's Promises*?
    - Do you want to read more in the series?

8. What is your impression of the author?

Deborah Armstrong
Book 4 in the
Davina + Quinn
series
Love's
Challenges

# Prologue

**Davina Thomas** didn't hear her son standing in the doorway to her office, and yet she felt his presence and the slight ache in her heart that came with knowing that he had awakened to the same nightmare. She kept her gaze on the family pictures covering her office wall while her right hand caressed the silky fur of the sleeping cat purring in her arms.

"It's been a long time," she said. "I thought the dragon had forgotten about us."

"Where would the fun be in that?"

Davina chuckled softly. "You're right. We don't want to get too comfortable in having a normal family life, do we?"

She turned her head to gaze at her son, Jack. He was the image of his father when he was twenty-five years of age. Shaggy dark brown bed head hair framed his perfectly chiselled face with blue eyes. His smile was all hers, though. Not the Hollywood smile Quinn Thomas could force quickly when necessary, but charming with the promise of mischief.

The dragon was all theirs, too—an inexplicable and unwelcome nightmare that warned them of bad things to come, always to Davina. She bore the scars from the dragon's bite—a gunshot wound and the reminders of battles won against cancer.

"It was the scariest and silliest dream I think I've ever had. The dragon was standing right here in this spot, and he was forcing you to put his picture on my wall. Right there." Davina nodded her head. "That's your spot."

"My spot?"

"That's reserved for your family picture of you with your ladylove and your children. The space beside it is for Stevie with hers, and David's is right below hers."

"Mom, I haven't found my ladylove."

"You will. Some day."

Jack came up behind her and hugged her. His cheek pressed against the side of her head with the silver streak of hair, her dragon's bite. They gazed at the family photographs that had been in Davi's office for as long as Jack could remember. His favourite was of Stevie and him as four-year-olds building a sandcastle on the beach with their father. Quinn told the knight's story with his ladylove and the dragon. Even then, the dragon had been a part of Jack's life.

"What was your dream about, sweetheart?"

"It was scary and silly, too, I guess. I was fighting the dragon. I was fighting him for her. I couldn't see her face, but I could feel her arms wrapped around my waist, holding me tight. We were riding Goliath. All the time, she was whispering in my ear, 'Don't hurt him, he's cute.'"

Davina laughed.

"Crazy. Right?"

"Definitely."

"So what do you think it means, Mom?"

"That we both had a bit too much to drink at your send-off party last night?"

"Seriously, Mom."

"Maybe, this time, the dragon's not the enemy."

# about the author

**Deborah Armstrong** hit the big 50, and became restless and couldn't concentrate on much. Her favourite escape was to read. Instantly, her daughter's romance novels became the ultimate magnet. Hours were spent devouring them.

That was then ... this is now. Deborah turned her restlessness into writing hot and spicy contemporary romance with a touch of country.

Deborah lives with her husband and five hundred cows on their dairy farm in Ontario, Canada. When she's not writing or working on the farm, she enjoys reading, travelling, watching movies, and spending time with friends and family, especially her grandchildren. She also proofreads and edits for fellow authors. Her writing muse tends to run on the liquid side: strong coffee, chocolate milk, and single malt scotch in no particular order.

Thrice each week, the local gym beckons. Cardio means book thinking time for unravelling plots and conversations for her current work in progress.

When Deborah's characters talk, she listens. Not surprisingly, they decide when and how to tell their story, talking to her at the strangest times. When she's driving, working out, or trying to fall asleep, they whisper in her ear and say, "this is what needs to happen next."

## Other books in the series

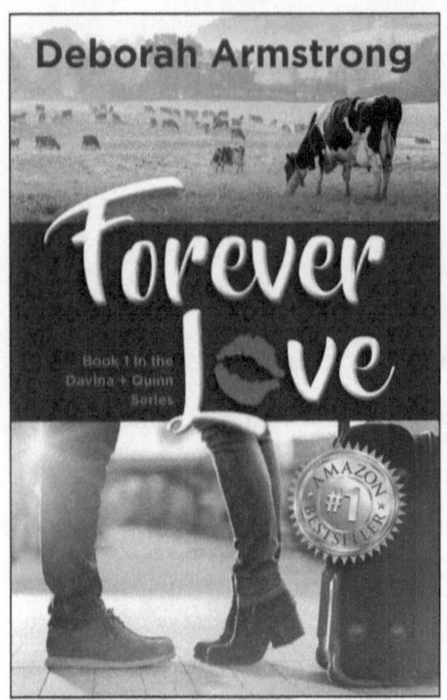


**Book 1**

**Book 3**

**Book 4**

**Novella**

# Also by Deborah Armstrong

# stay connected

**Deborah Armstrong** is a storyteller, creating fantasies and weaving them for your reading delight from her farm in Ontario, Canada.

If you are in a Book Club, bring Deborah to yours via Skype, Zoom . . .or in person! Whether it's a hot and steamy summer day or one kissed with a wintry landscape, have your Club gather their favourite snacks and beverages and discover the Davina and Quinn series. Deborah invites her readers to follow her on social media and to contact her by email. To work with her, visit her website and subscribe to her newsletter.

Website: DeborahArmstrong.ca

 WriterDeborah

 deboraharmstrongauthor/

 DeborahArmstrongAuthor

 deborah_armstrong_author/

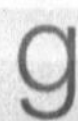 author/show/6467157.Deborah_Armstrong